BROTHERS AND GHOSTS

KHUÊ PHẠM is an award-winning Vietnamese German writer. A graduate of the London School of Economics, she worked for *The Guardian* and NPR's Berlin bureau before becoming an editor at the renowned German weekly *Die Zeit*. Specialising in long-form journalism, she profiled Kevin Spacey before his sexual assault trial and co-wrote an investigation into the Essex lorry deaths that earned her the nomination for Germany's version of the Pulitzer Prize. In 2012, she co-wrote *Wir neuen Deutschen*, a nonfiction book about second-generation immigrants in Germany. Her debut novel, *Brothers and Ghosts*, is loosely inspired by her own family, whose journey she traces over the course of five decades. Phạm lives in Berlin. Read more at khuepham.de/english.

CHARLES HAWLEY holds a bachelor's degree in political science from Whitman College and completed a master's degree in journalism at New York's Columbia University. In addition to working as a journalist, he is a literary translator for leading German publications including *Der Spiegel*, *Die Zeit*, and the *Süddeutsche Zeitung*. He has lived in Berlin since 2002.

DARYL LINDSEY studied journalism and German at San Francisco State University and Eberhard Karls Universität Tübingen. He works as a journalist and also as a literary translator for publications including Germany's *Der Spiegel*, *Die Zeit*, and the *Süddeutsche Zeitung*. He has called Berlin home since 2004.

BROTHERS AND GHOSTS

Khuê Phạm

translated by
Charles Hawley & Daryl Lindsey

SCRIBE
Melbourne | London | Minneapolis

Scribe Publications
18–20 Edward St, Brunswick, Victoria 3056, Australia
2 John St, Clerkenwell, London, WC1N 2ES, United Kingdom
3754 Pleasant Ave, Suite 100, Minneapolis, Minnesota 55409, USA

First published in Germany as *Wo auch immer ihr seid*
by btb, a division of Penguin Random House Verlagsgruppe GmbH,
München, Germany

Published by Scribe 2024

Text copyright © btb, a division of Penguin Random House
Verlagsgruppe GmbH, 2021
Translation copyright © Charles Hawley and Daryl Lindsey 2024

All rights reserved. Without limiting the rights under copyright reserved above, no part of this publication may be reproduced, stored in or introduced into a retrieval system, or transmitted, in any form or by any means (electronic, mechanical, photocopying, recording or otherwise) without the prior written permission of the publishers of this book.

The moral rights of the author and translators have been asserted.

Typeset in Garamond Premier Pro by the publishers

Printed and bound in the UK by CPI Group (UK) Ltd, Croydon CR0 4YY

Scribe is committed to the sustainable use of natural resources and the use of paper products made responsibly from those resources.

978 1 761380 12 9 (Australian edition)
978 1 915590 04 6 (UK edition)
978 1 957363 79 0 (US edition)
978 1 761385 56 8 (ebook)

Catalogue records for this book are available from the
National Library of Australia and the British Library.

The translation of this book was supported by a grant
from the Goethe-Institut

scribepublications.com.au
scribepublications.co.uk
scribepublications.com

THE NAMES OF VIETNAMESE CHARACTERS, CUISINE, AND CLOTHING IN THIS NOVEL ARE WRITTEN WITH VIETNAMESE ACCENT MARKS. FOR HISTORICAL PERSONALITIES AND CITIES, THE ENGLISH SPELLING IS USED.

For Phương and Thoại, who have travelled a much farther road than I have

KIỀU

Let me begin this story with a confession: I don't know how to pronounce my own name.

For as long as I can remember, I have felt uncomfortable introducing myself to anyone. The German people I grew up with tripped over my name's melodic sounds, while my parents' Vietnamese friends had trouble understanding my heavy accent. The Germans got around the problem by not addressing me by name at all. The Vietnamese would ask: 'How do you spell that?'

Once someone said: 'Are you sure about that?'

As a child, when we would go to the department store, I'd head straight for the toy section to try to find my name on the personalised pencils. At the hardware store, I would pin my hopes on the long, colourful keychains. If I could only find my name, it would prove that nothing was wrong with me, I would say to myself as I combed through hundreds of pencils and key chains. I would find 'Katrin', 'Kristina', and once — my heart skipped a beat — 'Kira'.

I never found 'Kiều'.

'Kiều' existed only in my family's world and in the title of a book on my father's basement shelves: *Truyện Kiều* (*The Tale of Kiều*). A work as important to the Vietnamese canon as *The Catcher in the Rye* is to English-language literature.

Of course, I was unable to read it.

Whenever my father was tidying up, he would pull out the book and say, 'Did you know that you're named after a famous young woman? Every schoolchild has read this novel! You're famous all across Vietnam!'

I believed everything my father told me when I was a child, so why should this be any different? I imagined walking through Vietnam and being approached by all kinds of people. I would constantly have to keep introducing myself, and each time I would have to pronounce my name. Followed by endless questions.

When I turned sixteen, I changed my name because I expected, falsely, it would give me a better chance at being accepted into Jeanette's circle of friends. When I was twenty, I had my passport changed as well, because I finally felt that I had some sort of power over my life.

For the last ten years, I've been a different person. Germans call me 'Kim'; the Vietnamese say 'Kihm'. It isn't perfect, but it is easier. Shedding my past never really bothered me. It really didn't.

Until I got that message.

*

The message, written in English, pops up on Facebook. Someone calling himself 'Sơn Saigon' has contacted me.

> *Is this you, Kiều? There's something I need to tell you and your father!*

There is only one group of people who know my true name; it's insider information limited to members of my large, nebulous family. My mother's side, who still live in Vietnam, is loud and includes many children. Whenever my relatives send photos, I'm amazed to find all sorts of new cousins whose names I can't remember even though, or perhaps because, they consist of only two letters. I don't really know my father's side of the family; I just remember a deaf aunt. All I know is that his siblings fled Vietnam after the war and ended up in California, maybe as boat people, maybe not.

Then there's also a great-aunt in England who got rich working as a lawyer for the cannabis mafia, and a cousin-in-law who was a poet and was flown out of Vietnam after the war to Canada by the PEN writers' club. And finally, my young cousin in France who appeared in that cheesy musical variety show my parents love to sing karaoke to: *Paris by Night*.

I only know these relatives from stories. They are just as unreal to me as the ghosts of dead ancestors for whom I light a couple of incense sticks on Vietnamese New Year's while going through the motions of praying. Once a year, they drift into my life only to vanish again after a brief greeting, like smoke.

So, who is this Sơn?

His Facebook profile photo shows a man with bushy eyebrows and a straight nose that reminds me of my father's. I have often heard Vietnamese acquaintances talk admiringly about its high, elegant form, which is why it's the first thing I notice about Sơn. His eyes are unusually round, making his face, despite his wrinkled brow, look rather boyish. He apparently lives in Westminster, California, where he runs an import-export business called Made in America. He must be my father's younger brother, the one who, according to family stories, was really bad at school but really good at playing cards.

I try to remember my father's family in the same way you might try to recall passages from a history book. I met them once, fifteen years ago — we took a trip to Vietnam and learned, by chance, that they also happened to be there. I have no idea why we never flew to California to visit them there. One time, when I asked my mother if there had been some kind of falling out, she thought for a second and then shook her head.

'Actually,' she said, dragging the word out in an odd way, 'everything's fine. But Dad's family is difficult. It's better if we just get on with our lives and let them get on with theirs. We send money, we don't have to visit them in California as well.'

Nothing more was said, and I didn't dare ask any further questions, sensing that I wouldn't get an answer even if I did.

There's something I need to tell you!

What does he want from me?

I snap my laptop shut, ready to plunge back into my everyday life in Berlin, a life that is German, orderly, and free of intercontinental family issues. My uncle hasn't spoken to me in fifteen years. It will hardly matter if I don't reply immediately, or indeed at all.

*

Two-and-a-half weeks later, I make my way to the light-blue house where my two siblings and I grew up. It's Christmas and, like every year, it puts me in a strange mood. Going back home means returning to the displacement of my childhood. My parents learned Christmas the same way they learned German grammar — as something you observed to be a part of this country. They've decorated the tree in the living room with a stuffed Santa Claus, wooden figurines they painted themselves, gaudily glittering baubles, and two strings of multicoloured lights. Only the fake snow is missing.

I sit down at my old piano and play Bach's 'Prelude in C Minor' from *The Well-Tempered Clavier*. The hammering of the notes blends with the clattering from the kitchen, where my mother is constantly messing about with her pots. How often did I fight with her over my piano lessons as I sat crying on this black stool? How often had I wished that I was growing up in a family that didn't have to become German because it already was?

The ski equipment in the basement, the BMWs in the garage, the framed family photos from Ibiza, Paris, and Halong Bay illustrate a history I heard people recount innumerable times during my youth: *Look at this family! They might be immigrants, but they've made it anyway!* It always bothered me when 'the Germans' — that's what we call them, as if they are a foreign, far-away people — congratulated us on my father's career, my mother's diligence, or the 'astonishingly good German' spoken by me and my siblings. Even as pride spread across the faces of my parents, I suddenly felt hurt. I was born in this country, why should I not speak its language perfectly? Over time, I have even come to speak it with my parents.

I miss my chord and my hands remain sitting there on the wrong notes. When the sounds from the kitchen die down, I close the fallboard. There is a black-and-white photo hanging on the wall above the piano, a picture my father took of my grandmother several decades ago. Slender and dainty, she is sitting in a taxi. Her curled hair is carefully pinned to one side, her Vietnamese silk dress, the áo dài, is embroidered with golden flowers. He took the photo long ago in Saigon, shortly before he left for Germany to pursue his university studies. Even though my grandmother is looking into the camera with a broad smile, her eyes wide open, there is something wistful in her expression.

My father once told me that my face reminds him of hers. I can see the resemblance mainly in my high forehead, which I conceal with bangs that I style in a variety of ways. I'm not quite as slim as her, a bit taller perhaps, and of course I never wear an áo dài, instead opting for black pants with monochrome tops. I think Asians in glasses look too nerdy, so I only ever wear contact lenses, despite my terrible vision. During my last visit to Vietnam, a lot of people thought I was a foreigner, not Vietnamese at all. Which, I have to admit, didn't bother me in the least.

*

As darkness falls outside the floor-to-ceiling windows, my siblings and I sit down at the table my mother has set with the heavy Rosenthal porcelain she normally reserves for German guests. She has even splurged on a white silk tablecloth from the famous KaDeWe department store, though she rarely spends large amounts of money, buying only marked-down products on principle. She's been living in Germany for half a century now, but having grown up extremely poor, she has never broken the Vietnamese habit of saving money wherever possible. Neither the BMW nor the large house has changed this habit of hers.

'A hundred euros! I thought about it for quite a while,' she says, gently stroking the lustrous material. 'I figured one of you could inherit it someday.'

We had spent the last several weeks discussing the menu for this evening's feast, and had ultimately settled on lobster, just as we had the previous three years. None of us is particularly fond of seafood, but lobster is quite festive, and it doesn't taste all that fishy, so we indulge once a year. Five of the creatures are lined up on a platter, glimmering orange-red. My father grabs a pair of garden clippers that he bought the Christmas before last because he didn't have any lobster pincers, finding the garden tools so handy that he's been using them ever since.

The phone rings in the bedroom.

'Don't answer,' my mother orders, standing up to serve the salad. An anger I recognise from countless arguments back when I was in school flashes in her eyes: anger that anybody would dare disturb our sacred family gathering.

The ringing stops and then resumes after a short pause.

'How rude,' my mother grumbles as she stabs her fork into the salad. My father, showing solidarity as always, clips a claw from his lobster.

Silence, then it rings again.

I jump up from my chair. Maybe it's an emergency. Or it could be my old schoolfriend Thomas, who is oblivious to the concepts of family rituals and holiday repose. I dash to the phone, just as I so often did as a schoolgirl to keep my mother from getting there first and launching into a tirade.

'Yes?' I say in an impolite tone. I *want* to sound impolite.

An unfamiliar male voice replies, asking in Vietnamese who this is.

'Kim, here,' I answer in long-unpractised Vietnamese. I haven't uttered a single word of the language since our last trip there five years ago and am not at all interested in speaking it now with this stranger.

'Who?'

He's clearly unfamiliar with my German name. I try again.

'It's Kiều!' I say, louder this time, drawing out the syllable.

'Who? I still haven't caught your name.'

'Kiều!' I repeat. 'Minh's daughter!'

'Oh, *Kiều*! Why didn't you say so in the first place?'

The conversation is hardly thirty-seconds old, and I've already been thrust back into the dark chamber that holds my most embarrassing memories. Suddenly, I can see a younger version of me desperately trying to make herself understood during my last visit to Saigon. I had suppressed that memory; you can see why.

Maybe I should hang up.

'This is your Uncle Sơn from California,' the man at the other end of the line says. 'I tried to reach you on Facebook, but you probably didn't see my message.'

He pauses, apparently having trouble expressing what he wants to say. Not knowing whether or how to apologise, I say nothing. There's static on the line. The connection is extremely bad.

'It's about your grandmother,' he says, eventually. 'She's on her deathbed. I really need to speak to your father.'

In another situation, another language, I would have said something at this point. Something like: *I wish I had gotten to know her better. Now it's too late.* But because I'm apparently not even capable of conveying my own name, I just mumble, 'Okay,' and, with my hand over the receiver, call for my father.

Your grandmother is on her deathbed. So that's what Uncle Sơn had wanted to say. Suddenly, I am overcome with guilt for not having responded to his Facebook message. I grab my phone, sink back into my chair, and start tapping around on it, even though I'm usually the first to reprimand others for doing so at the table.

The photos he has posted on his Facebook page over the last few months tell the story of a slow decline. He had taken dozens of pictures of my grandmother, with her body seeming to shrink from one album to the next. I had never realised just how severely people can shrivel up, and now I'm seeing it before my very eyes. Dark spots spread across her skin like tide pools. Her hair grows wirier, her eyes cloudier. The faces of the others also change: the early photos show my grandmother surrounded by relatives bravely smiling. Towards the end, though, their expressions start looking empty as well, as if the illness weren't just sapping the life out of my grandmother, but also hope from the rest of the family.

I scroll through the images with the distance of someone watching a silent film in black and white. Her suffering feels so distant to me. As sad as the photos are, they seem unreal. California is nine time zones and a world away. What happens there touches neither my day-to-day life nor — to be completely honest — my heart.

*

My father returns to the table after twenty minutes with a bottle of red wine. He wears his hair the same way all Asian men of his generation seem to: thick black hair shaved close in the back and on the sides and parted to the right above his forehead. Even to me, photos of the Chinese National Congress look like a single functionary was cloned in Photoshop and then multiplied a hundred times; I half-expect to find my father sitting in one of the rows. But he isn't a Chinese politician, he's a Vietnamese-German heart surgeon. When we go to the Philharmonic, he is sometimes greeted by others at the concert hall with a warm 'Professor! How nice to see you!'

He's holding an expensive bottle of Bordeaux in his hand, surely a gift from one of his patients. Of course, German families would never drink red wine with seafood, but we do.

'Well, how did it go?' I ask, trying to sound casual.

He looks at me over the top of his gold-framed glasses.

'How did what go?'

'Don't pretend you don't know! What did he say about grandma?'

I hold out my wineglass. He gently tips the bottle to slowly pour the wine, the muted splashing amplifying the silence of his thoughts.

'He said she's been on artificial respiration for two weeks. Her kidneys and circulation have failed. The doctors want to know if they should keep her on life support or not. Sơn called me to ask for medical advice.'

He is speaking in the matter-of-fact tone he uses with his patients.

'I'm afraid they've reached the limit of what can be done for a woman her age. She's had Alzheimer's for five years and had to be admitted to the hospital because she developed a serious case of pneumonia. Now her immune system has collapsed.'

My father has always been very rational. Even when his oldest friend was battling cancer (and survived), he never showed his feelings. I always saw his detachment as a by-product of his profession, a useful one, but I'm still surprised to see him maintain that distance even as his own mother is on the brink of death.

'And what do your siblings say?' I ask.

My father shrugs his shoulders.

'Sơn sounded very upset on the phone. They're all standing around her bed driving each other mad. They don't know how to deal with the situation and they're very emotional. They argued for a whole hour before calling me.'

He raises the wineglass to his lips, but then puts it back down without taking a sip.

'It's just like it has always been.'

It's almost as if he's more bothered by his siblings' bickering than by his mother's ill health. But perhaps his stoicism is his way of dealing with it; he is the eldest son after all. His gaze wanders to the photo of her in her silk dress above the piano and rests there for a few seconds.

'What did you tell them?' asks my brother, Tuấn, who is studying medicine and wants to become a doctor like our father.

'That they should cease all treatment,' my father answers.

'Really?' My brother's face widens in astonishment. 'You want to let your own mother die?'

'Tuấn, you're a man of medicine!' my father says, pushing his wineglass aside in exasperation. 'I spoke briefly with the doctor on the phone, and he described her condition. The chances that she'll ever return to health are almost zero. It's better to suspend treatment than to prolong her suffering. Sometimes you just have to make difficult decisions.'

'And sometimes people are emotional when their family is

involved,' interjects my sister, Lan, giving me and Tuấn that look that we used to use when conspiring against our parents. 'When are they going to switch the machine off?' she asks.

'Now.'

'You mean she's dying as we speak?'

'That's right.'

My father pushes his chair back from the head of the table and looks at us calmly. His face has taken on the colour of the lobster; it is probably Asian flush, though it could be something else. He clears his throat as if to speak, but then says nothing.

Silently, we pick at our lobsters. It's really strange to think that in a different corner of this world, a person without whom none of us except my mother would even exist, is dying at this very moment.

How are you supposed to act in such a situation?

How are you supposed to *feel* in such a situation?

I try to examine my emotions, but there's nothing there. No grief, no shock, and certainly no need to talk to anybody about this woman who I only met once in my life. A few months ago, my old Polish neighbour passed away. She used to bring me cake every now and then, and the idea that I would never again run into her in the hallway brought me to tears. Her death disrupted my daily life, but my grandmother's passing will have no effect whatsoever.

I realise I'm thirsty and reach for the bottle of water, knocking it over in the process. The white silk tablecloth soaks it up.

'Oh, Kiều! Why do you always have to ruin everything!' My mother jumps up and rushes into the kitchen to grab a towel. My mishap breaks the heavy silence that this emotional intrusion has laid on our family feast. My mother scrubs so violently as she mops up the spill that the tablecloth rips.

*

I finally see Dorian again the day before New Year's Eve. He spent Christmas snowboarding in France and he's wearing the yellow sweater I sent with him as a present. Standing behind the counter at his bar, Neue Heimat, he assembles an order of meats and cheeses. With his Alpine glow and dirty-blond hair, he looks so attractive and full of life that a strange feeling of pride washes over me.

His face lights up when he sees me. He kisses me softly and tells me all about how fine the powder was, saying I really must come along next time. He sets a plate on the counter for me, loaded with a hunk of baguette and homemade wasabi butter. A few regulars are sitting in the back corner, but otherwise the place is empty. Grainy black-and-white photos of friends hang on the wall. Along with cooking, photography is one of the things Dorian taught himself after deciding to abandon his maths degree. He's one of those people who is good at all kinds of things, and I envy him — not only for his talents, but also for not giving a shit.

'Sorry to hear about your grandmother. It must have been pretty heavy to get the news over Christmas dinner.'

He strokes my hair. I close my eyes and rest my head on my arms.

'Why should it make any difference if she dies on 24 December or 24 January?' I respond. 'Dead is dead.'

'I'm just saying. When my grandma died the year before last, it hit us all pretty hard. It was just before Easter, and when I went home over the holidays, the mood was pretty gloomy.'

I consider pointing out to him that for one, Christian holidays don't really hold much meaning for my family, and for another, my grandma was a complete stranger to me. But I let it go. My co-workers at the magazine where I work as a restaurant critic were also frightfully sympathetic. Grandmothers apparently have a special standing in other families. They are the campfire around which their descendants gather to share family stories.

Muttering half to myself, I say: 'The whole thing is more strange than sad for me. We don't hear a thing from our relatives in California for years, not a thing. And then suddenly my uncle gets in touch to say that my grandmother is dying. Apparently, she has left a letter for my father in her will, and he has to come to California so they can all open it. He told me that they haven't spoken properly for fifteen years, so what could she have possibly written in this letter from her deathbed? I don't want to speak poorly of the dead, but couldn't she just have told him whatever it is five or ten years ago?'

He laughs dryly. 'You sound annoyed.'

I shrug.

'I'm not. I just feel that my relatives' problems are not our problems, really. They were never part of my life and until very recently, they didn't seem to be part of my father's either. Why drag him into this now?

'I'm sure your father knows how to handle his family.'

'He does: by avoiding them. I barely know our relatives in California — there must be a reason for this. My father is the most conscientious person I know, but he's coming up with all kinds of excuses for why he can't go.'

'It's probably just his way of not having to deal with his grief. I mean, his mother did just die.'

My father, grieving? I don't think I've seen him cry even once in my life.

'I'm not sure that's how he works,' I mumble. 'Things are a bit different in my family.'

Dorian grabs a wineglass next to the sink and begins rubbing it with a dishtowel even though it's already dry. He has that well-meaning yet serious look on his face, the one he gets when he wants to share his insights into my soul.

'To be honest, I sometimes get the feeling that you're oversensitive about your family,' he says carefully. 'I think you worry about things too much. Every family has drama. Mine does too.'

He's gazing at me so innocently that I decide not to point out that there's a tiny difference between his Lake Constance relatives and my Vietnamese family. His parents are so liberal that he simply can't imagine how authoritarian mine used to be. To him, they seem so nice. They have such friendly smiles. Even when my mother let out a sigh the first time she met him and told him how much hope she'd once had for my future ('*You realise that she got the best A-levels in all of Berlin, don't you?*'), even then he didn't get it, first looking at me with surprise and then pride. His parents had also always believed in him, he said, and he loves them so much for it.

Love, I'd thought to myself. What a clichéd word to describe the relationship between parents and children. Had I ever used it in reference to them? Or they in reference to me?

I doubted it.

Since then, I have spared Dorian from the cultural conundrum that is my family, electing not to initiate him into our unwritten codes. He wouldn't even come close to understanding my parents' expectations, and I would never be able to explain the ways, both good and bad, that we operate emotionally. Even though I go out to eat every Friday with my parents and siblings, I only bring

Dorian along on birthdays. I want our relationship to work, so I don't throw too much at him. When we're together, I act as if my soul isn't so contorted, as though I'm not constantly trying to fit in, while constantly hiding my feelings of duty and guilt.

I smile at him.

'You're probably right. I'm just making it worse than it is.'

I grab the freshly polished wineglass and hold it out to him expectantly. He spins around to pull a bottle out of the refrigerator, opens it with a pop, and fills my glass. The wine is cloudy like unfiltered apple juice and silky smooth as it slides gently down my throat.

'It's a new orange wine that I had at a restaurant in France. I thought you'd love it!'

My thoughts wander back to the party at the Berlinale film festival where I met him two years ago. He was standing in the buffet line joking about the Thai curry, which was far too mild. When he told me where he worked, I knew it immediately; I had been to Neue Heimat a number of times and had put it on my list of places that I wanted to write about. (*'A bar where you can easily talk to strangers about the most recent Netflix series while sipping excellent whisky from Japan.'*) I didn't tell him that, of course, playing it cool as he told me he was a fan of my column.

He asked if I was at the party alone, and when I said yes, he blurted out, 'Fantastic! Me too!' even though two of his friends were standing in the corner. He was wearing a white T-shirt that revealed a coat-of-arms tattoo on his bicep when the sleeve slid up. I found him to be arrestingly free-spirited and not nearly as predictable as those other men who so annoyed me with their thoughts and observations about the beauty of Asia. When my wineglass slipped out of my hand at the dessert table, annihilating a dozen servings of mousse, he pulled me aside, laughing, and stopped me from immediately tracking down a waiter to apologise profusely for my mishap (I could hear my mother in my head: *Why do you always have to ruin everything!*). We spent the evening on a small balcony on the upper floor joking about the people below us. He told me about his dream of opening his own restaurant and, over the course of six hours, didn't ask me once where I was from. That's why I liked him.

*

When we leave Neue Heimat, the moon is already high in the sky and the air so dry and cold that I immediately start coughing. Wrapped in puffy down jackets, we look like giant quilted beetles as we trudge along the Landwehr Canal. Three guys in gold chains and tracksuit bottoms are sat on benches shivering, and they call over to us, but immediately turn away when Dorian shakes his head. He only smokes weed he grows himself and treats with a special fertiliser.

As we walk through the night, we each try to outdo the other's complaints about the Berlin winter. I insist that my DNA isn't made for this climate, and he surprises me by saying that he would much rather be living in Asia than here.

'I'm serious,' he says.

He stops, pulls back his hood and takes my hand in his, triggering an unexpected thought: Is he about to propose to me?

Even though I've always thought I don't care about marriage, excitement rushes through my veins. I've been both expecting this moment and not expecting it. I'm afraid of what I might answer with, yet I long to be asked. My throat begins tickling and I cough, loudly and violently.

'Scuse me, what?'

He laughs.

'I've spent a lot of time over the last few weeks thinking about the future,' he begins. 'I know that's a big word, but when you're standing way up high on a mountaintop, your life suddenly looks so small. Time feels so different. I'm almost forty. I can't keep going on like this forever. It's great to enjoy life and to have a job that's pretty much a hobby. But I have to do something else. Something bigger. It's time.'

I'm waiting for him to finally get to the point, but I'm also trying not to be impatient or unromantic.

'And what were you thinking about doing?'

His voice grows deeper.

'It might sound crazy, but I'm thinking of moving to Tokyo for a while.'

'To *Tokyo*?'

Surprised by the intensity of my own disappointment, I gasp for breath. How did I arrive at the ridiculous idea that he was about to propose? And how did he arrive at the ridiculous idea that he could live in Tokyo?

'You can't speak any Japanese! You've never even been there before!'

'But it's the culinary capital of the world!'

'So what?!'

If Dorian wants to move to Tokyo, that means he wants to leave Berlin. And if he wants to leave Berlin, that means he doesn't care about leaving me behind. Or am I missing something?

'How do you think that's going to work?' I ask, though in reality, of course, I mean: how do you think that's going to work *with us*?

'David wants to open a restaurant there and is looking for a partner. He has already started talking to an investor, some scion from the Toyota family, a young guy, but super-rich. It would be a once-in-a-lifetime opportunity!'

Of course. He's hanging onto David's coat-tails. David, who does all the work, just like I do all the cleaning and the shopping, and book all of our dinners out and joint trips, so that Dorian can skip lightly through life, pursuing his dreams.

'Would you be against it?' he asks.

I lift my shoulders as if I were some kind of wind-up doll. The fact that he even has to ask the question tells me everything.

'If it's important to you, I'm not going to stand in your way,' I reply, hurt.

'Cool,' he sighs with relief. 'I was really hoping you'd support me.'

He steps closer, takes me into his arms, and presses his cheek to mine. It's cold, then soft. I can feel his warmth in the frigid air.

'Maybe you could take some time off and come visit me for a couple of months, hmm?'

'We'll see,' I say coolly.

He now realises that something's not quite right and kisses me softly on the lips. He speaks quietly into my ear.

'I'm going to miss you a lot, Kim! But I'll only go for a year, two at the most, and then I'll come back. You know that I've always dreamt of doing something like this!'

We start walking again and he keeps talking about the Toyota heir and the timeline, which David has already put together, and neighbourhoods they might want to live in. About the many Michelin-starred restaurants in the city and real wasabi, about Japanese toilets and the correct way to board a Shinkansen. He sounds like a travel guide, which heightens my sense of annoyance.

He keeps talking and I continue to say nothing. Either he's intentionally ignoring my disappointment, or he hasn't noticed how intense it is, which is just as bad. During the entire walk to Neukölln, I wait to see if he'll interrupt his flood of words to ask the question I want to hear. But when we finally find ourselves standing in front of our door, I know that it's not going to come.

*

It's the middle of the night and I'm suddenly wide awake. Light from the city is filtering in through the white fabric of the window blinds, floating through the room. I hear a hammering, and quickly realise it's my heart. Despite the cold, I'm sweating as if I've just finished running a marathon. My clock reads 4.37 am; beside me, Dorian's body rises and falls in peaceful rhythm. As usual after there is tension between us, we smoked weed until we no longer cared and fell into bed for a bit of make-up sex. Now I feel the darkness engulfing me, like somebody has switched off the light inside me.

I slide out of bed and shuffle into the kitchen. Even though my expectations are low when I open the fridge, I'm still disappointed: a bottle of Sancerre, a half-dozen eggs, a yellowing head of broccoli. Nothing that I can just stuff into my mouth.

I pull up a kitchen chair and climb onto it. My hand starts feeling around the top shelf of the cabinet, where I keep the unhealthy stuff. Plastic rustles when I find the instant noodles, the salty, shrimp-flavoured kind. I rip open the silver foil and pull out the light-coloured noodle brick. I should put the kettle on to make soup, but boiling water is a lot of work when it's half past four in the morning and all you're really trying to do is keep the darkness at bay.

I grab my phone.

Earlier that evening, when I was still drinking my orange wine in Neue Heimat, my father had sent me a photo on WhatsApp. It showed a gaunt woman with wiry curls, the colour of her áo dài matching the greyish white of her hair. Wrinkles criss-crossed her face like rivulets, her cheeks daubed with rouge. Her head was resting on a shimmering white pillow, exuding the universal look of the recently deceased: peaceful and waxen, as though they are just beginning to float away.

'She was very beautiful as a young woman,' my father had written, as sentimental as he gets.

I bite into the dry block of noodles and wash it down with the Sancerre. I can feel the hard noodles growing softer, limper on my tongue before melting away. My mouth is filled with a tangy blob that doesn't taste much like anything, but in the darkness of night, my expectations are modest. I shuffle over to the leather couch in the living room and slouch into a lying position so the night can consume me.

'What about the funeral?' I had written back to my father. 'Don't you want to fly over?'

Since my talk with Dorian, I had wondered if perhaps my father was more crushed by his mother's death than he was letting on. He'd been absent-minded for several days, constantly writing back and forth with Uncle Sơn.

'I have to give the keynote at a conference next week,' he replied. 'But I've sent money.'

'Okay.'

'The funeral will be pretty big, and all the siblings will be there except me. I have asked Sơn to film everything and send it to me. They find it extremely regrettable that we can't be there.'

We? I wondered, the fear of getting dragged into family drama rising within me.

'Well, what if you and Mom go to California next summer?' I suggested. 'You could go there on vacation!'

'I don't think she wants to.'

He didn't write anything for a bit, then sent another message — a question I didn't want to be asked, not from him at least.

'Do *you* want to go to California?'

'Me? Why would I want to go?'

'If you agree, it will be easier for me to convince your mother. You know how she is. We could visit our relatives together. They've been asking about you.'

I knew he was right. If I came along, she would too. And if she came along, it wouldn't be so hard for him. Still, I didn't answer. I wanted to believe that our family was just like any other; a family where everyone took care of their own affairs and where children in their thirties were seen as adults.

Ping. A new message from my father appears on my phone in the darkness. Apparently, he can't sleep either.

'It would mean a lot to the relatives if you came. They're going through a tough time. Maybe you could convince Lan and Tuấn to come as well.'

Now that we have passed the age of threats and punishments,

my father often resorts to appealing to family loyalty instead. And as much as I don't like to admit it, I'm rather susceptible to such manoeuvres. I am the oldest child after all.

'It would mean a lot, Kiều! ☺ ☺ ☺'

I look at his message, tense and bewildered. I have never seen my father use smileys before.

THE STORY OF MY FATHER (PART I)
MINH

Saigon, 1968

On his seventeenth birthday, Minh was given a T-shirt emblazoned with a big yellow smiley, the phrase *Don't worry, be happy* written beneath it. One of his mother's regular American customers had brought it to the tailor's, and Minh had proudly accepted the gift and immediately put it on. He sat in a white plastic chair like a king on his throne, wearing the T-shirt, slightly disappointed that it was too dark for the others in the garden café to see him well.

The café was located on a peninsula wrapped by the Saigon River in an affectionate embrace. Tall palm trees and bamboo stalks lined the path to the riverbank, the wind rustling in their leaves. The deep blue of the evening was illuminated only by a few lanterns, and Minh could hear crickets chirping and frogs croaking, almost like he wasn't in the city at all. His mother was sitting on his left, while Sơn was playing cards with the twins on his right.

A man with a thick moustache and yellow shorts approached

them, pushing a food cart. On the left side of the cart was a large pot of soup, across from a translucent container packed with meatballs. He was selling hủ tiếu bò viên, a noodle-meatball soup, and when he heard it was Minh's birthday, he let out a gleeful 'Oho!'

He fished three dice out of his pocket and held them in front of Minh's little face, which was dominated by the big glasses he wore.

'Do you like games?'

Minh nodded.

'Then let's play.'

The rules were easy and difficult at the same time. Each player alternated rolling the three dice all at once. If there were doubles, the dice in question were cast aside and the eyes of the third were counted as the score; no doubles meant a score of zero. Totals would be compared after each round. In the first round, Minh could win two meatballs, four in the next, eight in the one after that, and so on, but if he did not win a round then all the meatballs he had previously accumulated would be lost.

'Got it?' the man asked.

Minh immediately realised he had nothing to lose. Either he would win some free meatballs, or he would pay for them like everyone else. It was an opportunity he couldn't refuse.

The man pulled up a red plastic stool to sit on and placed another between them as a table.

Minh rolled first: four, four, three.

The man rolled: five, two, five.

Two meatballs were his.

He also won the second round. His younger siblings, who had lined up in a semicircle behind him, cheered him on like it was a football tournament. The man spread his legs, leaning all the way forward for each roll, his tongue peeking out of the corner of his mouth. Minh was exhilarated, but extremely focused. Four meatballs became eight. Then sixteen. The T-shirt with the smiley was apparently a good-luck charm.

'One last round,' he shouted.

He gently jiggled the dice in his open hand, giving them just the slightest nudge as they rolled onto the table. His siblings gasped.

Two, two, one.

If the man rolled doubles now, Minh would lose. He arched his back and took shallow breaths. The dice fell onto the table with a clatter.

Six, five, four.

Minh jumped up as if he had just scored the winning goal in a championship match, his siblings dancing around him. He threw his arms into the air.

'Thirty-two meatballs! Unbelievable!'

The man gave him a good-natured pat on the back. Grabbing a thick wire from the side of the cart, he opened the door of the see-through box. He threaded meatball after meatball onto the wire, so many that he had to twist the wire into a big coil. When he was finished, the cart was empty, save for four balls. Minh held the coil of meatballs above his head like a trophy.

He was seventeen years old and filled with the sense that whatever he wanted in life, he would get.

Minh may have still had the smooth, innocent face of a child, but he was bursting with the vigorous self-confidence of a young man. His slender body had become lean and defined through years of taekwondo. He wore his bushy hair parted to one side and needed thick glasses to correct his severe short-sightedness.

Not long ago, he had seen the great French philosopher Jean-Paul Sartre on television wearing black horn-rimmed glasses, so he had bought a pair for himself. At school, he could often be seen rushing through the halls with a book in his hand, his soft face brimming with importance because he was again on his way to meet his older friends to discuss French existentialism in the café while smoking forbidden cigarettes. He loved debating back and forth with them, seeing himself as a man of thought and discussion.

He was the eldest son in a family of seven from Saigon, who had achieved a decent level of prosperity with their tailor's shop. Their close ties with an influential businessman, who often commissioned Western-style suits, had helped the family secure a house in the centre of town. It was on an avenue lined with lush tamarind trees that was once called Rue Catinat. After the victory over the French colonisers, it had been renamed Đường Tự Do, Liberty Street.

With its white French façade and pale-green shutters, the building blended in seamlessly with the surrounding neighbourhood and its elegant stores, restaurants, and hotels. At street level, the tailor's beckoned with suits and áo dài draped on mannequins, perfectly tailored garments made of the finest silk: collars so erect that they elongated the neck; dress slits high, and so tight that every woman appeared svelte and graceful; trousers so wide that they softly fluttered around the legs. Behind the store was the kitchen, and above it the living room with its wide balcony. One floor above that, Linh and Sơn shared the larger of two rooms because, at thirteen and seven respectively, they were the second and third oldest. The twins, Hồng and Hùng, who were only five, slept in the smaller room. On the top floor, Minh's room was on the left, his parents' on the right.

Being addressed as 'older brother', anh, by his four siblings gave

Minh an early self-confidence that the others didn't possess. He was the only one in the family to receive pocket money. He set the rules for his siblings and reached for the cane when they disobeyed. He was also allowed to use his father's moped while he was away in central Vietnam, fighting in the war as a colonel in the South Vietnamese army.

*

A few weeks after his seventeenth birthday, at the dawn of the Year of the Monkey, Minh was jolted from his sleep in the middle of the night by a loud boom. Still in a daze, he opened his eyes. It was the first day of the Tết New Year celebrations and he had spent the evening on the balcony with his brothers and sisters looking out at the bustling street, lavishly decorated for the festivities. Mr Giang from next door had given them a string of Chinese firecrackers and had stood next to his father laughing, both men overjoyed that they had been granted leave and were able to spend the holidays at home.

Minh wondered drowsily what was happening outside. Were the fireworks still going?

He rolled onto his side and pulled the pillow over his head; the fan whirred softly beside his bed, blowing cool air through the blue mosquito net. He slipped back into sleep, but not for long.

Boom! There it was again, louder and more menacing than before. A rumbling sound like heavy thunder, only shorter and deeper.

He bolted upright.

His father burst into Minh's room, naked to the waist, clutching a pistol in his right hand.

'There's something going on out there. Quick!'

Minh jumped up, grabbed his glasses, and ran downstairs to gather his brothers and sisters. They rushed into the living room and stood by their mother, who was pressed up against the balcony door.

Minh saw spotlights slicing through the night sky. In the distance, he heard a rapid rattling sound, a bit like the string of firecrackers from earlier, except that it was intermittent — and interspersed with dull roars, sometimes from the north, sometimes from the west.

Bombs? Here in Saigon?

'Turn on the radio,' his mother whispered. Minh ran over to the sideboard and turned up the volume. Strangely, the Vietnamese station was playing nothing but Beatles songs — but the man presenting the news on Voice of America sounded agitated.

'... *a surprise offensive in a number of cities. In Saigon, Viet Cong fighters have attacked the airport and infiltrated the American Embassy, where there are reports shots have been fired. The offices of Radio Saigon have been occupied. The communists tried to play a recording of the North Vietnamese President Ho Chi Minh, which an employee of the station was fortunately able to prevent. Some fighters have advanced to the Presidential Palace ...*'

'How dare they attack during the holidays!' Minh's father railed. 'A three-day ceasefire, that was the deal! Bloody barbarians!'

Adrenaline coursed through Minh's veins. Even though it was pitch black outside, he was wide awake. The idea that they were surrounded by danger made him jittery with fear, but he was also brimming with curiosity. He had never seen a communist before, and wondered if these people really were as savage and cruel as his mother said.

He pushed his siblings out of the way to stand next to his mother and opened the balcony door a crack, allowing the cool night air to rush in. The whispering of his siblings only increased his resolve, and he took a step out onto the balcony. Then another, and another until he reached the balustrade and could get a better view of the street. It was littered with the shreds of red paper from the spent firecrackers, but was otherwise completely empty. The black power cables that hung between the tall masts were swinging gently. Far off in the distance, a cloud of grey smoke rose from the sea of buildings.

'There's no one here,' he said, his voice betraying his mild disappointment. 'Everything is quiet. You can go back to bed.'

*

After his siblings returned to their rooms, his father came out onto the balcony and stood behind Minh, lighting a cigarette. Since his promotion to colonel last year, he seemed to have aged beyond his years. Although he was only forty, deep wrinkles criss-crossed his forehead and his hair had begun going grey. He had lost weight, and his high cheekbones only served to accentuate his slenderness.

Minh didn't know what exactly his father was doing in central Vietnam. His parents had never said it in so many words, but he understood that the war wasn't to be mentioned. It was bad enough that the communists gave them no peace. Talking about them wouldn't change anything.

His father's intermittent, brief, and difficult-to-decipher letters had made him none the wiser. The two underlying messages were always the same: first, the enemy was devious but inferior. And second, the older children were not to neglect their homework just because there was fighting in uncivilised parts of the country.

His father's voice jolted Minh from his thoughts.

'So, how are your brothers and sisters doing?'

He spoke as casually as if he were inquiring about last week's weather. Whenever he was home on leave, Minh's father would ask him about his younger siblings. Minh was, after all, the man of the house in his father's absence.

'Everything's just fine — they listen when you tell them something,' Minh replied. 'I've taught Linh to read a bit, and Sơn's marks have improved some.'

'And what about your own marks? Will you do well in the baccalaureate? You know your mother and I are counting on you!'

Minh dreaded this question. Even though he supervised his siblings with a certain zeal, he couldn't stand talking about his own academic performance. He was good in school, but not great — blessed with talent, but also with arrogance. He found memorising the dates of Vietnamese dynasties or English sayings by heart trivial. Yes, there certainly were better, more dedicated students than him at the prestigious French lycée he attended. But he also didn't want to upset his father by telling him this.

'You don't have to worry about me. Final exams are in six months, so I still have plenty of time to study.'

'Well, that's fine then. You see, I have a plan for you after you graduate.'

His father blew smoke into the night air, and Minh longingly watched it dissipate. The conversation was making him nervous, and he would have given anything for a cigarette.

'I met a doctor up there,' his father said. 'He's very impressive — a hard-working, respected man.'

'A doctor?'

Minh thought back to when he was five years old and had had to fetch a doctor because Linh had been suffering from severe febrile seizures for days. The man had given her an injection and said that it was very potent new drug from China. It made her fever and the seizures disappear — but also her ability to hear. She was only one year old at the time, so she never learned to speak. And because she couldn't talk, she would never go to school and never find work.

Even today, twelve years later, Minh would shudder when he pictured the man drawing his syringe and injecting it into his sister's soft thigh.

'He's a surgeon, to be precise,' his father continued. 'He recommends that you study medicine and eventually open your own clinic. It's not easy, but if you were successful, the whole family would benefit. Your brothers and sisters could be assistant doctors, Linh could become a nurse — you don't have to be able to talk to care for people. It would be perfect, don't you think?'

He looked at his eldest son expectantly.

'Our family has had some bad experiences with doctors,' Minh reminded him.

'He was a black sheep! Nothing like Professor Xanh! It is a *very* good job, with *excellent* prospects. Just think about it. Whether there's war or peace, people always get sick!'

'I'm not sure that's what I'm really interested in,' Minh replied cautiously. He knew he shouldn't contradict his father, but he had to try. There wasn't a single vocation he despised more than the medical profession. He saw its practitioners as charlatans who made false promises to people in distress to bilk them out of their money.

Did his father really want him to become one of them? And to spend his life in a place that reeked of disinfectant and disease? The mere thought of it gave him the creeps.

'What kind of attitude is that, Minh?' His father's voice grew deeper and more threatening. 'You should be grateful that we're sending you to medical school. Don't forget, this isn't just about you. At least one of you five *is* going to be a doctor. You're the eldest son, so it's up to you to set a good example!'

*

After the communist fighters in Saigon had been killed, their own dead buried, and the rubble cleared away, peace once again returned to the city. The newspapers described the Tết Offensive as a heavy defeat for the enemy. In Saigon, they said, the communists had suffered far greater losses than the South Vietnamese and Americans combined. In Huế, the Viet Cong had slaughtered thousands, revealing their true, murderous colours. Now the fighting was over, the South Vietnamese and American soldiers strutted confidently through the streets in their green uniforms, assuring the shocked population that they had pushed the rebels back to the North.

Minh wasn't particularly interested in these developments. He only paid fleeting attention to who was fighting against whom and where. His father's plans weighed heavily on him. He knew there was no way out, but that made him all the more unconvinced. Still, as long as he passed his final exams and was admitted to university, he wouldn't be drafted into the army. That was the main thing.

A short time later, Mr Bảy, the businessman with the penchant for Western suits, approached his mother: might she be interested in letting a room to an American? The man in question was a guard at the American Embassy and had been living there. But now he had to move out because the building, which had been attacked, was to be renovated. He was willing to pay a decent amount and had only one condition: he needed a refrigerator. Business-minded as she was, his mother offered up Minh's room immediately. It was the largest in the house, so it could command the highest rent.

The American showed up three days later. Minh had pictured him resembling the fair-skinned, blond actors he knew from the movies. But to his surprise, the man was black. He stood in front of the tailor's, a cigarette in one hand and a dark-green canvas duffel bag in the other. He looked to be about twenty and towered over Minh, stocky yet muscular and athletic. His hair was closely cropped and his eyes alert, accentuated by arched brows. Two chains protruded from his sleeveless jungle-green shirt, a worn dog tag hanging from one and a crucifix from the other.

Minh's mother, clutching a wad of dollar bills, beckoned to her son. She had curled her hair and put on the light-green silk blouse that went so well with her jade earrings. 'We had a bit of bad luck,' she said. 'White Americans are strange enough, how are you supposed to trust the black ones? But money is money, I guess.'

Minh wasn't sure whether it was because of the rent payments that would now be coming in or the shock of the Tết Offensive, but his mother had started making her own plans for his future. She had opened an account at the French bank in District 1 to deposit money for his studies. Instead of staying in Vietnam, he was to head to a university overseas, where he would be safe if the South Vietnamese government decided to draft students into the army.

Minh liked the idea. The thought of leaving the war behind and seeing the world — he was thinking of beautiful Paris or, if that didn't pan out, perhaps some high-rise city in America — made the prospect of his tedious medical studies almost bearable. He flashed the American a friendly smile.

'Chào em,' the soldier said in greeting.

'You speak the language?' Minh replied in Vietnamese.

'Hell no!' the American laughed. 'All I can say is "Hello" and "How much is it?" My name is John. Great to meet you!'

Minh shook his hand. What difference did it make if he was black or white? At least he had taken the trouble to learn two sentences in Vietnamese. That was more than most.

He led John through the shop's rear exit into the kitchen and, from there, up the stone staircase. Behind him, he could hear the American cursing as he kept bumping into the walls with his bulk. The stomping of his boots thundered through the entire house.

They reached Minh's old room, with its bright-green walls and black-and-white patterned tiles. He was filled with a certain remorse: it was a lot bigger than the windowless cubby-hole he would be sharing with Sơn from now on, with Linh having moved in with the twins.

On the wall was the Beatles poster he was so proud of, and lining the shelves were the French novels from Book Street that he had spent so much money on — volumes like *La Peste*, *L'Étranger*, and *Le Petit Prince*. Next to the bed was the small refrigerator he had lugged up the two flights of stairs the day before and astutely stocked with a beverage that was a favourite among both Vietnamese and American men.

'Beer?' He opened the fridge door.

'Absolutely!' John grabbed a can and took a long swig. 'What about you?'

Minh hesitated. On the one hand, he would have loved a beer. On the other, he was confident his mother would be along shortly to make sure everything was alright.

He shook his head.

John heaved his duffel bag onto the bed, unlaced his boots, and began unpacking his things. Everything that he pulled out of the duffel — the jeans, the sneakers, the black notebook — looked expensive to Minh.

'Where are you from?' Minh asked in English, realising how different it felt. In Vietnamese, there is a distinction between older and younger, so he would have addressed John as 'elder brother'. The English 'you', on the other hand, put everyone on the same level, something Minh found a bit alienating, but also quite pleasant.

'I'm from California,' John replied. 'I wanted to go to college on a basketball scholarship, but I was too short. So here I am.'

John laughed. He was quite different from the Vietnamese men Minh knew. More laid-back.

'What's it like in California?' Minh asked, resisting the urge to add: *Like in the movies?*

'Nice. Beautiful beaches, pretty girls, the weather is about the same as here. But no monsoons.'

'And what do you think of Vietnam?'

'You want the truth? I think it sucks. Saigon's okay, but for the guys going into the jungle, it's hell. At first, they told us we were here to defend freedom. But honestly, they have no idea what's going on here! I lost two buddies when they attacked the embassy. The Viet Cong fighters died like flies, but they don't care. They just send a thousand more to their deaths, and then another thousand! I don't know what we're doing here, but it doesn't have much to do with freedom!'

He shook his head. His nose was shiny. Everything he said sounded quite a bit different from what the Vietnamese papers were writing. Minh drew closer.

'What about you?' John asked. 'Do you want to fight too?'

Minh blushed. 'Actually, I'd rather go to university.'

'Smart boy!'

John lit a cigarette, inhaling deeply. But he didn't blow the smoke out the way Minh did when he smoked with his friends as they dabbled in philosophy. Instead, John formed his lips into an 'O', grey rings of smoke rolling out from his lips. *Pfff. Pfff. Pfff.*

He held out the pack. Real Pall Malls, from America. Minh pulled one out.

They chatted about the differences between Western and Vietnamese women, with the conversation consisting largely of John talking and Minh nodding every now and then, as if he knew what the American was talking about. Apart from the time he had gone on a walk with one of Linh's deaf friends, his experience was limited. He was shocked when John told him about the Vietnamese women in certain bars who prowl around like cats, purring innuendos so explicit that Minh didn't even dare translate them in his own head.

'Let me show you something.'

John pulled a notebook out from among his things and opened it. He said he'd been keeping a diary since he arrived in Vietnam so that he wouldn't forget any of the unbelievable things he had experienced here. A Polaroid fell out from between the pages. It had been taken on the rooftop terrace of an expensive hotel and showed John dancing with a Vietnamese woman in a long red dress. Her hair cascaded down her back in waves, and her face was carefully made up. She was far more elegant and modern than the Vietnamese women Minh secretly gazed at on the street. She seemed unattainable, a woman for foreigners.

'Isn't she stunning? The best singer I've ever met. I was madly in love with her, but she never let on what she was thinking. Maybe she just wanted me for my money. Not that I have that much, but here in Vietnam, even a hundred dollars makes you a king. I spent two weeks looking for her after she stopped answering my calls, asking about her at every bar. At one point, I found a friend of hers. "Where's Kim?" I asked. And you know what her friend told me?'

He laid the photo between the pages and closed the notebook.

'It turns out she wasn't actually called Kim! The woman I was so in love with hadn't even told me her real name!'

The next day, Minh headed over to Book Street and bought himself a black notebook of his own, though the pages were thinner than the ones in John's diary. He could already see them filling up with the outline of a novel beginning in Saigon and ending in Paris.

But time passed so quickly that he rarely found the time to write in it, and sometimes entire weeks would pass between his entries. He had to study for his final exams — this time, he was really trying his best — and he was attending language courses for French and English in the evenings. Plus, he wanted to spend a bit of time with his friends, who regarded his approaching departure with a mixture of pride and envy. None of them had the money or the connections to go abroad. Some had even been drafted into the army already.

He wrote in his journal:

> I'm not afraid of travelling overseas, but these final days at home feel like when, the moment before death, you see your life flash before your eyes and realise how much you love it. Yesterday I went to Airplane Phở with Sơn and bought him an XL bowl. The fan was broken, of course, and homeless children kept coming in. But wasn't the broth amazing? Had I ever tasted such tender meat? I even enjoy going to the market with Mother now. The woman who cackles as loudly as the chickens she sells, the man who keeps an eye on my Honda — none of them will ever leave the country or see the wealthy West. When I come back one day, they will still be standing at their market stalls or watching over the mopeds of shoppers. How will I see them then? Will I still love Vietnam as much as I do now, on the eve of my departure?

*

On his final day at home, he packed his suitcase as carefully as if it were his last trip, not his first. With the help of his mother, he had chosen a brown model with golden clasps from the Chinese quarter of Cholon. He carefully laid his light-coloured summer suit on top of his darker winter suit, stacking six white shirts next to them along with two pairs of plaid pyjamas.

His mother's favourite tailor had spent three weeks on his outfits, and another week on the dark-blue winter coat, made of the heaviest material they could find at Bến Thành Market. He packed the dried meat and homemade rice cakes into plastic bags, placing two dictionaries next to the food. One was Vietnamese–English and the other English–German. Learning the language like that was a bit cumbersome, but he had been unable to find a Vietnamese–German dictionary in all of Saigon.

That he was heading to Germany and not to France or America was due to his marks. As the official at the Study Abroad Office had told him, those spots were particularly sought after and only given to graduates with better academic performances than Minh's. 'I can offer you Germany instead,' the official had said. 'You don't even have to pass a language test before you arrive.'

Minh had immediately accepted. He preferred this third-best option over no option at all. He couldn't imagine anything worse than admitting to himself and everyone else that his plans to study overseas had failed before they had even begun. He didn't know much about the country, but figured it couldn't be all that bad. After all, Einstein had come from Germany, hadn't he? Plus, he seemed to recall that Germany wasn't too far from France. What difference did it make if he was in this part of Europe or that part?

His brother Sơn walked into the room and asked if he needed any help packing. He was wearing his blue-and-white school uniform and had just been to the barber, his bangs falling diagonally above his round eyes. His childish voice was quivering.

'Do you think you'll see snow in Germany?'

'Sure! It's extremely cold in winter there, so it'll probably snow.'

'Do you think you could send me some?'

Minh laughed.

'I don't think it's quite that easy.'

'Because it's so expensive to send packages to Vietnam?'

'Because the snow would melt on the way here.'

'Really? Snow melts?'

Sơn sat down on the bed and began thinking out loud about what Minh could send him from Germany instead. Perhaps sweets. Or a toy. Although he couldn't really grasp the true implications of Minh's move, he understood with his seven years that Minh was going abroad to bring the family honour and wealth. Over the past several weeks, he had told his entire school that his brother was going to get on a real airplane and travel to Europe — and happily received all the congratulations and compliments as though they were meant for him.

Minh laid the last items into the suitcase, snapped it shut, and slid his feet into his new leather shoes. He was wearing his best clothes for the day, a black suit with a white shirt. His passport was in his jacket pocket, the plane ticket tucked away in his pants pocket. He almost felt like he was starting a new job, a managerial position.

He took a deep breath, lifted his brown suitcase, and made his way down to the living room where the others were waiting. His glance fell on a stack of books that he had grabbed out of what was now John's room yesterday. His Camus, his Sartre, his most valuable possessions. He didn't, of course, want to move to Europe without his European books, but his suitcase was already full of suits and rice cakes.

His mother called up to him that his taxi to the airport would be arriving any minute.

'Sơn, I need you to help me!'

His brother giggled.

'You want me to come with you so you're not so lonely?'

'Dream on! You need to stay here and keep an eye on something for me. Something important!'

He looked around their small room and picked up the box his new shoes had come in. It was made of black cardboard and was just big enough for his books. He quickly lined them up in the box, their spines facing upwards, and then, since there was still a bit of room, he hesitantly set his journal in the box as well. He was pretty sure nobody would read it. He put the top on the box, taped it shut, and wrote his name on it with a black felt-tip pen: MINH.

'Can you hide this box for me? In a place where no one will find it? When I return, I want it back.'

'Why don't you just leave it in John's room?'

'Because I don't want him or anyone else snooping through my stuff. Will you do this for me? You can have my T-shirt with the smiley on it!'

Sơn grabbed the shoebox, wrapping both his arms around it. With a serious expression on his face, he assured Minh that he could count on him. He then bent down and shoved the box under his bed. He looked up at his brother. 'Every night,' he said solemnly, 'I will guard your books like a dog.'

In the living room, his siblings were standing with John as if they were guests at a wedding, looking festive in their best clothing and full of excitement for the happy occasion. His father, who was on leave to see Minh off, made a brief speech, which Minh would primarily remember for the word 'proud'. To his surprise, his father gave him a heavy black SLR camera. The right side of it was dented and the colour had been scraped off on the corners, but Minh could tell that it was a premium model. He had seen it in the hands of war photographers.

'You'll need this camera in Germany,' his father said as he handed it over. 'Take lots of pictures and send them to us!'

Minh thanked him sheepishly and smiled at his siblings. Out of habit, he admonished them one last time to pay attention in school, but then, a sudden feeling of relief came over him. On the one hand, he was embarking on this journey on behalf of his family, but on the other, he felt liberated from all the duties that weighed on his shoulders as the eldest son. In Germany, he would live in student accommodation with others his age — with nobody around to watch his every move, criticise him, or ask him for help with homework. On his own for the first time in his life. This wasn't just the start of his university studies. He would be entering a new world, a world that was foreign, modern, and peaceful.

As he was saying goodbye, John handed him a magazine with an orange border. *Der Spiegel*, it read in white letters, with an image from Vietnam on the cover. 'Friends of mine at the German Embassy got it for me,' John said. 'You can read it on the plane! If you can't understand the words, you can look at the pictures.'

Minh watched as his siblings waved goodbye and saw the sad look on John's face as the taxi left Liberty Street and headed off to the airport. His parents, wearing their finest clothes, were sitting in the back seat holding hands. Rarely had his mother looked so beautiful. Her curled hair was pinned to one side, and she was wearing a red áo dài with golden embroidery.

He turned around in the passenger seat and pointed his camera at them, smiling with a mixture of happiness and sorrow. *Click*, went the shutter, and then a second time. *Click*.

If I go now, he found himself wondering, when will I ever come back?

The sun had already begun its evening disappearing act as he gazed at the city passing by outside the window. He would miss the hustle and bustle so much, the piquant aromas of street-food stands and the feverish bargaining of vendors, the incessant honking of mopeds and the chattering of pedestrians. The taxi wound its way through the throng, crossed the broad, filthy canal, and finally approached the no man's land in front of the terminal.

One day, he would return to this airport, but he would no longer be Minh, the schoolboy, but Minh, the doctor. He could feel his heart beating in his chest.

When he bid farewell to his parents at the gate, his mother's eyes were gleaming with pride and sadness. He hugged her briefly as his father patted him on the back. Because they were unable to find words to express their emotions, they simply stood in silence. As he turned to go, he heard his mother calling out hesitantly: 'Don't forget where you came from!' He didn't look back.

Minh had four lay-overs and twenty-five hours of travel ahead of him: Bangkok, Karachi, Paris, Munich. He had never left his country before, but he wasn't afraid, just impatient. He climbed the steps to the plane quickly, ticket in his right hand and *Der Spiegel* in his left.

KIỀU

The night before our flight to California, I see myself descending steep, narrow stairs from a plane. The grey concrete of the tarmac below me contrasts sharply with the turquoise of the sea, whose waves crash against the edge of the runway. I am enveloped in a salty breeze; the sun hovering high overhead warms the air. I reach the bottom of the staircase and step onto American soil. A gleaming black limousine is waiting for me, a car just like the ones I see on television when the American president arrives for a visit. The door opens, revealing one leg and then another. A man with black hair climbs out of the car, his back slightly rounded and his face half-hidden behind a cowboy hat. He sweeps it from his head with his right hand.

'*Chào chú Sơn.*'

The greeting is one of the simple Vietnamese phrases that I can still remember. I try to pronounce it, but the words refuse to come out, instead echoing around inside my head.

I try again, in a futile attempt to ask how he is doing.

'*Chú Sơn có khỏe không?*'

Again, I hear my voice loud and clear in my inner ear, but Uncle Sơn remains unmoved.

I open my mouth wide and start shouting, the same phrases over and over, but it's as if I have been muted. My uncle is standing right in front of me, but my words aren't reaching him. Something is wrong with my mouth — maybe it has sealed shut or disappeared completely. I grab my face in a panic, clutching my lips and pulling them apart, knuckles striking hard against my teeth.

I bite down.

The pain catapults me out of sleep and I jolt upright. My eyes search through the shadows in the room, and I locate the familiar silhouette of Dorian sleeping on his right side, his back to me, the cover gently rising and falling to the rhythm of his breathing. I groggily sit up and switch on the small lamp on my bedside table. It's 2.42 am.

I have to get up in three hours to catch my flight. I wipe the hair from my forehead with my right hand but stop suddenly, gazing at a perfect impression — red and pushed into the skin on the back of my hand — of my front teeth.

*

Despite its charmless architecture, a remnant of the bygone West Germany — the octagonal control tower, the light-coloured linoleum floors, and the black-and-yellow information boards — Tegel Airport exudes the promise of liberating the people of Berlin from their grey day-to-day lives. The departure lounge is bustling with activity, but I'm so tired that my brain has become cotton gauze. The other travellers, with their bright clothing and unbridled anticipation, are nothing but heavily pixelated stripes to me. My arms, dragging along one white and one blue suitcase, are growing weak with effort. A vague sense of envy wells up inside me: while everyone else is flying off on holiday, I am heading straight into my nightmare.

'Kiều! We're over here!' My mother's shrill voice rises above the clamour of summer travellers. She, like them, has a breezy sundress on, black with pink roses. Her name means 'flower', so she loves to wear patterns like this.

'Do you have the presents with you?' she asks in lieu of a greeting.

I point to the blue suitcase. 'That one's full of them.'

In preparation for this trip, we had long telephone conversations about the issue of gifts. In Asian culture, handing out presents is as central to family visits as the tree is for Western Christmas. It's a mixture of tradition, joy, and torture. A caring gesture, but also one that shows that you 'made it' abroad. With four uncles and aunts, along with their spouses and children, the presents couldn't be too expensive. But it was still important to bring along quality products from Germany for all.

Initially, my mother had planned on buying jewellery from the shopping channel along with wallets, sunglasses, and bathing suits that she found on sale at the Karstadt department store, as she usually did for visits to her family in Vietnam. But this time I wouldn't let her. I didn't want us to embarrass ourselves by bringing along cheap gifts to America. The discussion ended with me buying 400 euros worth of Nivea anti-ageing day creams, shampoos for men, and serums containing hyaluronic acid. The saleswoman did her best to keep her composure, but I could tell from the expression on her face that my overflowing shopping basket was anything but normal.

My mother furrows her brow at the suitcase. 'You think that's enough?'

I decide not to point out that this custom of distributing presents has something of a colonial aftertaste, and go to stand next to my father. He's wearing the fishing hat I find so embarrassing, and sandals with Velcro straps. In his right hand, he's holding our Lufthansa tickets to Frankfurt, where we will get our connecting flight to Los Angeles. He is humming quietly. When I mention that this obsession over gifts merely serves to show just how unequal our extended family is, with some enjoying the privileges of the West while others are subject to the restraints of the developing world, he holds up his left hand to share another one of his theories.

'The members of a family are like fingers. Some are longer, others are shorter.' He moves his fingers back and forth as if playing an invisible piano. 'Everything has its natural order. Don't you worry about it.'

His hand sinks back to the ribbed surface of his hard-shell suitcase, his fingers drumming on the TSA lock. How different we are. When I think about our relatives, I feel guilt at having grown up knowing only peace and a middle-class life. He, on the other hand, doesn't seem too bothered by the notion that everything should be the same for everybody.

*

As I sit down next to my parents on the plane, I once again pull up Sơn Saigon's Facebook profile. My mental preparations for this trip have so far consisted primarily of denial. At the beginning of the year, in response to my father's polite persistence, we decided to take a family vacation to California, all five of us. However, at Easter my sister sent an email from Munich, where she works as an event manager. Her boss, she wrote, had appointed her the head of a film festival and she wouldn't be able to take any time off over the summer. A few weeks later, my brother called: one of his residency rotations had been cancelled, so he had to drop his summer plans in order to apply to other hospitals. I was the only one without an excuse, so my mother booked three flights to Los Angeles for August. Two weeks of vacation with my parents. Even worse, two weeks of vacation with my parents visiting foreign relatives.

We never actually talked about what we would do in California, nor did we discuss the ominous letter that was included with my grandmother's will. Why was it so important for my father to be there when it was opened? What might my grandmother have written that she couldn't have told the family while she was still alive?

I have since learned that my relatives arrived in America as refugees. But it remains unclear how they got there, and when. My parents have been rather vague on the issue, as though it makes them uncomfortable. Their relationship is such a mystery to me.

I scroll through my Uncle Sơn's timeline to learn a bit more about him. I see beach photos from California, oversaturated images of Vietnamese dishes, and countless dog pictures. Then I see a post I hadn't been expecting.

It's a video of Donald Trump standing on a stage next to Melania and Ivanka, his hand raised in victory. It is from the morning of his election, 9 November 2016 — a day I remember as one of the darkest moments of the past year. But Uncle Sơn shared the video, adding a smiley and the word 'Finally'!

I continue scrolling and find a gushing Breitbart article about a

Trump rally in California, a withering analysis of Hillary Clinton, and a CNN video on which he'd commented 'Fake News'.

My uncle, a Trump fan?

I slump back into my seat as the sign illuminates above me. I have never met a Trump supporter before, nor had I ever intended to. All my friends and colleagues are united in their contempt for the American president, a view they consider to be just as self-evident as their conviction that women should have the same rights as men and that beating children is barbaric. Just as it is a law of nature that the sun rises in the east, it's clear that Trump represents a danger to democracy. But my uncle in America seems to be blind to that fact.

For the hundredth time, I regret ever having agreed to this trip. Why didn't I find an excuse not to go like my brother and sister? Why can I never say no to my parents?

Through the window, I see the grey of the runway racing past before we gently tip backwards and leave the ground behind. My father presses his fingers into his ears, his jaw grinding to relieve the pressure. We rise into the weightless blue of the sky, gliding through clouds that float around us like cotton candy.

A perfect take-off.

'Did you know that your brother likes Donald Trump?' I ask.

No answer.

My father's eyes are closed, his cheeks gently expanding. His nose scrunches up before widening as he exhales. As he drifts into sleep, his snoring rises from our row and seems to fill half of economy class, but nobody seems particularly bothered. Everyone is filled with anticipation about their approaching holidays.

After my mother also falls asleep, I dig a small bag from the pharmacy out of my backpack. While waiting at the gate, I had told my parents that I wanted to pick up a travel guide, then secretly ran to buy a pregnancy test instead. I can't really imagine being pregnant — or, perhaps, I don't *want* to imagine it — but my period is two weeks overdue, and as a grown woman, I ultimately have to face the fact that sex can actually lead to babies.

Bag in hand, I clamber over my parents' seats and walk down the aisle to the restroom, which is so tiny that I can hardly move once I'm inside. I rip open the pink packaging (why do all women's products use this repulsive colour?), pull out a tiny strip that feels not even an inch thick, and then wonder how I'm supposed to pee on it. According to the instructions, you're meant to dip it into a container full of urine. I could, of course, ask a stewardess for a paper cup. But to call from the restroom while holding a pregnancy test? No thanks!

I sit down on the toilet, jam my hand between my legs, and try to concentrate on peeing straight down. No luck, the warm stream dribbles onto my fingers. Outside the door, I hear an agitated man talking to a woman.

'I'm really sorry, but the other toilet is clogged,' she says, probably a stewardess. 'I'm sure that this restroom will be free shortly.'

He then calls out: 'Can you please hurry? I have stomach cramps!'

Great.

I pull the strip back out from between my legs, hold it up to the light, and reflexively begin waving it back and forth. It's supposed to take three minutes before the result shows up. I clean myself up and pull up my sweatpants, but don't flush yet — I don't want to raise any hopes outside the door. When I look at the test again, I see that two stripes have formed in the middle. I grab the instructions and read through them twice.

Positive.

This is one of those moments when reality hits you so hard that you stagger out of your own body and see yourself from a distance.

I watch as I idiotically wave the strip back and forth again and hold it up to the light, willing the second stripe to fade away. For some reason, I had always assumed that unplanned pregnancies only happen to other women, that this kind of a thing would never happen to me. I see myself bury my face in my hands, sink down onto the toilet seat, and pull up my legs so that my feet are resting on the front half of the oval. I wrap my arms around my legs and lay my head on my knees, closing my eyes.

I think back to the time right before New Year's when Dorian and I were walking along the Landwehr Canal, how he took my hands in his and told me about his grandiose Tokyo plans. The disappointment I felt surges through me once again, but this time there is a bitter aftertaste. Dorian is definitely not the kind of man you can imagine having a baby with, not the sort who could deal with all the responsibility that entails. He is full of enthusiasm, but often just floats through life, and there is nothing he hates more than duties and obligations. For my part, I have never wanted to be a mother. Nothing is worse than the assumption that women need to have babies in order to find their purpose. I have never wanted to exchange the life I have for a cliché of a woman's life; I have other goals than merely finding a man to marry me, get me pregnant, and take care of me.

Dorian and I often joked about those in our circle of friends who moved back to their hometowns after having their first child to relive the small suburban lives of their parents. It was definitely not for us, we would tell ourselves as we gazed into each other's eyes over our wineglasses. But we never talked about what our future might actually look like. We were too young and free to spoil things with grown-up problems. We just ignored it, as if tomorrow would never come.

And now, here I am, sitting in an airplane restroom holding a pregnancy test in my hands with two pink stripes on it.

I feel myself growing nauseous, the bread roll I scoffed down on the train to the airport rising in my throat. My saliva grows bitter as I kneel in front of the toilet, eyes closed. Outside, the man with stomach cramps is growing impatient, knocking on the door and demanding to know how much longer I need.

'I'm feeling sick!' he calls out. I would love to jump up and pound on the inside of the door in response, if only I had the strength to do so. But I don't. I listen to my heart hammering in my chest for a couple of seconds before saying quietly to the wall: 'Me too.'

Slowly, I take a deep breath and let it out. The pressure in my stomach begins to subside, and when I blink, I realise how wet and sticky my eyelashes are. Once the saliva in my mouth begins to taste normal again, I get to my feet. The test slips out of my hand and falls into the toilet, floating limply in the pale-yellow liquid. I push the flush button weakly, and with a roar, the strip vanishes into the void.

*

Darkness has already descended upon California by the time we're finally sitting in our rental car and leaving the giant letters L-A-X behind us — almost twenty hours after we started our journey in Berlin. The Chevrolet roars as my father accelerates onto the freeway, moves left into the car-pool lane, and makes a few disparaging remarks about the quality of American cars. 'Los Angeles 18 mi', reads the bright green sign in front of us, but LA isn't our destination.

After half an hour, the navigation system guides us off the highway onto a wide street that, despite being lined with tall palm trees, nevertheless radiates the drabness of a suburb. Low-slung houses with wide garages. Strip mall after strip mall. Gas stations, supermarkets, funeral homes. So, this is Little Saigon. An endless expanse of concrete dotted with palm trees.

When the GPS announces that our destination has been reached, we find ourselves in front of a wide driveway with a neon 'Motel' sign. I can see a fenced-in swimming pool on the left, and on the right, a yellow, two-storey building with brown doors that could easily be mistaken for a prison.

'Is *that* our hotel?' my father blurts out as he stops the car. I check the email on my phone hoping for a mix-up, only to realise that I really did book this motel for our stay, and even paid for two weeks upfront after reading the enthusiastic reviews on TripAdvisor.

Defeated, we lug our suitcases up to the room, which is decorated with a brown carpet, beige walls, and two tacky paintings above the two beds. The air conditioning has cooled the room down to what feels like ten degrees Celsius.

Welcome to America.

I fall onto the bed on the left and crawl under the covers. My mood has plummeted to such depths that I just want to go into hibernation and wake up in a different reality. Why can't all the bad news I'd received since take-off be fake news? Why can't things be like they were yesterday?

I hear the muffled ringing of my father's mobile phone.

'Ah, Sơn! How are you? We just got here.'

[...]

'It's okay,' he says with a laugh, 'very American.'

[...]

'You made phở? Wonderful! I'll speak to them.'

With a dark foreboding, I flip down the covers and look into my father's expectant face. All the relatives have gathered at Uncle Sơn's house, he explains. My aunts have prepared noodle soup and want to have dinner with us.

'Should we drop by for a bit?' he asks.

'Now?' My mother blurts out the question like a rebuke. 'It's ...' she looks at her watch and starts converting the time ... 'almost ten!'

'They've been waiting for us since seven,' he says.

'But there wasn't even a plan!' she retorts.

'He thought we would drop by no matter what, and he got everyone together. Hùng came all the way up from San Diego with his child!'

Hùng, I think to myself, who is Hùng again?

I imagine a bunch of strangers lined up on a sofa. They've dressed their children in their best clothes and cautioned them to be nice to their relatives from Germany. In anticipation of our arrival, certain that we'll be exhausted from our journey, they've made soup for us. This is, after all, the first time my father has ever visited them in California. The last time some of them saw me was when I was fifteen, and others haven't met me at all. It dawns on me that they'll be extremely disappointed if we don't do them the small favour of going over to eat a bowl of phở. It happens to be my father's favourite dish. They certainly did their best to prepare a warm welcome.

My father seems to be reading my mind. He turns to me. 'What do you think?'

I look into his hope-filled eyes and into those of my mother, whose expression makes it clear that she is prepared to compromise. I know that if I go, she will too. And if we all go, everyone will be content. This is one of those moments when a small gesture becomes a big one. Then I start thinking of my uncle's posts on Facebook and of the phone call at Christmas. *Who? I still haven't caught the name.*

'I'm really tired,' I hear myself saying. 'Can't we just visit them tomorrow?'

I may be thirty years old, but I'm still a kid. Too petulant to pull myself together for the waiting relatives. Too selfish to put my own feelings aside for the good of all. My father glares at me in silence for a few seconds, then sighs and starts talking into his phone again.

'Sơn? There's a problem with our room, and we need to take care of it right away.'

[...]

'I think it will be too late after that. You've already waited so long. Just eat without us.'

[...]

'Don't worry! We ate on the plane. Besides, we're totally beat. The connecting flight from Frankfurt was delayed, we sat on the runway for two hours.'

[...]

'*Alright.* We'll go out to eat together tomorrow, okay?'

My father tries to hide his disappointment and presses his lips together. I turn onto my side so I don't have to look at him. I hear him set his mobile phone on the nightstand, and shortly afterwards, the shower goes on in the bathroom.

MINH

Ebersberg, 1968

Three days after landing in Germany, Minh, dressed in his best suit, arrived at the pale-pink home of a paediatrician who had invited him for a 'welcome dinner'. Her grey hair pulled back into a bun, she was wearing a pearl necklace and a pair of wire-rimmed glasses along with a light blouse over a loose beige skirt and sandals with wide straps made of leather. Her roundish figure gave her a cosy appearance. Had they been in Vietnam, he surely would have addressed her as 'grandmother' or 'aunt', but Minh found it difficult to guess the age of Europeans, and he didn't dare ask. Her name was so complicated that he decided to simply avoid using it: Frau Schmidt.

He grew even more self-conscious as he followed her through the living room and discovered not only a brown piano, but also several framed photos of light-skinned, blond-haired people who must be her relatives. Everything about her home struck him as distinguished: the grained wood on the ceilings and floors, the green-tiled fireplace, the red-and-white checked fabric hanging in front of the freshly cleaned windows. Outside, green fields stretched across rolling hills dotted with white houses and their red roofs. In the distance, the jagged outlines of the Alps shimmered in the September sun, which was shining brightly yet absent the blazing heat he was used to from back home.

How beautiful this country was.

He was still groggy from the long journey, but he was also exhilarated by this strange new world. He couldn't sleep at night because of the time difference (why hadn't anyone warned him?), and during the day, he felt like he was floating through a dream. Ebersberg, a small town in Bavaria with one church and a bunch of farmhouses, looked like a postcard. Everything was so charming, clean, and quiet that it seemed almost unreal. From his room on the first floor of the Goethe Institute, he looked down onto a lake with a silver slide in the middle of it. The air, warm and dry, smelled of hay. He went through two rolls of film in just the first three days.

When they reached the kitchen, he saw a young woman with a round face and a flat nose seated at the table, her shoulder-length black hair tucked behind her ears. When he was introduced to her, she seemed pleased, and immediately started talking. Her name was Hoa, and she was also from Vietnam. She had two small silver studs in her ears in the shape of flowers, likely in reference to her name.

Hoa was a year younger than him but had already been learning German in Ebersberg for three months. Unlike Minh, she was here on a scholarship from the South Vietnamese government and was renting a room from a blind man who she helped around the house. Because she had started taking German classes back in Vietnam, she was already able to speak entire sentences and understood quite a bit about the country. With her flared jeans and embroidered hippie blouse, she looked stylish and laid-back. Minh glanced down at his black suit: had he overdressed?

The doctor said something unintelligible in her foreign, severe-sounding language and motioned for him to take a seat next to Hoa on the bench. She placed two glasses on the table, poured cold milk into them, then added two spoonfuls of a dark-brown powder that he thought might be a kind of light coffee until he smelled its strangely sweet aroma.

Again, she said something he didn't understand. The way she raised her voice at the end of the phrase indicated that she was asking him a question. He could think of nothing else to say, so he uttered the first German words that came to him from today's class: '*Sehr gut!*'

The doctor raised her eyebrows. She said something that sounded like a question to Hoa, who responded in an apologetic tone. Their words flowed past Minh in an incomprehensible stream. His admiration for his tablemate's ability to speak this language grew and grew as the lively, light-hearted conversation bubbled between the two and he heard Hoa say: '*Aber Frau Schmidt!*'

He sat next to them sipping his milk, a spectator. The fact that the doctor kept trying to include him in the conversation with short, simple questions didn't make things any easier. He never answered her directly, instead always turning to Hoa, his new acquaintance and translator.

So this is what it means to be foreign, he thought to himself. You suddenly feel so small and irrelevant.

To his relief, the doctor got up to set the table. He knew his mother would sometimes spend two days in the kitchen before visitors came; only the best was good enough for guests, she would always say. He could hardly wait to see what Frau Schmidt had prepared. He watched in anticipation as she took two plates out of the refrigerator and placed them on the table. Slices of pink meat were piled on one, slices of yellow cheese on the other. His stomach tightened as the smell hit his nose.

'Can you tell her that I'm not very hungry today and will only take a bit from the appetiser?' he asked Hoa. 'I don't want her to think I'm being rude.'

'What do you mean by appetisers?' she replied.

'The things she just took from the fridge!'

Hoa laughed brightly. 'You really don't have a clue, do you? Germans eat the same thing in the evening as they do in the morning. They just have different names for it.'

Minh shook his head in disbelief.

'*This* is dinner? A few cold cuts and cheese?'

'From what I've seen so far, most people seem to like it. We're used to eating hot meals two or three times a day. But they don't know it any other way, so they don't miss it.' Hoa shrugged. Three months in this country, and she already seemed as if she'd been studying Germans her whole life. She poured some more powder into her brown milk.

'Believe me, anh, they are very different from us. It won't be easy for you to get used to them.'

For a brief, agonising moment, Minh thought of the grilled pork skewers they ate at home with rice noodles and fresh herbs, and the tender slices of beef that would be cooked in hot phở broth, his favourite dish. But he forced himself back into the present. He was now a guest in another culture and would have to adapt to German customs and somehow come to terms with them.

'Okay?' Frau Schmidt pointed to the plates and raised her right hand in the universal sign that even he understood: thumb and index finger together, the other fingers spread.

He nodded a bit too emphatically. '*Sehr gut*,' he said.

After another trip to the kitchen, Frau Schmidt returned with a basket containing some sliced dark-brown bread. The slices were as large as his hand, but half as thin as his fingers. It was baked with grains much coarser and larger than sesame. Hoa explained that it was fresh rye bread and that it was how you could tell the quality of the *Abendbrot*, with toast or pre-packaged white bread being far inferior. This rye bread, she pointed out, came from the bakery near the big fountain in the village centre, and was vastly better than the fluffy, tasteless baguettes they ate in Vietnam.

Minh leaned forward and sniffed. The bread smelled good. Nutty and aromatic, unlike anything he'd ever had before.

The doctor asked how many slices he wanted. He looked at the bread and at the thinly sliced, pink meat. How on earth was he supposed to satisfy his hunger with this meagre meal?

He raised his hand and spread five fingers in the air.

*

Now that he was in a foreign country, Minh realised how attached he was to the Vietnamese language. It had given him solid ground on which to stand, whereas here, he felt like he was in constant free fall. Learning German proved unexpectedly difficult for him, and he often felt stupid and awkward. The gulf between the two languages was so vast that he even had trouble copying down sentences or unfamiliar letters like the umlauts 'ä', 'ö', and 'ü' or that strange double-s letter, 'ß'. He also didn't understand the grammar. In Vietnamese, neither verbs nor nouns change form, so he had to painstakingly learn the meaning of conjugations and declensions.

The worst, though, were the articles: 'der', 'die', and 'das', three versions of the word 'the'. Why was the noun for kitchen feminine, but the one for living room neutral? Why were the world and the Earth feminine, but the globe and the planet masculine?

Forming a German sentence, *pronouncing* a German sentence, seemed to him like climbing a rock wall with his bare hands. The risk of slipping and making a grave mistake was far greater than the probability of arriving at the top unscathed. Most of the time, he preferred to just sit in silence.

Language, which had allowed him to spin the boldest theories from the depths of his thoughts in Vietnamese, now blocked his path to completing the simplest tasks of everyday life. Everything was suddenly so tedious: finding the way to the bus stop, buying a ticket, understanding the scheduled departure time, getting off at the right stop, finding the way back. Outside the sheltered world of his language school, with its classrooms and single bedrooms, he felt disoriented and lost. He, who had always been able to impress others with his stories and ideas, no longer knew how to act.

If there were Germans around, he hardly dared open his mouth. Their large bodies towered over him, and the matter-of-fact way they spoke, loud and full of laughter, intimidated him. In Vietnam, he had always admired Western students, but now he preferred to avoid them. It wasn't that he didn't want to meet them. He just didn't want to lose face.

Hoa, who was far less self-conscious than he, often teased him about it. 'You need to lose that silly pride of yours,' she said. 'You'll never learn the language if you're too afraid of making mistakes!'

After that first meeting, they saw each other almost every day. Sometimes they would visit Frau Schmidt and listen to her complain over cocoa and cold cuts about her son Werner, who was studying in Berlin and rarely called her. Or they would walk along the lakes to Bavarian pubs, where white-haired men were playing cards. To the astonishment of the locals, the two of them would frequently share a single serving of pork roast.

Minh felt more at ease around her than with anyone else. He wasn't shy about being himself and shared his most private thoughts with her — feelings and observations he would have written in his journal if he hadn't been so consumed by learning German. He sometimes wondered if their closeness only had to do with the fact that they both came from Vietnam, or if there was something else there. Sometimes she would give him a look he couldn't quite decipher.

*

After the first few weeks of gliding more or less silently through Ebersberg, Hoa came up with a dare. If he could muster enough courage to go into the small store on the market square and buy the ingredients, she would make him rice soup.

He had seen the store several times while walking through the city. It had four aisles, and a woman in an apron sitting at the check-out counter. Exasperated by all the cheese, goulash, and white sausage he'd been eating, Minh immediately agreed. Surely, he told himself, he wouldn't have to talk as much as in Vietnam, where shopping always involved extensive haggling. In the days leading up to his visit, he practised the one, pivotal sentence over and over again: *'Wieviel kostet das?'* How much does this cost?

'Kos-tet,' he would say in front of his mirror, flicking his tongue against the inside of his mouth. How could anyone come up with such a difficult word?

The store was located in a white building with a bright red roof and black-and-white slatted shutters. MÜLLERS MARKT stood in large copper letters above the arched entrance. A little bell rang as he entered. The woman at the check-out looked up, and for a brief and terrifying moment, the thought occurred to him that she might approach him and ask what he needed. But he had only practised that one sentence. Apart from cola, he couldn't name any of the groceries he wanted.

Fortunately, at that very moment, a mother with two children approached the check-out with quite a number of things, taking up all the cashier's attention. Quickly and quietly, as if trying to sneak out of her eyeline, Minh made his way into the aisles, disappearing behind the high shelves.

The sight of the food calmed him, and he soon found himself wandering the aisles like a tourist. The cans and jars were lined up so neatly in front of him. He admired how sanitary the pots of white yogurt and milk bottles looked in the large, whirring refrigerator. How neatly the price tags had been affixed to them. Everything was so different from Saigon, where shopping was done in noisy, bustling markets, and there were no such things as refrigeration units and set prices.

After walking through the aisles four times, he placed a frozen chicken, two onions, a bag of rice, pepper, salt, gummy bears, and two bottles of cola in his red shopping basket. He approached the cashier, his heart pounding. She had pushed her thin glasses up into her short brown hair and looked at him in a way that seemed especially stern. He glanced around and saw a man with a large white dog in front of the canned foods, but Minh was the only customer at the cash register.

His body tensed up.

'Grüß Gott!' the cashier said without raising her eyes.

In a seamless motion, she retrieved each item of food from his basket, tapped the price into the cash register, and placed everything into a thin beige fabric net. Like some miracle of human efficiency, she had rung up his purchases so quickly that the moment Minh had been dreading was over before he knew it. Without saying anything, she pointed to the amount displayed after the 'ka-ching' of the cash register: 8.38 marks.

In his attempt to be just as quick and efficient as she had been, Minh fumbled his coins and they clattered onto the floor. As he bent down to pick them up, he half-expected the cashier to admonish him with her brusque German words, but she remained wordless and still as a statue.

He paid, exhaled — and was annoyed at himself. On the one hand, he was relieved that she hadn't spoken to him. On the other, though, he had once again managed to avoid exchanging words with a German. On his way out, he clenched his fist and said loudly and forcefully: *'Danke!'*

Surprised, she looked up.

'Enjoy your weekend, young man!' she proclaimed.

*

The colder and windier it got, the more intense Minh's urge to leave the small world of Ebersberg became. After three intensive courses, his German had improved enough for him to start thinking about moving elsewhere and pursuing his studies. He chose Berlin because the university there was affiliated with a large hospital and had a good reputation. Frau Schmidt ordered her son Werner to pick him up when he arrived so he wouldn't feel so alone.

The city gave Minh a rather gruff welcome at Zoologischer Garten train station, where swarms of people immediately swallowed him up in their clamour and bustle. He waited on the platform for half an hour before finally dragging his suitcase down a flight of stairs to a phone booth to call Werner, who answered in a breathless frenzy. He said something about a crisis and promised to take Minh out for a beer soon, adding that Minh should have no problem finding his way to his student accommodations. It was quite simple, Werner shouted hurriedly down the receiver. 'You just have to go one stop on the S-Bahn.' He didn't wait to hear Minh's hesitant question about what exactly an S-Bahn was.

Minh now found himself standing in front of the station like a piece of uncollected luggage. He raised the collar of his winter coat against the steady drizzle, feeling abandoned, just as he had when he brought Hoa to the train station in Ebersberg a few weeks earlier. She had moved to Heidelberg in early September to study economics at the university there. After they embraced awkwardly and said goodbye, she had looked at him, almost as though she was expecting some kind of word or gesture from him. But he had been overcome by uncertainty and simply grabbed her by the shoulders. The moment he uttered his parting words, he realised how stupid they sounded: 'Don't forget to study hard!'

He looked around. Compared to Saigon, Berlin seemed pretty quiet. Women in colourful coats and men with shoulder-length hair walked past him, smoking, before turning into a large street lined with shops. A double-decker bus, taller than any vehicle he had ever seen, roared down the wide boulevard and disappeared under a train viaduct. His gaze fell on a cinema with a huge movie poster plastered onto the front of it and a church with a shattered, light-green spire. It reminded him of the ruined buildings he had seen in the days after the Tết Offensive. And he suddenly remembered hearing, at the Goethe Institute, about a great war in Europe, and about a powerful, murderous leader named Hitler.

How strange that the Germans still hadn't repaired this church. Perhaps they weren't quite as orderly as he had thought.

He pulled a piece of paper from his coat pocket on which he had written down the address of his student hall. 'S Tiergarten', it read, but the words were so mysterious to him that he might as well have been holding a note written in Russian.

A man in a blue uniform approached wearing a dark cap, a baton in his belt. Minh patted his coat pockets: Where had he packed his passport with his visa for Germany again? Where was his wallet? He wasn't sure if the German police officers also conducted random checks to collect bribes, but he wanted to be prepared just in case.

'Can I help you, young man?' the officer asked. His voice was deep, and his dialect sounded quite a bit different from the one Frau Schmidt spoke.

'I'm from Vietnam, and I am in Germany to study,' Minh replied. Fortunately, they had practised this sentence so often at the Goethe Institute that it rolled off his tongue smoothly. 'I have a visa.'

'And where are you heading?' the man continued.

Minh held out his note. 'I need to get to S Tiergarten,' he said. 'But I don't know the way.'

The policeman glanced at the address and took a step back. His gaze wandered from Minh's Sartre glasses to his tailored wool coat and back to his soft, boyish face. Then he turned towards the station entrance and motioned Minh to follow him.

The man strode purposefully ahead, back into the station and up the stairs to a track that looked exactly like the one Minh had arrived at an hour ago. What was the policeman up to? Was he taking Minh to the station for questioning?

Chattering groups of people were standing next to them and waiting. The station concourse echoed with the noise of people and trains, arriving and departing. A red-and-yellow train came to a stop in front of them, emitting a piercing signal as its doors opened automatically. The people next to them started moving.

'Get on here and get off in one stop, okay?' the policeman said, giving him a gentle nudge.

Minh nodded. He took a big step and entered the crowded carriage.

'Take care of yourself,' the man called after him. 'These are wild times in Berlin!'

*

Three days later, Minh found a spot in the last row of Lecture Hall C at the Free University of Berlin; he was filled with a mixture of tension and joy. One minute before the start of the introductory seminar, the lecturer stalked into the room and positioned himself behind the tall wooden lectern with the air of an officer about to conduct roll call. Tall, white-haired, and wearing rimless glasses, he scanned the students seated in the uncomfortable wooden seats before him. Without averting his gaze, he popped open the buckles of his black leather bag. The students fell silent.

Without any greeting, he began to speak.

'How many of you want to become doctors so you can save people from dying every day?'

Hands stretched hesitantly into the air. Minh, sat so far back, wasn't sure what the professor had said, but the words 'people', 'death', and 'save' were all familiar to him. He placed an elbow on the desk in front of him and raised his index finger half-curved, half-extended into the air.

The professor's gaze swept right over him, coming to a stop on a boy in the front row with parted blond hair and a blue sweater from which a white shirt collar peeked out. The lecturer stepped towards him, and Minh saw the boy straighten up and jut his chin forward.

'Why don't you tell us why you're here and what you expect from your studies,' the professor said.

'I read in a newspaper that you are about to become one of the first doctors in Berlin to transplant a heart,' the student said in a confident manner Minh found deeply impressive. 'I want to do that too.'

The professor folded his arms in front of him.

'And you think it's really that simple?'

The student's hand fell from the air.

'You think that all the mysteries of medicine are open to you just because you managed to enrol in this programme?'

The lecturer bent over deeply, clenched his hands into fists, and propped them on the boy's desk. He lowered his voice, but he could still be heard by all those in the lecture hall.

'Do you even know how the heart works? How many times it beats per minute? How many litres of blood it pumps through your body? How many litres of blood it was already pumping through your body when you were still an embryo in your mother's womb?'

The student recoiled, his back pressed up against his wooden chair. His voice trembled.

'I already have the textbook, but I haven't had time to look at it in detail yet ...'

The professor straightened up again. 'Then I would advise you to start reading before you set out to perform a heart transplant,' he said coolly.

He adjusted his glasses with his thumb and forefinger, then stalked briskly back to his lectern. The white chalk screeched loudly as he wrote in large letters on the board: 'The Foundations of Medicine.'

After the seminar, Minh trailed after the others to the dining hall, where he heard his fellow students complaining about the professor and his authoritarian manner. Apparently, he had a dubious past, which they discussed at the table in animated whispers. The blond student claimed that the professor had worked for a Nazi doctor, assisting with euthanasia experiments. His seat-mate countered that she had heard from a fourth-year student that he had 'only' been a soldier in the Netherlands. Minh focused his eyes on his bland canteen food but listened attentively.

Back in his room, he looked up the words he hadn't understood, but the reason why the other students had spoken about these things in such dark, whispering voices still eluded him. Hadn't the professor's alleged actions taken place years ago? Didn't terrible things always happen in war? Why did these young Germans care so much about what had transpired more than twenty years ago? Why couldn't they just let the past be the past?

There were thousands of students at the Free University of Berlin, but Minh felt more alone than ever. In class, he remained so silent and reserved that even after several months, he still hadn't gotten to know any of his lecturers or fellow students. Though his appearance stood out, he remained lost in the crowd. In the eyes of others, he was the quiet foreign student who always smiled but never said anything. They took note of the formal suits he wore, but they didn't really notice him.

The cold of the approaching winter heightened his sense of alienation. In the mornings, he dreaded taking the five-minute walk to his S-Bahn station because his Vietnamese wool coat turned out to be neither rain nor snow repellent. In the evenings, he would return exhausted to his student hall, where he would prepare a slice of bread with cold cuts and cheese in the communal kitchen, before taking it back to his room and eating it joylessly as he sat in bed.

He would go to bed in his wool sweater and socks at around ten, when the lights were still on in the rooms on either side of his and conversations and rock music still filtered through the thin walls. Every night, he attempted to fold the large, thin blanket over itself to provide him with more warmth, but it always ended in disappointment.

The relentlessness of the Berlin winter refused to loosen its grip.

More and more often, he would fall asleep thinking that perhaps coming here hadn't been such a great idea after all. What did he have to offer the Germans, anyway?

*

Frau Schmidt's son Werner hadn't tried to get in touch with him again. Minh had rung him several times, but even though he had always sounded enthusiastic on the phone, it had never been possible to meet up.

Werner was studying a subject called 'sociology' and had to constantly take part in events he called 'sit-ins' or 'teach-ins'. He also talked about the German Students' Committee and Socialist German Students' Union meetings he had to go to. Minh understood that Werner had important things to do. So he was quite surprised when he was called to the telephone downstairs in the common room one evening. A certain Werner wanted to speak with him.

'Hello? This is Minh!'

He paused for a moment. He always felt particularly self-conscious when speaking German on the phone. A few of the older students were sitting on the sofa in the corner watching TV. Minh turned his back to them.

'I'm sorry I didn't get back to you, things are really busy again,' Werner poured forth. His voice was as bright as a child's, and he sounded excited. 'We're in the process of organising a big anti-war conference.'

'Great,' Minh replied, wondering if he had somehow missed something. What war was Werner referring to? Germany seemed so peaceful to him.

'We want to mobilise all of Berlin,' Werner continued. 'Berlin against imperialism! You must know all about this kind of thing, being from Vietnam, but we in Germany also have to stand up against the reactionary powers! The Springer publishing house, the Berlin Senate, this whole authoritarian mindset! There are way too many people who are just following along like sheep and need to wake up!'

His voice grew louder with each sentence, to the point that he was now shouting his words into the receiver. One of the older students looked up from the TV and glanced over.

'Absolutely, great!' repeated Minh, who was drawn in by his enthusiasm even if he didn't understand exactly what Werner was saying.

'I knew you would get it,' Werner replied. 'I mean, considering where you're from, you must know what it's like to be oppressed!'

He laughed hoarsely.

Minh heard a rustling noise through the receiver, then the muffled sound of Werner shouting something to someone. Apparently, he had a visitor. After an unintelligible exchange of words, Werner's voice could once again be heard clearly through the receiver.

'I was wondering if you could help us,' he said. 'We could really use you.'

'Me?' For a moment, Minh wondered if Werner was joking. 'What am I supposed to do?'

'Why don't you come over? I am sitting with the planning committee right now. We're preparing the agenda for the big Vietnam conference next week.'

Minh looked at the clock on the wall: shortly before 10.00 pm. Tomorrow morning, he had another seminar with the strict professor, and he had intended to get up at 6.00 am to prepare for it. He stared out the window into the black, rainy night. Part of him just wanted to crawl into his bed and hide from the cold world outside.

At the same time, though, he had never been invited to anything by a German student before.

'Sure' he said, trying to sound enthusiastic. 'Which S-Bahn do I need to take?'

*

An hour later, he was standing soaked and in a foul mood in front of a construction site in Schöneberg. Following Werner's instructions, he slipped under the barrier and waded through the mud towards an old, pre-war residential building. A flickering light shone from a ground-floor window, softly illuminating the grey, crumbling masonry. Neither the door of the building nor that of the flat was locked.

He found himself in a hallway that reminded him of a basement: the brick wall was unplastered, exposed pipes stretched beneath the ceiling, and an unlit light bulb hung down from a cable. A Beatles song a student in his dorm liked to listen to was blaring loudly from the room to his left: 'Lucy in the Sky with Diamonds'.

Minh covered his left ear with his hand and pushed the door open with his right.

'Werner?' His voice wobbled with nervousness.

Three faces looked up at him. One man with light-brown curls, another with a bowl cut and a cap, and a woman with blond hair and glasses. They were sitting cross-legged on the floor, smoking a single hand-rolled cigarette, passing it between one another. A black desk lamp was standing on the floor next to them, casting its light on a few sheets of graph paper that had something written on them in felt-tip pen. On the wall hung a map of Vietnam and its neighbouring countries. Next to it was a shelf full of books with old, fraying covers.

'Are you the Vietnamese guy?' the woman asked.

The curly haired man jabbed his elbow into her side.

'Geez, Gundi, he has a name!'

He looked different than in the photos Frau Schmidt had shown Minh. His hair was longer, his face gaunt. In his worn-out sweater and corduroy bell-bottoms, he looked like he hadn't eaten enough in weeks. He stood up and approached Minh with his arms outstretched.

'Welcome, brother!' Werner proclaimed.

That night, Minh came to understand why Werner called his mother so rarely. He and his friends were fighting for a freer world, which left little time for anything else. They wanted to rid the universities of professors they considered to be 'authoritarian assholes', they hated the Springer-owned tabloid *Bild* for its 'reactionary agitation', and they were so deeply emotionally involved in the war in Vietnam that it made Minh feel guilty. He, the one actually from Vietnam, preferred to block out news of his homeland.

They lowered their voices when speaking about their mission of bringing the revolutions from Vietnam, Cuba, and Palestine to German soil. They peppered their sentences with complicated words and phrases that he was unfamiliar with and found difficult to remember: *the global struggle against US imperialism. Solidarity with the working class. The hegemonic power structure of the media.*

'We cannot forget that the war over there is our war too,' Werner proclaimed, pointing to the map with INDOCHINA written across it. 'His oppression is my oppression too.'

He nodded to Minh as if they had survived an accident together. Minh nodded back out of politeness, but he neither understood what Werner's situation had to do with his, nor could he see the connection between the political situation in Palestine and that in Vietnam.

Where was Palestine, anyway?

Minh promised himself he would start reading more news. He did leaf through the newspapers in his student residence from time to time, but since his German still wasn't totally up to snuff, he usually only read the short articles on the back page. Sometimes he would try to study the articles towards the front, but it was a tedious undertaking because he had to look up so many words.

The woman, Gundi, popped open a bottle of beer and took a gulp. She was wearing a wool, black-and-white patterned sweater and spoke a lot like the people in Ebersberg had. The previous weekend, she had travelled home for her grandmother's funeral, apparently her first visit to her hometown in two years.

She was upset that her mother had been so 'submissive' and her father so 'repressive'. It was only when she spoke about the return trip that her voice brightened again. She had apparently stopped in Frankfurt on the way back to attend a lecture by a famous professor. He had a name that sounded like a Greek god, and when Gundi mentioned him, Werner whistled in admiration and pulled a book from his shelf. *Dialectic of Enlightenment*. Yet another jumble of worlds that Minh didn't understand.

'And now I'm thinking about donating the 10,000 marks from my gran to the Vietnamese,' Gundi proclaimed, setting down her bottle. The man with the cap next to her looked at her in alarm.

'I thought we were using it for a trip through Africa!'

'Don't be like that, Thomas! It's my money, so I can do what I want with it! Should I use it so the two of us can travel the world for a few months? Or should it go towards liberating a country from imperialism? Everyone can do their part, us too!'

'But it's *your* inheritance. Why shouldn't you use it for yourself?' Thomas took off his cap and began kneading it in his hands. 'Besides, you don't even know what the Vietnamese would do with it. They might use it to buy weapons!'

Gundi shrugged her shoulders.

'If they think that's what they need.'

'But we're pacifists!'

Minh remained silent as he sat next to them, smoking. He was surprised to see how much time Werner and his friends spent thinking about Vietnam. It never would have occurred to him that people abroad could be interested in his small country. But it remained unclear what they hoped to gain from their involvement. None of them had ever set foot on Vietnamese soil and yet they seemed to have so many opinions about the place. He understood neither whom the money from Gundi's grandmother was to go to, nor what she meant by 'liberation from imperialism'.

Two or three times, the others asked him questions, which he answered vaguely to conceal his own confusion. The whole thing baffled him as much as it flattered him. At some point, his attention to their revolutionary back-and-forth began to fade. The herb they were smoking was making him groggy and lethargic. He let his head sink onto Werner's shoulder, closed his eyes, and fell asleep.

*

On the morning of the Vietnam Conference, Minh was awoken by an icy draft that stalked through his room like a malevolent ghost.

He rolled out of bed, walked over to the window, and opened the curtains. The sky was milky grey, with shapeless clouds sliding lazily past each other. Looking down from his window, he saw white flakes floating from the sky like a slow, gentle rain, some collecting on the bare crown of the tree that stood outside his dorm, now covered in a layer of snow.

He opened the window and stuck out his right hand. Small, wondrous ice formations landed on his outstretched palms, melting immediately and turning his skin red. The cold was more piercing than he had thought it would be, but the sensation of touching snow warmed him from the inside.

Do you think you could send me some?

Enchanted by the magic of the moment, he wondered if there might be a way to send a few snowflakes home to his brother after all. He would just have to find a way to freeze them, put them in a package and wrap them up well enough to survive the tropical heat on the other side of the world.

He shook his icy hand and laughed. Then he took his camera from his closet and started snapping pictures, first inside and then outside. If he couldn't send snow to Sơn, then he could at least mail him a couple of good photos.

*

By the time Minh found himself hurrying up the steps of the underground train at Ernst-Reuter-Platz two hours later, the white snowflakes had turned into hard grains of ice. They pelted down from the sky, turning the roofs of the cars into drums. He lifted his new black leather bag over his head like a shield and struggled along the wide, deserted street until he was standing in front of a spaceship-like building with several rows of black windows.

In front of the entrance to the Technical University of Berlin, directly beneath the white letters bearing its name, a red-and-blue flag with a yellow star was hanging. It seemed familiar to him. He paused, taking off his glasses and cleaning the wet lenses. It was the flag he had seen so often on the Vietnamese news, that of the communist Viet Cong who were terrorising his country.

What a strange mistake. Werner needed to know about it.

From the end of the corridor, he could hear a marching song, with a number of people loudly singing along. The music was coming from the large auditorium; the conference had already begun. He hurried down the hall. A poster hanging on the closed double doors read: *'The struggle for the Vietnamese Revolution is part of the struggle for the liberation of all people from oppression and exploitation'*. Next to it was a placard of a Vietnamese soldier, his machine gun held high.

Minh carefully pushed down the door handle.

The lecture hall looked as big as a stadium. To his right, he saw hundreds of students sitting in the rows of seats layered upwards like a grandstand. To his left was a stage, where five men were sitting behind a long row of tables, their severe expressions and the stacks of papers in front of them making it look like they were about to pronounce a government declaration. Standing at the very front, microphone in hand, was Werner. He was wearing a black beret and a red-and-blue T-shirt.

His gaze fell on Minh.

Minh felt his scalp begin to itch. How had he ended up being so late — it was embarrassing! Why hadn't he just stayed home rather than disrupt this event? He shielded his face with his hand and crouched as he walked to the row of chairs at the very back. He found a seat as far from the stage as possible.

The music fell silent.

Werner held the microphone to his mouth and began to speak. 'The other day, dear comrades, I had a long conversation with a friend from Vietnam. He told me how much he had to go through to get here. He told me of his escape, of his desperation! He told me about this illegal war! His country needs all the support it can get. Each of us can do our part. Each of us *must* do our part!'

He paused, pounding his right hand on his heart. 'I am thrilled he could be with us today.'

To Minh's horror, Werner held out his hand to point to his seat at the very back.

'Minh, brother, we are in this together!'

To his right and left, Minh could hear people shifting in their seats. In front of him, the audience turned around to get a look, hundreds of pairs of eyes. After a few seconds, a man on the podium shouted, 'Solidarity with the Vietnamese people!' A woman in the third row held up a placard reading 'Vietnam'. Up on the stage, Werner began slowly clapping. The students in front of him joined in. Minh heard whistles, and then cheers.

He just sat there, frozen.

KIỀU

Driving through Little Saigon the next day, we pass by an expansive shopping mall watched over by a Buddha and three marble statues wearing long capes: the gods of happiness, prosperity, and longevity. The entrance is lined with white columns supporting light-green winged roofs, just like a pagoda. I roll down the window to take a picture.

'What's that flag hanging there?'

Between the columns is a yellow flag with three red horizontal stripes. It reminds me of the Spanish flag, but the proportions are all wrong; the red stripes are much thinner than the yellow ones. My father glances over.

'That's the flag of South Vietnam.'

'But the Vietnamese flag is red and has a yellow star,' I object.

'It does now, but before the war, North and South Vietnam had different flags. This one is the flag of the former republic in the South. The one you're talking about is that of the communists from the North. There was also a red-and-blue flag with a yellow star, which was the symbol of the Viet Cong.'

'Complicated.'

He sighs.

'The war was *very* complicated.'

Just as I am about to ask him to explain, he turns up the car radio. I know about the Vietnam War from school, of course, and I am familiar with the images of Ho Chi Minh and the naked girl running from napalm. What I do not know, though, is what the conflict did to my father and his family. Neither he nor my mother have told me anything about it of their own accord, and I've never thought to ask, nor have my siblings. The Vietnam War is something that takes place in the history books, or in black-and-white documentaries. It couldn't be farther from us or our lives in Germany.

I look back at the flags until they dissolve into yellow-red stripes in the setting sun. South Vietnam may have been defeated in the war, but in Little Saigon, it apparently lives on. The ghosts of the past still seem to haunt the present day, as if they have unfinished business to take care of.

*

Outside, everything fits the Western mould, though dotted with Vietnamese symbols. While the stores may look typically American, they have names like Saigon City Market Place or Hanoi Corner. The restaurants advertise bánh xèo pancakes, xôi sticky rice, and bánh mì sandwiches. The pharmacies have Vietnamese names, as do the laundromats, the bubble tea stores, and massage parlours whose services are so cheap that it seems criminal ('*1 hour — $15 dollar only!*'). I only see a few people walking down the streets, but all of them have black hair and Asian builds that often seem a bit frail compared to Caucasian ones. Here, though, they are among their own, so they don't all just look short. Some are stocky and athletic, others look petite, while others even seem tall.

One lane over, an Asian family with two girls drives by in a pickup. The mother has dyed her hair brown and pinned it up loosely, the father is wearing black architect glasses with a white T-shirt and blazer. I watch them in envy. Who would I be if I had grown up here?

When I think back to my childhood, I see a black-haired girl living in a light-blue house, growing up with the melodic language of her parents. Innocently, I repeated the words with which they rocked me to sleep, tender with happiness at their firstborn child. When I was little, I didn't know that my family's world was different to the one around us — that I was growing up on a planet shared by only five people: my mother, my father, my sister, my brother, and me.

I began to see it in preschool. There I met Paul and Sarah, who would play with colourful building blocks as I watched in silence. Their parents were tall, blond, and always joking with the childcare workers. My parents were short, black-haired, and always late; when they finally came rushing to get me, I'd be sitting outside the door trying to recreate Paul and Sarah's building block castles.

As I got older, I could see how different we were. As I grew smarter, I studied how others behaved. For every German word I gained, I shed a Vietnamese one. I forgot the songs I had sung as a toddler and joined the Germans at school as they sang theirs. I wanted spaghetti for dinner, not phở. When my parents had their Vietnamese friends over and sang karaoke, I rolled my eyes. I was always expected to play the piano. My parents always bragged about my marks. My only solace was that the other Vietnamese kids had to endure the same. Together, we stood there cringing as our parents boasted about our exam results or performance in a maths contest.

My German friends seemed to be free from that pressure to achieve. They received money for a B in maths; they started asking their parents for cigarettes at fifteen; and on weekends, they were allowed to stay out as late as they wanted. On the rare occasion they did argue with their parents, it was always followed by a family conversation and words like 'sorry' and 'love'. I never knew this sort of talk from home, so I was bewildered by people sharing their feelings so openly. But being confused was also strange, so I said nothing.

I wanted the differences between my family and their families to disappear because our world was small and unusual while theirs was big and universal. 'Put on something decent, you know how much the Germans mistrust us foreigners!' my mother used to say with a mixture of fear and menace. I can still hear her today.

We were ready to be anything, except who we were. There was no place for us in the Germany of the 1990s. Strangers would stop my father to ask if he had any smuggled cigarettes to sell. Over time, I forgot how to pronounce my own name. Caught up in their immigrant ambitions, my parents let it happen. I was supposed to make it in Germany, whatever the price.

Kiều came from a small world, but Kim understood the big one and had no trouble navigating it. She knew how to please Germans, how to become one of them.

It's only here in Little Saigon that I start to wonder if things could have been different.

*

We drive further down Bolsa Avenue, turn onto a wide side street and then into one of the huge parking lots. A man standing in front of a restaurant starts waving to us from a distance; at first, I don't recognise him. He looks different to his Facebook photos, his hair is grey, and his beard is thin and wiry. With his round eyes, a green T-shirt, and plaid shorts, Uncle Sơn looks like a prematurely aged teenager.

He lets out a laugh when the three of us are standing in front of him, then swings his arms towards my father, as if to perform a half-hug. Finding themselves face to face, they look at each other awkwardly: two brothers reunited by the death of their mother after fifteen years of separation.

'You look like our old man,' my father says in greeting.

'Oh, come on! I'm just old,' Uncle Sơn snorts.

'You're younger than me.'

'You wouldn't know it by looking at me!'

He giggles like a little boy.

As the four of us walk into the restaurant, the sound of eating and slurping washes over us. In Germany, lobster restaurants tend to be expensive establishments with starched white tablecloths, silver cutlery, and waiters who oddly tuck their left hand behind their backs when serving. This place is like a train-station bistro.

The room is large and devoid of decoration, aside from a red Chinese daily tear-away wall calendar and a giant plastic crab mounted on another wall. Families of eight, ten, twenty people are sitting at round tables with Lazy Susans in the middle and covered with paper tablecloths. They are chomping away loudly, laughing, and spitting. Towers of empty bowls are stacked next to plates and glasses as greasy fingers shoot up into the air, waving and snapping at the waiters who are dashing about.

Uncle Sơn had proposed the restaurant in the newly established WhatsApp group this morning, immediately triggering a family dispute. Other relatives countered with suggestions of their own, everything from Vietnamese hotpot to Korean barbecue to 'very good, very cheap steak'. They were arguing as if they were competing at a debating society, driven by passion and the will to conquer others. My father had translated the constant stream of messages for me, since I couldn't read the Vietnamese phrases popping up in the chat. The twins, for example, complained that there would be too many Chinese families dining at Special Seafood who had 'no manners'. Uncle Sơn countered that the Chinese simply knew where to find the best food.

As the afternoon's discussion spilled over into questions about dessert, parking, and how broad the circle of relatives should be, Uncle Sơn finally announced in capital letters that he would be making the goddamned reservation and would be picking up the tab. And with that, the battle was won.

'Sơn? Good to see you!' A waiter sporting 1990s aviator glasses and the inevitable Asian side-part winds his way through the tables to us. Although he is older than my uncle, he addresses him respectfully as *anh*. Ignoring the shouts coming from left and right, he leads us to a long table in the back located next to four large aquariums. More than a dozen lobsters are swimming around — large orange-and-black creatures with heavy claws that seem to have their antennae pointed at us.

Uncle Sơn raps his knuckle against the glass.

'What a beautiful creature!' he says, letting out a throaty laugh. 'So nice and meaty.'

My father takes a seat at the head of the table, while Uncle Sơn sits to his right and pulls up a chair for me. Panic begins building up inside of me: what should I talk to him about?

If he was someone I didn't know, some random interview partner, tons of questions would spring to mind. But this isn't a stranger that I'm meeting as a journalist, it's my uncle. Deep down, I'm itching to ask him about the death of my grandmother or about his life in general in recent years. But I feel paralysed by the thought of conducting such a conversation. I wouldn't even know how to start it. With a remark about the warm California weather, perhaps? Or his mother's funeral? Is it even appropriate to talk about death at a restaurant?

A simple joke would save me from my awkwardness, but I'm unable to find the right words. I haven't spoken Vietnamese for so long that it takes great effort to remember the most basic expressions. I can feel my tongue lying heavy and motionless inside my mouth.

More people file into the restaurant and sit down at our table: Uncle Hùng with his wife from San Diego, her skin bleached by whitening cream. Cousin Vinh carrying a to-go cup from Starbucks. Aunt Hồng, who has come straight from her job at a nail salon and is dragging her shy husband behind her, their sixteen-year-old son trotting along after them as he stares into his mobile phone. There are close relatives, ones who have married into the family, new faces, and ageing faces. Dizziness overwhelms me, and the corners of my mouth begin to ache from smiling. It's like a traumatic speed-dating event I went to a few years ago, after which I had eight new phone numbers but also nausea.

*

The lobsters look different to what I thought they would. Instead of being served on their own, they are presented on a bed of glistening noodles — a Chinese specialty apparently popular in Little Saigon. The waiter pushes three large platters across our table, and my mother and Aunt Hồng stand up to serve the others. In contrast to Germany, where everyone gets their own plate with their own dish, we each have a bowl and share all the food that is on the table. Eating is our way of communicating and showing affection. Just as Americans say, '*I love you*,' the Vietnamese say: '*Have you eaten yet?*'

Uncle Sơn stabs the mound of fried noodles with his chopsticks, pulls out a clump, and flops it into my bowl. He grabs a chunk of lobster lying on top of the pile with his fingers, pulling out the meat and setting it on top of the noodles. The aroma of soy sauce and chilli fills my nose, spicy and greasy at the same time. Even though I do like lobster, I am suddenly overcome by a revulsion more intense than I've ever experienced.

I shove my bowl away and turn towards Uncle Sơn to get a breath of slightly less scent-laden air. Unfortunately, he takes it as an invitation to talk.

'How old are you again?'

To my relief, I can grasp what he is saying, he speaks in a Vietnamese dialect similar to my father's. He seems to expect no less of me — everyone here, the waiters, the guests, my aunts, uncles, and cousins, are speaking Vietnamese, even though we're in America.

My mother leans over from the other side of the table, the flower pendant on her necklace dangling over a large soup bowl like a cable car.

'She's thirty now. Can you believe it?'

'Really?' he responds. 'When I last saw her, she still had braces!'

He breaks a bright-red claw apart with a crack, juice spurting out. I turn away so I don't have to look at the moist, reddish-white meat.

'Are you married yet?' he asks.

I feel my cheeks growing warm as half-formed sentences tumble through my mind. 'I believe in love, but not in marriage' is how I once put it to my mother. That was, of course, long before that terrible evening when Dorian *didn't* ask me to marry him, although I would probably say the same thing now just because of that.

If they were white Americans, I would tell them about my scepticism of the church and the high rate of divorce. If I were sitting with German friends, I would talk about my relationship, which, like any relationship between modern, free-spirited people, could turn into anything, or into nothing at all. But here, in this Vietnamese lobster restaurant, my lips remain sealed.

I lack the vocabulary for a discussion like this, but also the will to try. The only words that I can still remember in Vietnamese are the first words that I learned. I can say things like 'That tastes good', or 'I'm tired', but I am unable to express myself. Trapped again in the small world of my childhood, I sit before my relatives in silence like a little girl.

We are separated by just a few inches. A few inches and a light year of sentences unspoken.

'She's dating a German,' my mother says, sighing so loudly that it can even be heard over the clattering of the dishes. 'Marriage isn't on the cards anytime soon.'

Damn right, I think to myself, but of course I don't say it out loud. I haven't told her about Dorian's Tokyo idea nor about the pregnancy. Besieged by her incessant questions about our 'family plans', I have put up a wall of defiance and never tell her anything. I have to protect myself from her. From her and her desire to transform me into a mother like herself. I witnessed how she gave up her career so my siblings and I could have home-cooked food when we returned from school each day. I saw how she spent her days in the light-blue house as my father pursued his career in the hospital.

Wasn't I supposed to make it in life and achieve more than just that? What were the piano lessons for? The top marks in high school? My career in Germany?

'What about children?' my Aunt Hồng chimes in. 'The clock is ticking.'

I can tell by their looks that they see me as damaged goods. Their eyes scan the oversized white tank top I've stolen from Dorian, the black jeans, and my face, free of make-up. My bangs hang low over my face; this morning, my mother had rolled her eyes at them again.

Uncle Sơn feels the need to put in his two pennies' worth. 'At thirty, you should really be thinking about children.'

'Tell me about it!' my mother says, emboldened. 'I keep trying, but she's so stubborn!'

Under normal circumstances, I would brusquely tell my mother to mind her own business now. But it would be inappropriate in front of all these relatives. A loss of face for both of us. So I just sit there listening as they continue talking about me as if I weren't there. Back when I was in school, I would also have to stand there as my mother chatted with an acquaintance, comparing my marks to those of her son. I was her trophy then. Now, I'm the problem. Aunt Hồng's advice: persuade the German to start a family as *soon* as possible. Uncle Sơn offers to look around for a Vietnamese man who grew up in California and isn't too fussed about age.

My mother eagerly takes in all of their suggestions, but fears that I won't play along. 'She's very German.' It sounds like I have some infectious disease.

The longer they talk about children, marriage, and family, the more terrified I become. I imagine what it would be like to have a child with a man who wants to move to the other side of the world. I would spend my days caring for the crying baby, changing diapers, and calling Dorian via Skype in Tokyo, holding the laptop camera over the sleeping child, and beaming: 'Look, did you see their fingers move?'

As I would transform into a mother, he would be consumed by guilt. Sooner or later, we'd split up because he'd have to devote all his time to the restaurant, while I'd be unable to forgive him for forcing me into the role of waiting wife. As a single mother, I would first cut my hours and then maybe quit working altogether: Could there be anything more important than the child's wellbeing? I see my future flashing before me like some bad movie. My adult life would end before it had even started.

Uncle Sơn nods at me in a way that's probably meant to be encouraging. 'My wife and I were unable to have children, even though we wanted to. Don't waste the opportunity! You'll regret it for the rest of your life!'

He grabs my bowl and places a little more lobster on top.

My stomach starts to churn, and nausea wells up inside me. I try to breathe in slowly, but my stomach clenches, pushing a mash of food upwards. The saliva on my tongue has a sour, acidic taste. I press my lips together and squeeze my eyes shut, my hands clawing at the edge of the table.

I can hear everyone falling silent.

'Here, Kiều!'

Uncle Sơn quickly grabs an empty soup bowl and holds it out to me. I throw up, relieved and deeply ashamed at the same time; I spit, cough, and collapse in my chair. Once I have calmed down, my relatives look at me with a blend of shock and concern. I search for the right words to defuse the situation, but my empty mind fails to remember the Vietnamese expression for 'sorry'.

MINH

Heidelberg, 1969

On the long bus ride from Berlin to Heidelberg, Minh began feeling so nauseous that he almost threw up. But now that he was standing in front of Hoa, all of his discomfort was gone. She was wearing a long winter coat made of light-brown leather with a broad, fluffy collar along with heeled black boots. They embraced awkwardly, and as they pulled back, he realised just how intensely he had missed her, and was suddenly overwhelmed with longing.

'It's been a while,' he mumbled.

'There was so much going on,' she responded.

They began making their way towards the Old Town, crossing a river by way of a red-brick bridge, behind which he could see a castle perched on a hilltop like a bird's nest hewn from stone. The narrow streets were lined with colourful, pointy-roofed buildings, the bare branches of the trees stretching out like arms. Considering it was November, the day was surprisingly cold — sunny, yet so chilly that their breath formed small white clouds as they exhaled. Minh took a deep breath.

'I ran into Frau Schmidt's son in Berlin the other day. Remember? She would sometimes talk about him.'

'That Walter guy? The one who doesn't visit her anymore?'

'His name is Werner, but yeah, that's the one. He's ...' Minh paused as he tried to find the right words. '... a political activist. Very passionate about Vietnam.'

He had been thinking about Werner a lot in the last few weeks. Minh was by now convinced that the red-and-blue flag with the yellow star at the entrance to the Technical University had actually been intentional. Werner and his friends were communists. They were siding with the enemy.

'Vietnam? What is he saying about Vietnam?'

Hoa looked at him expectantly, and Minh stopped walking. Even though they were speaking Vietnamese, he lowered his voice and leaned towards her.

'I think Werner is a supporter of Ho Chi Minh!'

He straightened up, expecting her to be just as shocked as he was, but she didn't say a word. Absentmindedly, she began telling him about a Christmas market she wanted to take him to, one she had recently been to with Peter. The way she said the name got Minh's attention. Without noticing his disquiet, she turned into a narrow lane leading to a large square in front of a church. It was filled with wooden stalls selling food and carved wooden ornaments, red-cheeked market-goers wandering among them. The scent of candied sugar and grilled sausage filled Minh's nose, and he suddenly realised he was starving.

'Isn't it beautiful?' Hoa turned back to him and spread her arms like a tour guide enchanted by the wonderful sights of her own city. 'I have to say, I've really fallen in love with this country!'

She seems happy, he thought with a pang.

She disappeared into the crowd and returned with two mugs filled with a steaming red drink. They found a table to stand at and clinked their mugs together. Minh wanted to ask about Peter, but he didn't know how to, so he started talking about Werner again. You have to be very careful around Germans, he said in his best big-brother voice. A lot of these students may seem nice, he warned, but they are actually dangerous radicals.

His head began to itch beneath his wool cap. He took it off and started scratching.

'The question is *why* the Germans think like that,' Hoa said, her face disappearing into her mug.

'How should I know? Werner said something about war crimes committed by the Americans. He has probably fallen for communist propaganda.'

Hoa put down her mug and lit a cigarette. It seemed she had started smoking here. In silence, she watched the people at the Christmas market as they bought gifts and sweets.

'I also heard something about war crimes. It didn't come from the communists — my aunt told me. She lives in central Vietnam, in Quảng Ngãi province. Before I came to Germany, she mentioned a village that the Americans had attacked and completely destroyed.'

Minh was growing increasingly agitated. Was he the only person in this country who recognised the danger? Had she been brainwashed by her new German friends?

'It was probably a village full of Viet Cong spies,' he countered. 'You know that the communists control large parts of the population in the countryside.'

This visit wasn't going the way it was supposed to, and he didn't understand why. In the weeks leading up to the trip, he had often pictured them strolling through the snow, telling each other funny stories about Germans. The two of them against the world, just like it had been back in Ebersberg. It always made him wistful to think about their time together, and he regretted the way they had parted.

He took another sip of his mulled wine. Now cold, it tasted like sweet fruit juice.

'I don't know exactly what happened,' Hoa finally allowed. 'My aunt told me about it right before I left, and I had too many other things on my mind to ask her about the details.'

They finished their drinks, and each ordered a bratwurst with mustard. She told him about her new waitressing job in a club and about the two friends she went to the movies with on Wednesdays when tickets were cheaper. He limited his stories to his strict professor and how incredibly demanding his medical studies were. She mentioned Peter once more, when telling him about a famous hill in the area that Germans liked to hike. Minh was too proud to ask further questions. Even though he had planned to spend the entire weekend in Heidelberg, he decided to take the last train back to Berlin that evening.

When they said their goodbyes on the platform, she smiled at him so buoyantly that his heart grew heavy. He gathered his courage, kissed her on the cheek, and fled into the train carriage, saying: 'I'll write you!'

*

Two days later, he bought himself a fountain pen and dark-blue ink at KaDeWe and hurried home to try out a few potential openings with his fancy new writing utensil.

Dear friend
Good morning, sister
My dear Hoa

Because nothing sounded quite right, he decided to go casual, the way Germans did. *Hello Hoa*. It had a modern ring to it.

He wrote that it had been really nice to see her and that the mulled wine had tasted exquisite.

He wrote that it was wonderful that she had found so many friends, male and female, in Heidelberg.

He wrote that it wasn't easy to get used to Germany, but the two of them would manage.

He stopped, waiting for the right thoughts to deliver the right words to his fountain pen. Words that would ensure that she would never again want to lay eyes on Peter, his nemesis, whose existence had ignited in Minh a burning sense of losing something that should be his.

He wrote: 'You and I share a special connection that no one else will understand. We're from the same country. We speak the same language. Sometimes I wonder if it was our fate to meet in Germany. I didn't realise it back then, but now I know how important it is to find someone like yourself when you're in a foreign country. I keep thinking back to our time in Ebersberg. It was wonderful discovering this country together. Was it the same for you?'

He paused again, wondering if he had said too much, or not enough. He hadn't yet told her, for example, that his heart filled his chest whenever he thought of her.

And that he spoke to her.

And that he dreamt of her.

And that he could hardly eat.

And that he could hardly sleep.

He wrote: 'I'm thinking of you, and I hope that we can spend more time together in the future.' He closed his eyes so he wouldn't have to look at what he had written.

*

It took so long for her to answer that he began doubting himself. Day after day, he would ask the caretaker in agony if he'd received any mail, but day after day, he'd head back up to his room empty-handed.

By now, he was certain that his words had scared her away — that he had crossed the line between what was acceptable, and what was not. He had been too open about his feelings, pushing her into a corner that she could only escape by responding with feelings of her own.

But she didn't answer.

And because she didn't answer, her silence was constantly on his mind. It expanded to occupy his entire consciousness. Sitting in his lecture hall, he would think: Why hasn't she answered? Sitting in the canteen, he would think: What a stupid letter! Sitting on the S-Bahn, he would think: I should have never written about fate. Lying in bed, he would think: She never wants to see me again.

He had laid himself bare, and now he was freezing. She clearly loved the German guy. And Minh? He had embarrassed himself by showing his feelings.

Still, the hope wouldn't die. Every day, he would give it another try at the caretaker's office.

No, there's no letter for you.
Again nothing. Sorry.
If something comes, I'll bring it to you. I promise.

Shivering, he would drag himself back upstairs. He would never fall in love with a woman again. But in the unlikely event that he did, he promised himself to never show his feelings.

*

One evening, Minh was watching TV in the common room with a few other students when the main anchor opened the evening news with a serious face. Grey hair parted to the side, he was wearing rounded, wire-rimmed glasses. Developments in Vietnam, he intoned, were unsettling.

'According to reports in American newspapers, there was an attack on civilians in the South Vietnamese village of My Lai. Around 500 people were killed by American soldiers. Although the residents did not fight back, their homes were burned down and all the people killed, including many women and children.'

The anchor set aside the sheet of paper he had been reading from and looked straight into the camera. 'Clearly, it was a war crime.' Minh sank back into the sofa as bodies with twisted arms and legs appeared on the screen, captured in grainy, black-and-white photographs. He had always seen the Americans as protectors and friends. Could they really have killed all these people? *His* people?

The story of Hoa's aunt sprang to his mind. When she had shared it with him, he had dismissed it as propaganda. Now he felt stupid.

Over the next days, he read everything he could find about the massacre in My Lai. German newspapers reported on the incident with long features accompanied by horrific pictures. It turned out to really be the village where Hoa's aunt had lived. The attack had taken place back in March 1968, but the American military had been covering it up. The news magazine *Der Spiegel* devoted a fifteen-page cover story to the massacre — which took Minh, dictionary in hand, six hours to read. The article accused the American government of waging a war it couldn't win. Why, it asked, was the US lying to the world?

The more Minh read, the clearer it became to him that there were many questions that had never crossed his mind: Why had the Vietnamese communists formed in the first place? What was in the 1954 Geneva Accords, which had led to the French withdrawal? Why were the Americans defending the country? What were the chances of reunification between the North and South? What were the chances for peace?

He wondered why these questions only occurred to him here in Germany. Perhaps you can only see the shape of things when you look at them from a distance, he told himself.

*

The next Sunday, Minh headed to the flea market on Berlin's 17th of June Street and spent two marks on a well-worn copy of a French standard work called *Indochina*, soon devoting his undivided attention to the tome. Using a pencil, he underlined the dates that seemed important to him: the beginning of French colonisation in the nineteenth century; the division of Vietnam along the 17th parallel in 1954; the resolution by the Geneva Conference to hold elections two years later. And the subsequent refusal by President Diem of South Vietnam, a protégé of the Americans, to hold those elections.

Suddenly, the war in Vietnam seemed like a game of chess played by the great powers, with his small homeland serving as the board. He now understood that his uncle spoke French so well because he had worked for the old colonial government, and that their old neighbour from Hanoi had moved south in 1954 to escape the communists. The more he read, the greater his sense of betrayal. He had always thought that people made decisions because of their personal hopes and anxieties, but now it dawned on him how often their actions were determined by geopolitics. He signed up for a student subscription to *Der Spiegel* and began struggling his way through the long articles about his homeland in each weekly issue. He read about villages that had been completely destroyed: straw roofs engulfed by flames, chickens and water buffalo slaughtered, surrounding rice fields befouled by blood and body parts drifting in the water.

He read about vast tunnel networks and secret pathways that the Viet Cong had built into the mountains of Laos and Cambodia to smuggle fighters and weapons from the North to the South.

He read about the South Vietnamese president, Thieu, who was disliked and corrupt; about the American president, Nixon, and his fight against the anti-war movement; about the futile peace talks in Paris that dragged on year after year.

Most of all, though, he saw the pictures of the eighteen-, nineteen-, twenty-year-old soldiers, hundreds of thousands of whom had lost their lives in the swamps, forests, and streets of his homeland. Men of his age. Boys like him. Their bodies lying on the ground like garbage, faces disfigured by bullets, arms and legs twisted grotesquely in death. Now it had ceased to matter whether their lives had begun to the north or to the south of the 17th parallel.

Why did they have to die in this squalid war while he sat in his student residence reading books?

*

Four months later, Hoa was suddenly standing at the front door down below, as if they had agreed to meet up to study together. The air smelled of spring and she was wearing a denim jacket, her expression somewhere between delight, embarrassment, and anxiety — a look he couldn't recall ever having seen on her face before. Her left hand was wrapped around the handle of a large red suitcase, her right clutched a pack of Gauloises Red. Surprised, he led her up to his room.

'Thank you for your letter,' she muttered, as though he had written it yesterday and not several months ago. Hoa opened her mouth as if she wanted to say something more, but then slumped down on his chair without a word. Her legs were bouncing, her hands rubbed up and down her thighs. Outside, dusk was slowly bringing the day to an end.

'I need your help,' she began. 'I didn't know where else to go.'

He wasn't sure if her surprise appearance was a good sign or a bad one. Her long silence had hurt him at first, but then his sadness had hardened into anger; intentionally or not, she had forced him into the role of a beggar, which he found deeply offensive. At the same time, he was happy to see her again, and he felt a certain gratification at the fact that she had turned to him — and him alone — in her time of need. Peter was apparently no longer part of the equation.

He took a seat on the bed across from her and turned on the bedside lamp. Hoa sat there wringing her hands.

'Out of the blue, the money for my studies stopped coming in,' she began. 'At first, I thought there was some mistake, so I went to the bank to ask. That's how I found out that the Study Abroad Office had suspended my scholarship. Then, something arrived from Vietnam.'

She opened her suitcase and fished out a crumpled light-blue airmail envelope with diagonal red-and-blue stripes on the edges.

'There was no letter, just this.'

She carefully pulled a folded newspaper article out of the envelope and handed it to Minh. It was page ten of a South Vietnamese newspaper from the month before last. In the side column was a short article marked with an X.

> On Monday, 2 February 1970, the Military Court sentenced overseas student Phan Ánh Hoa in absentia to 20 years in exile for treason. If she returns to the Republic of Vietnam prior to that, she will be penalised with seven years of forced labour. The convicted is a student at the University of Heidelberg in Germany, where she has engaged in pro-communist activities. She has screened propaganda films under false pretexts and sought to politically incite other students. A courageous compatriot notified the South Vietnamese authorities. The traitor's stipend, generously granted by the government, will be suspended immediately.

Minh let the paper slide out of his hands onto the bed. The lamplight cast a shadow of Hoa's profile on the wall — her flat nose, long hair, and round face. He thought back to the carefree girl that he had first encountered in Frau Schmidt's kitchen not even two years ago. Now she was being portrayed as a criminal. Twenty years of exile. A traitor. A foreign agent. She sounded like a villain straight out of a James Bond movie.

'What did you do?' he whispered.

She heard the slight quaver in his voice and looked over at him, shoulders slumped. Hoa, too, had read the reports about My Lai, but in contrast to Minh, she hadn't withdrawn to read even more. Instead, she had set up an event at her university. She and some German students had shown film clips from My Lai, and she had spoken about what she knew from her aunt. Interest in the evening had been significant, and a couple of Vietnamese students, fresh from the homeland, had also been sitting in the audience. One of them must have reported her to the embassy.

'So who sent you this anonymous letter?' Minh asked.

'My father reads this newspaper every day — I'm sure it was him. He probably didn't write anything so as not to put the family in danger. It's bad enough that they're related to me.'

'Do you think he's mad at you?'

Hoa shrugged her shoulders. 'Maybe. Maybe not. My parents don't have much money. Their main concern is probably not getting into trouble themselves. It's obvious that the South Vietnamese government wants to threaten me. The message is clear: Don't come back!'

'Shit.'

'That's one way to put it.'

'Are you scared?'

'I was at first. I couldn't sleep the first few days. I kept thinking the whole time that I could never go back. I just lay there and dreamt about sneaking back into our house to surprise my father. But whenever he turned towards me, I would wake up. Maybe he wouldn't be happy to see me at all. I can't escape the feeling that he doesn't want me to come back either.'

She grabbed the page of the newspaper and slowly crumpled it up.

'I never thought the South Vietnamese government would feel threatened by someone like me. I'm just a student overseas, I only wanted to tell the truth. I was naive, I guess. Maybe the best thing to do is to keep your mouth shut and not say what you know.'

Hoa's banishment was the best thing that had happened to Minh in a long time. They shared his room for a week, heading to the Free University in the mornings and cooking together in the shared kitchen in the evenings. At night, they would sleep reversed in his narrow bed, her legs bumping against his back and his feet against her head. Every time their bodies brushed each other, his heart would skip a beat. Sometimes, when he was still dozing, he would think about turning around and taking her in his arms as they slept. But something kept holding him back.

She got herself a waitressing job, and Minh found a room for her on the third floor. But they still saw each other every day, almost like it had been back in Ebersberg. Now, though, he gave her things to read. The French book on Indochina, the *Der Spiegel* story on My Lai, a report by a German doctor called 'My Years in Vietnam'. Minh remembered how she had once mentioned that *The Tale of Kiều* was her favourite book, so he began looking for it all over Berlin, finally discovering it in a library that bore the impossibly German name Stiftung Preußischer Kulturbesitz. To his surprise, they had the Vietnamese original on their shelf: *Truyện Kiều*.

Kiều, he thought to himself, what a beautiful name.

One evening, he found Hoa in her room hunched over a clattering black typewriter, carefully typing letter after letter with her index finger. She quietly pronounced the words as they appeared on the page. Next to her was a notebook, in which something had been written by hand.

'Where did you get that thing?' Minh asked.

'From Werner,' Hoa responded without looking up.

'Werner? I didn't even know you were friends.'

'You were the one who told me about him, remember? I got in touch with him when I needed help writing a protest letter. And he immediately got me a typewriter.'

'What do you mean, protest letter?' Minh asked as he took a seat on her bed. 'Are you part of this clique now too?'

'Oh, come on!' Hoa fired back. 'They disbanded a long time ago. The group dynamics weren't right.'

'The *what*?'

Hoa turned towards Minh, rolling her eyes. 'What do I know! They didn't get along. Werner didn't give me much detail. He said something about violence against property and violence against people.'

Minh shook his head. 'I never understood Werner and his friends. I didn't even understand them when they were talking about Vietnam.'

He stretched out on her bed, arms behind his head.

'Do you really think you can change anything with a letter? What are you trying to protest against?'

'There's a case just like mine in Munich, some guy from Da

Nang. They want to take away his scholarship because he took part in a discussion about America's role in Vietnam. I'm afraid we're being watched by the South Vietnamese authorities. We have to defend ourselves, Minh! We need to teach the embassy that they can't push us around like children.'

Impressed, he let out a low whistle. Apparently, the fervour of the German students had rubbed off on her.

'Werner suggested that I send a German version to *Der Spiegel*,' Hoa continued. She pointed to the notebook next to her. 'He wrote down a few phrases for me. They sound good.'

'Are you setting yourself up for trouble again?'

'I'm not scared anymore. What can they do? Banish me? I can't go back anyway!'

She turned away from him and started typing again, a cloud of frenzied concentration. Minh flipped though his anatomy book for a bit, but the clacking of the typewriter made it impossible for him to focus. He looked over at Hoa, bent over her desk, full of defiance. Suddenly he felt like a coward for only silently asking himself questions and not daring to discuss them with anyone else. Maybe he should be taking some action too?

He sat up, climbed out of bed, and stood behind Hoa. The hammering of the return lever punctuated her outrage line by line: *We — refuse — to — tolerate — any — interference — in — our — affairs.*

He grabbed the notebook lying on the table next to her. And suddenly, an idea came to him: 'Let's write a third letter when you've finished this one. A letter that we can send to all Vietnamese students in Germany. Maybe we can join forces!'

*

Shortly before Christmas, Minh and Hoa organised their first demonstration. The air smelled of sweat and gingerbread as they linked arms with Werner, holding each other's gaze to gather courage for the march.

Hundreds of people were lined up behind them, holding posters and flags — exuding an energy of unanimity that warmed the army of protesters and set them in motion. Leading a demonstration turned out to be far easier than he had thought it would be. All Minh had to do was put one foot in front of the other and give his anger free rein. How much longer was he supposed to stand aside and watch as his homeland was bombed to bits in the name of freedom? How many more images of mangled corpses was this war going to produce?

The ruined tower of the Gedächtniskirche jutted into the cold blue sky as they trudged through the slushy snow. Christmas shoppers, standing in front of brightly lit stores, stopped to watch. Some began clapping in support. Others chanted 'Ho-Ho-Ho-Chi-Minh ...' Someone at the back of the demonstration joined in. Then someone in the front. The name rolled through the ranks.

'Ho-Ho-Ho-Chi-Minh ...'

And Minh, his cheeks flushed, joined in.

Ever since he and Hoa had written that protest letter, his life had taken a new direction. The Vietnamese students they had befriended had sent the letter to their friends, inspiring Minh to set up an association. Two people turned into eleven, then twenty, and then more than fifty. They cooked together and studied together, focusing not just on the history of Vietnam, but also on the theory of communism. They read Mao, Marx, and Ho Chi Minh; they spoke of exploitation, revolution, and independence. His transition to the other side had been so gradual and profound that Minh didn't think much about it. He felt like he had woken up from a political hibernation. It wasn't just their shared origins that tied him to his new friends; it was also the fight for a greater purpose. Now that they had seen the light, they had to help others see it as well. Minh felt like he had finally found a home in Germany. He finally felt important. German students began inviting him to their parties, while pastors and philosophers wanted to engage him in discussion, their voices filled with respect when they asked him what was 'really' going on in Vietnam.

This is what it must feel like to find your calling in life, Minh thought. You suddenly feel important and special.

By the time they reached the Amerikahaus, behind the railway arches at Zoologischer Garten station, his voice had grown hoarse and raw. When Werner called him up as the next speaker, he trembled with nervousness. Yesterday, he had practised his lines in front of the small mirror in his bathroom. Today, he was looking out at a sea of red-and-blue flags emblazoned with yellow stars. Elevated by the euphoria of the crowd, he stepped up onto a plastic crate. Turning his back on the red-white-and-blue façade of the building, he took a deep breath. Werner handed him the megaphone. It lay heavy and expectantly in his hands. Faces turned up to him full of anticipation. German faces. Vietnamese faces.

Hoa's face.

'Enough of my homeland being bombed back into the Stone Age,' he shouted. 'Enough of the war that is tearing our families apart. Enough of Americans slaughtering our people. Why the hell are they in Vietnam? When are they finally going to stop the senseless killing?'

The wind carried his words down to the street, to the supermarket, and through the railway arches, where the homeless looked up from their bottles of beer.

How loud he was.

He ordered US president Nixon to cease all fighting and fully investigate all war crimes. He called for South Vietnamese president Thieu to step down for the good of the entire country. He insisted that the German government provide more humanitarian support, and entreated his fellow students, German and Vietnamese alike, to stop believing the lies of their governments. He issued demand after demand until his voice failed him completely and he was swallowed up by the cheering of the masses.

He lurched down into the crowd, looking for her. Her eyes were glowing.

'I could have listened to you for another ten hours,' Hoa whispered.

Her hand brushed his, warming his insides. He saw the snow falling on her hair and felt her standing there next to him, breathing next to him. He smelled her skin, taking it in. Quietly, he mumbled to her: 'Do you really think they understood me? With my accent?'

Laughing, she kissed him.

*

Using his deep-blue ink, he now penned another letter. He wrote to his parents to tell them that he had met a woman and was going to live with her in a small apartment in the residence hall. He wrote that they would doubtlessly like Hoa, as she was Vietnamese, but also at ease in the West. He wrote that he could imagine getting married to her one day and returning to Vietnam together. He included a photo with the letter, a portrait that he had taken of her shortly before the demonstration began.

'Hoa also sends her greetings,' he wrote.

The answer to his letter reached him two months later. It included a thin sheet of paper filled with his mother's handwriting. It wasn't what he had been expecting:

> Your father and I heard about your new friends in Berlin. We are surprised by what others have told us. Have you forgotten that you shouldn't get involved in things that don't concern you? Have you lost track of why you are in Germany? From a distance, it is difficult to understand what is going on in Vietnam, and it is easy to confuse friends and enemies. Don't ever forget what kind of family you come from. Focus on your studies and stay away from distractions. We are doing well, but we are very worried about you!

She had folded the photo of Hoa in two and put it in the envelope along with her letter. A single sentence was written on the back:

> She isn't good enough for you.

KIỀU

When my father announces that Aunt Linh plans to show us where my late grandmother is interred, I don't know what I should be more afraid of: A Vietnamese cemetery and my ignorance of how to behave in such a place. Or my deaf aunt and my inability to talk to her.

'So where is this cemetery?' I ask, as if knowing the street name would affect my dilemma in any way.

He pulls out his mobile phone. Another twenty messages are waiting under the heading DINNER TONIGHT in the extended family's WhatsApp group. His finger stops.

'Hoa Nghiêm Temple, 13041 Nelson Street.' He pronounces the street name with a demonstratively American accent.

We've been in California for a week now, and in that time, I've noticed a remarkable change in my father. After seeming a bit reserved for the first couple of days, he has quickly adapted to the extended family's routine. He often hums to himself in the car, and if someone makes a suggestion, his standard response is 'yes'. His Vietnamese has acquired a greater depth, but he also peppers his sentences with American phrases like '*alright*' or '*Let's do it!*' just as his siblings do.

Every day, we meet his brothers and sisters for coffee, lunch, dinner, or a combination thereof. Even though they haven't seen each other in more than a decade, they get along well. So well that it's almost like they're trying to make up for lost time.

Strangely, though, that important conversation — the one where they talk in detail about the last year with my dying grandmother, or the fifteen years before that — still hasn't taken place. The absence of a heart-to-heart discussion is so palpable that I can't help thinking: a German family would surely have spoken about these things by now.

Instead, my relatives talk about her in anecdotes and asides. 'At the end, she thought she was a young girl in Vietnam again,' they'll say, for example, as we're standing in line at a Vietnamese bakery to pick up some bánh bao dumplings. Or, as we wander the streets of LA's Chinatown looking for the best dim-sum restaurant: 'We took care of her at home for a long time, and Linh washed her, fed her, and rocked her to sleep like a baby.' Or, when we stop to buy some 'I Love Little Saigon' T-shirts at the night market in front of the shopping centre with the red-and-yellow flags: 'Before she died, she was pining for home, but we didn't know how to make her wish come true.'

Their pain surfaces briefly but is never completely laid bare. They provide us with enough of a hint as to how difficult it must have been for the family as my grandmother became more forgetful and fragile. But they also spare us from uncomfortable questions — questions about my father and his duties as eldest son.

Why did he never visit his mother in all those years? Why had he told me so little about her? Does he regret not having gone to see her one last time? Did he ever think about his siblings, who had to bear the burden of care and grief without him?

The German in me can sense the constant presence of such questions, filling every empty crevice between the chitchat and sightseeing. The Vietnamese in me knows why they aren't talking about it: no one wants to disrupt the family harmony and taint this visit with hurt feelings, accusations, or difficult questions. Why delve into the ugly details of the past when the present is so fleeting and precious? Why talk about something when it can be covered in silence?

*

I'm in for a surprise when we reach the temple. I had imagined a spot with a garden, a wooden bridge, and perhaps a small gazebo. But the place where my grandmother rests could easily be mistaken for a company cafeteria. The building is unadorned, a yellow concrete structure, with the only hints at Buddhism being the curved roofline and the red letters above the entrance proclaiming it a school of the Dalai Lama.

My aunt emerges from the open door and starts waving when she sees us. She rushes over to my father, who is still smoothing out his cotton shorts, wrinkled from the car ride. Clutching a black quilted Chanel handbag, she's wearing a Marilyn Monroe dress and zebra-patterned flip-flops. Her eyebrows have been drawn in high arches and her lipstick is a soft pink shade. An ageless beauty. Standing opposite her, you feel like you're in a Hollywood film.

She pushes her sunglasses back into her hair and hugs my father in that peculiar Vietnamese way: quickly and with no physical contact. She then pats his belly, grimaces, and gives a thumbs down.

We've been eating out so often here that he's starting to develop a noticeable bulge beneath his T-shirt. He shrugs with a *shit happens* expression on his face, prompting a laugh. In her own wordless way, she too evinces that dry Vietnamese tenderness that requires no verbal expression.

I know from Uncle Sơn that Aunt Linh hardly left the house when she was a girl. There weren't any schools for deaf children in Vietnam at that time, and because my grandmother was worried about her safety, Linh wasn't allowed out by herself. She learned a bit of reading and writing from her siblings, who would point to objects and write the corresponding words on a chalkboard. Otherwise, they communicated with her by moving their lips in an exaggerated manner when they spoke, or through gestures. Linh spent her youth cooking for the family and sewing clothes for her doll. Later, much later, she would tell her siblings that throughout her childhood and youth, she had dreamt of only one thing: to attend school.

That dream came true for her in America. It's here that she was able to learn sign language and train to become a beautician. Here is where she met a man who wanted to marry her and was willing to move into a house next door to her mother. In contrast to the family, he studied sign language so he could properly talk to her. Who knows if she could ever have achieved this normal, middle-class life in Vietnam, a place she never wanted to visit. Here, in California, she seemed content to spend her free time at the mall and around the family. Although her mother used nothing but the simplest gestures to communicate with her daughter right up to the end, the two saw and 'spoke' to each other every day and night in the months before her death. And as her mother faded, the other relatives would say, 'Aunt Linh is the only one who can still understand her.'

*

When we enter the temple, we are greeted by the sweet smell of incense. We walk past a low-ceilinged hall divided into rows of wooden seats. From behind, I see the backs of worshippers who have tied white cloth ribbons around their heads in honour of the deceased. We keep walking until we reach a bright room filled with the scent of orchids. A golden Buddha is enthroned on a pedestal upfront.

I haven't been to many funerals, so I always feel a bit awkward in cemeteries. Here, in this temple, though, I'm even more disoriented. Neither the Vietnamese characters nor the religious symbols hold any meaning for me. The walls are decorated with metal-framed wooden plaques encasing bronze images. Some of the people pictured are young and made up as if for wedding portraits. They seem like figures from another era, doll-like and surreal.

I look for my grandmother's face, but I can't find it. Absently, I stare at the wall.

Aunt Linh's gaze meets mine, and wordlessly, she seems to understand. She grabs my arm and pulls me to the other corner of the room and I stumble after her, relieved to be led. She delicately taps against the glass of a display case, behind which a dozen black urns with golden adornments and black-and-white photos stand next to each other.

'*Ma.*' Her lips push the word out of her throat. It's the Vietnamese word for ghost or, pronounced with slightly different intonation, for mother. She holds up her index finger to indicate that she's not finished. Then she reaches into her handbag and pulls out the small pad she always carries with her. In deep concentration, she places the ballpoint pen on the paper: '*I miss her so much.*'

On the far left, I recognise the woman with curly hair and a dark áo dài. Her portrait is framed by a wreath. *Nguyễn Thị Liên* is written in large silver letters below. Born on 2 March 1936, in Saigon, Vietnam; died on 24 December 2016, in Westminster, California. She was eighty years old.

Only now, standing in front of her urn, do I realise that I have just learned my grandmother's name for the first time. For me, she was always just bà nội, my paternal grandmother. The only name I knew her by was her position in the family hierarchy. I never even wondered about her real name. And I never asked.

*

On the way back from the temple, I am as silent as my aunt, who we bid farewell with hand gestures. I am ashamed to be so ignorant about my own family history, and it adds to my guilt that I only realised this today.

A question Germans often asked me in my youth pops into my head: '*Where are you from?*' I tended to be rather sensitive about it because it sounded like a rejection to me. Between the lines, I could hear their confusion as to how a young woman with black hair could speak their language as well as they did.

I knew it wasn't racism, but it was their way of letting me know that, despite my best efforts, I was different and always would be. A misfit who constantly had to explain herself and her odd existence. A rare creature that had been released into the wrong habitat and had lost contact with its herd.

Because it bothered me, I refused to give them the answer they wanted and told them the truth instead. '*I'm from Berlin,*' I'd usually say. Or, if they kept pushing, '*from North Berlin, to be more precise.*' I would see the disappointment in their faces, their frustration over my rebuff, their refusal to let it go. After a brief pause, they would clear their throat and ask: '*I mean, what are your roots?*'

In my mind's eye, I could see a tree growing, roots stretching deep into the earth and gathering nourishment from the soil. The breadth of its trunk, the shape of its leaves — yellow, red, or green and serrated — all that could be explained by the roots. It was like an image out of a gardening book, simple and descriptive, but completely inadequate for describing the tangled paths that make up who I am.

'*Where are you from?*' For the first time, it occurs to me that there might be another way of framing this question.

Not as a question that can only be answered with the name of some country of origin, but as a search for all those who came before me and left their visible and invisible traces along the path to the present. My parents, my relatives. The ways in which they deal with life, or don't deal with life. Even if I don't remember a single sentence uttered by my grandmother, that too says quite a lot. About her and about all the other nebulous people who are part of me.

*

As I am lying on my motel bed that afternoon, I get a WhatsApp message from Uncle Sơn. To my surprise, he has only sent it to me, and he has written it in English.

'Look what I found while cleaning!'

It's a photo of a photo. I'm wearing a denim skirt and a spaghetti strap top; an embarrassed smile reveals the metal grill of my braces. Uncle Sơn is standing next to me with mirrored sunglasses and yellow flip-flops, his arm around my shoulders. The photo must have been taken fifteen years ago in Vietnam. In the background, the tamarind-lined avenue in Saigon where my father grew up can be seen.

Suddenly I remember how we went to the old house on the last day of our holiday because my dad had learned that his family from California were staying there. A distant cousin who managed the building on behalf of his relatives had told him. When we arrived, she slid open the gate and let us in, saying the others were already waiting. In the living room, we met my uncle and grandmother, who had just arrived from America and would be in town for four weeks.

I remember my Uncle Sơn constantly jumping up to bring something or clear things away while my parents sat at the table drinking tea with my grandmother. She had been living in California for many years, but my father seemed strangely uninformed about her life there. For some reason, the conversation was mostly about money. 'Are you receiving the transfers from Germany?' he asked her. 'Is it enough for the rent and Linh's education?' I understood that something else was being negotiated here, but I didn't know what.

My uncle returned at some point with a deck of cards and asked my siblings and I if we would like to play. He taught us a Vietnamese game called tiến lên, and the longer we played, the more we liked him. He let us win from time to time and liked to joke around, which was very different from my father, who was strict and serious.

Finally, Uncle Sơn clapped his hands and asked if anyone else was hungry. He had heard about a good new restaurant nearby and wanted to introduce my dad to someone there. As we stood outside on the street waiting for a taxi, he put his hand on my shoulder and told me I looked like a young version of my grandmother.

'But you're more of a quiet type like your dad, aren't you?' he remarked. Someone grabbed a camera and snapped some photos of us. I found it all quite embarrassing, of course.

I had completely forgotten about our encounter in Vietnam, but now I could see everything again so clearly, like a movie playing in the cinema of my imagination.

'What a funny photo!' I write to Uncle Sơn. 'A long time ago.'

He replies immediately.

'You had those braces back then!'

'Please! Don't remind me!'

'Hehe.' I can almost hear him giggling like a little boy.

'How was the temple today?' he enquires.

'Strange,' I answer.

'Why?'

My finger floats in the air. Now would be a good time to ask him the questions that haunt me when I can't sleep at night. We're chatting so casually and comfortably that I'm sure my uncle wouldn't hold it against me. I slowly start typing.

'When I stood in front of the urn, I found myself wondering why it is that we live in Germany while you live in America. How come we've never visited you? Was there a fight in the family? Did grandma say anything about it before she died?'

I re-read my message to make sure it doesn't sound too serious or personal. Then I tell myself: If I can't even ask my own family personal questions, then who can I ask?

Ping. A new message from Uncle Sơn.

'Have you decided where you want to eat tonight? The steak restaurant I told you about is really good. Tell your father not to listen to the others. They don't know anything!'

Quickly, and with a sense of relief, I delete everything I have just written.

'Steak?' I reply. 'I LOVE steak!'

THE STORY OF MY UNCLE
SƠN

Saigon, 1975

Sơn saw himself desperately sprinting away from a group of men. They were waving a red-and-blue flag with a yellow star, their faces twisted in hatred as they came after him with giant strides. 'Grab the boy!' called a slender, bearded man who looked like Ho Chi Minh. 'Grab him and cut his hair off!'

Sơn screamed.

And woke up.

Heart thumping in his chest, he sat up in bed and wiped his brow. The weak light of the moon shone through the window, casting soft shadows onto the walls of his room, and on the Beatles poster that his brother Minh had put up ages ago. Next to it was another of a beach in California that John had given him. The clock on his bedside table read 3.24 am.

Sơn grabbed his pillow and headed for his parents' bedroom, pushing the door handle down slowly so as not to wake them. Even though they would certainly scold him in the morning, he snuck in, laid his pillow on the floor, and nestled his head into it. Curled up like a cat, he closed his eyes. In the darkness, he could hear his father snoring.

Ever since refugees had begun pouring into Saigon, Sơn had been having trouble sleeping, frequently waking up in the middle of the night. With their torn shirts and empty eyes, they looked to him like ghosts haunting the city. But they weren't ghosts. They were the relatives of neighbours, suddenly appearing huddled on the sidewalk with their clothes, pots, and fears. They were women and children who slept in the large temple near his school. They were former soldiers, their arms and legs torn to pieces, who would limp across the street to ask him for money. In hoarse voices, they would speak of the homes they had left behind as they fled from the communists; of the bloody corpses they had passed on their long escape; of the hostile army, conquering one city after the next on its inexorable march towards the capital.

Sơn's teachers and classmates also talked frequently about the Viet Cong, in whispers at first, but before long their voices grew louder and louder. Rumour had it that the communists buried their enemies alive. Allegedly, they first planned to put wealthy families on trial in their people's courts before then sentencing them to death. It was said that the women would only be allowed to wear black and the men would be locked away in prison. The fingernails of the girls would be cut short, as would the hair of the boys.

Why, Sơn wondered, did the communists punish children? What kind of hateful people must they be?

Whenever he woke up in the middle of the night, such questions would swirl around in his head. He would lay awake brooding in the dark for hours at a time. There certainly were a lot of South Vietnamese soldiers who had been wounded, like his father. But the Americans were strong and powerful, weren't they? And they were fighting on the South's side and would never leave them to the enemy. That's what he would tell himself as he lay on the floor next to his parents' bed before finally falling back into a restive sleep. But during the day, when his father, arm in a sling, would sit on the balcony listening to Voice of America, Sơn was never able to screw up the courage to ask him what he thought of the situation.

*

One morning, a report came on the radio saying that the communists had attacked the Saigon airport during the night. Sơn ran out into Liberty Street when he heard it. In the pale-blue sky, he could see American helicopters circling as they evacuated their people, while down on the street, black buses were fighting their way through the traffic. The city was clogged with people trying to flee Saigon. So it was true. The enemy had arrived.

He ran screaming back into the house only to be slapped in the face by his mother. 'Pull yourself together, damn it!' she yelled. 'We have to go. We have to get out of here!'

They quickly packed what they could carry and ran for it. His father led the way, carrying a leather satchel full of money and documents, his mother close behind him, holding Linh's hand. Hùng was lugging a suitcase full of clothes, and Hồng was hauling a bag full of rice and noodles. Sơn cradled an album full of family photos in his arms. They ran past the Continental Palace hotel, from which the American correspondents had checked out that morning. Past the National Assembly, which had seen two presidents come and go in just the last two weeks. Past the hospital, where wounded South Vietnamese soldiers were being brought in like supplies to a factory that is unable to shut down its machines.

They finally reached the American Embassy, but they were too late: the black gate in front of the boxy white building was closed, and there was a sea of people in front of it spilling out into the surrounding streets. Heavily armed American soldiers were standing on a wall next to the gate. Every now and then, they would reach down to pull people out of the crowd, one at a time, flopping like fish on a line. 'Take me! If you can't take me, at least take my child!'

His father waved his documents wildly in the air above his head, still believing that papers might be able to save them. 'I was a colonel in the South Vietnamese Army, you have to let me into the embassy or they'll kill me!'

His mother was waving dollar bills in the air, still believing that they had some value. 'I'll give you $1,000 if you let me and my family in! $1,000!'

They screamed, begged, and pleaded, but the men on the wall didn't respond. At some point, Sơn's mother turned to him and said: 'You speak English! Do something!' She grabbed him by the shoulders and shook him.

Sơn let the photo album fall to the ground, grabbed the suitcase out of his brother's hands, and emptied it onto the street. He quickly rifled through the clothing and found the American T-shirt printed with *Don't worry, be happy*. Its smiley beamed into the wind as he raced back down Thống Nhất Boulevard and turned left into Mạc Đĩnh Chi, desperately looking for the side entrance to the compound.

Where was the place where the cars would drive in again?

Everywhere he looked, there were people — arms, legs, hands, heads. It made him dizzy. Somebody shoved him and he fell awkwardly onto his right leg as someone else trampled over his T-shirt and then onto his foot.

He gasped in pain.

He pulled himself back to his feet and felt a burning sensation. But he limped onwards, the snarled traffic on his right and the sea of people on his left. He fought his way forward and finally found the entrance, but it too was closed. A red-haired man was standing on the white wall that surrounded the building.

'Mister! Please help me!'

Sơn was five foot two, fifteen years old, and his voice was cracking. The man on the wall didn't hear him.

Sơn fought his way further into the crowd, pushing his slender body between the others, slowly making his way towards the wall. He could see the barbed wire they had stretched out above it and the sweat on the face of the red-headed soldier.

He jumped up and down, ignoring the pain it caused.

'Help! I'm all alone!'

He held up his T-shirt and began waving it around like a flag.

'I love America!'

The man on the wall glanced in his direction. He squinted, hesitated for a moment, and then leaned down. He waved Sơn over and stretched out his hand. Other hands immediately went for it.

'Only the boy with the T-shirt!' the redhead yelled. 'Let the boy with the T-shirt through!'

He began pulling Sơn up, his biceps bulging. A man next to Sơn grabbed him, hanging off his injured foot.

'Just the boy!' the soldier yelled. 'Let go or I'll shoot!'

Sơn came to rest on the wall right next to the barbed wire. Someone else lowered him down on the other side into the embassy compound. He could hardly keep his balance, but whether it was because of his euphoria at having made it or the pain he was in — he wasn't sure. Everything had gone so fast. It was all too much.

'Get to the helicopter,' the soldier yelled to him. 'Quick!'

Sơn heard the loud clattering of a helicopter landing somewhere nearby. He limped ahead.

Next to the parking lot lay the severed trunk of a gigantic tamarind tree, its lush branches spread out across the ground, leaves still glowing an opulent green. A huge helicopter was descending out of the sky right where the stump of the tree was still protruding from the soil. MARINES was printed on the belly of the bulbous, green aircraft, clearly visible as it sank to the ground.

The wind from the rotors knocked Sơn down.

He struggled back to his feet and limped onwards. Past the helicopter taking the first batch of people to the airport. Past the swimming pool where the next group was already waiting. He headed straight for the gate that was holding back the crowd of people peering at him from the outside, their eyes hungry with envy.

He threw himself against the white bars and yelled: 'Mom! Dad! Where are you?'

*

He was still lying there hours later, long after he had lost his voice and darkness had fallen. His ears were ringing from the constant clamour of the helicopters as they landed and took off. His heart was numb from the hope the noise awakened each time he heard it: *This helicopter is the one that will take us all away from here. This time I'll make it for sure!* But the hope was always followed by disappointment. For the thousandth time, he stared into the sea of faces, all looking exactly alike. His family was drifting somewhere out there. He looked at his hands — red, filthy, full of blisters — and wiped them across his tear-stained face.

Had he lost everything? Was it over?

Using the bars of the gate, he pulled himself up into a standing position, but his wobbly legs gave out and he collapsed back to the ground. Again, he picked himself up, this time onto his knees. He carefully set his hands into the gravel and began making his way forward on all fours.

Suddenly, somebody heaved him up from the ground and carried him piggyback over to the swimming pool, setting him down next to the edge. The water stank of urine and the lawn was covered with rubbish. He saw American soldiers with their Vietnamese girlfriends, embassy employees, military advisers. He saw Vietnamese officers and interpreters with signs pinned to their shirts — all of them with their families and children. Up in the sky, he could see the blinking lights of the American helicopters.

So many people and so few helicopters.

He rolled onto his back and spread out his arms, ready to surrender himself to his fate.

*

'Sơn, why are you lying here all by yourself?'

The voice was speaking English, but somehow it sounded

familiar. He blinked his eyes open to see John's broad face hovering over him. Could it really be true?

Sơn slowly lifted his head, wrapped his arms around John's neck, and allowed himself to be picked up like a baby. Finally, he wasn't alone any longer. Tentatively, he came to stand on his feet unaided.

'Are you alright, Sơn? Say something!'

John looked at him through tired eyes. He had returned to Vietnam two weeks earlier for his second tour and had dropped by the tailor's shop a few days before to give Sơn the poster of the beautiful California beach. With a twinkle in his eye, he had said that he hated the war, but loved Sơn's mother's cooking, which was the real reason behind his return to Saigon. Of course, she insisted that he stay for dinner. That evening, John had been loud and funny, telling stories about America. And even though Sơn's parents and siblings hadn't understood everything he was saying, they had all laughed together.

Now, though, John looked exhausted. All of his light-heartedness had vanished. The sleeves of his uniform were stained, his face glistened with dusty sweat, and he was unshaven, a patchy beard developing on his chin.

'You have to pull yourself together to get out of here. Got it?' John said. 'Stay strong, my friend!'

Sơn's eyelids grew heavy, and slowly they closed. He began whispering.

'I'm so tired, but I have to stay awake and wait for my family! So that we can take a helicopter to America together!'

Again, he sank to the ground. Over the last several weeks, his difficulties sleeping had led to an exhaustion that built up inside of him like water behind a dam. His arms and legs felt so heavy that he could hardly move them. He wanted so badly to sleep. Just for a moment. If he could just close his eyes for a few seconds.

John knelt down to him.

'Where is your family? I don't see them!' He bent down lower, speaking directly into Sơn's ear.

'Are they still outside? Didn't your family make it in?'

Sơn turned his head to the right and then to the left. Tears ran down his cheeks, leaving trails in the dirt on his face.

'Shit!'

John stood up.

'I'm going out to get them! Stay here and rest. I'll come get you once I've found them. Wait here for me, got it?'

Sơn heard John's heavy footsteps as he left. He closed his eyes, laying his head in his arms and curling up on the ground. John would take care of him. Everything would be okay. His breathing slowed as he fell asleep. He dreamt about escaping from the communists. They wanted to cut off his hair, but he flew away from them, shooting up into the sky in his smiley T-shirt like Superman: *Don't worry, be happy.*

*

He woke up because something had changed, but it took some time before he realised what it was. The noise of the helicopters had stopped, the clattering was gone. He sat up and looked around. The Vietnamese families with their children were still there, but there were no more soldiers on the top of the walls. Something was wrong.

He peered into the darkness, examining the shadowy outlines

of those still present. He saw women, men, and children. But the brawny outline of John? That he didn't see. He counted to a thousand, and because John still wasn't there, he kept on counting, until he reached 3,000.

Where were the American soldiers?

Sơn pushed himself to his feet and limped towards the embassy building. The windows were brightly lit, but when he went inside, it was completely empty. Cigarette butts were still glowing in ashtrays, and he lifted one into the light: Pall Mall.

He saw a fire escape and limped over to it.

'John! Where are you?'

His call echoed across the compound, amplifying the panic in his voice. Fear welled up inside him, pushing him up the next flight of stairs, and then the next. When he reached the third floor, he found himself standing in front of a wooden door — only the roof was still above him. He tried pushing down the door handle, but it wouldn't budge. He shook it and pulled it.

He could hear voices speaking English behind the door, all hectically talking over each other, filled with anger. One of them sounded like John.

'John, is that you? It's Sơn! Open the door!'

He pounded on it and tried shaking the handle again.

'I've been waiting for you outside! Let me in!'

The voices behind the door fell silent.

Then he heard steps.

He kept pounding. 'John, is that you? You said you'd take me with you! Where have you been this whole time?!'

A deep, throaty voice answered. It wasn't John's. 'I'm sorry,' the voice said.

'Let me talk to John,' Sơn called out. 'He'll help me!'

'There is no John here,' the voice said. And again: 'I'm sorry.'

Sơn started screaming: 'But John! You promised me!'

The sudden roar of rotors quickly swallowed up his shouts. Sơn could hear a huge helicopter landing on the roof, and the people behind the door rushing into it in a hail of rapidly barked orders. He threw himself at the door, but it had been blockaded from the inside. He pounded on it, screaming, but nobody heard him. Above him, people were flying off to freedom, but he was locked away like an animal. He howled as the helicopter took off again and flew away.

A deep silence returned.

He sank down onto the stairs. Outside the window, he could see the helicopter's blinking lights recede into the distance. He was suddenly aware of the cold and started to shiver. Snot, thick and slimy, ran out of his nose as he wept into his T-shirt.

'John,' he whimpered. 'Don't leave me behind with the communists.'

*

As night gave way to a new day, Sơn began to realise just how alone he was. A new era had dawned, an era of lost hopes. So this is what it feels like to be betrayed, he thought to himself. You suddenly feel so empty.

The morning sun shone weakly onto the rubbish dump that had been American territory until the night before. Women who had been telling their children about the new lives they would live in the USA just a few hours earlier were now carrying chairs out of the embassy. Men who had been unable to get their families to the helicopters were now clutching statues, glasses, and bronze plaques, their faces as grey as granite. Silently, they went about exacting their meagre revenge.

Sơn dragged himself home, sensing along the way that his pain had moved to a different place. Walking proved not to be a problem, but breathing had become difficult.

When he got home, he collapsed into his mother's arms.

We thought that you —
But I was —
We were standing there and —
The bars of the gate. They were so —
Everywhere, I looked everywhere for hours —
John was there, he wanted —

They stood there, clutching each other, for an hour or maybe a minute, he didn't know. Then his mother slowly loosened her embrace. She was wearing black house clothes. Her eyes were red.

*

He somehow managed to drag himself upstairs to wash the filth from his body. Then back downstairs and onto his moped. His mother got on behind him; she wanted to get to the French bank to withdraw their savings before the bank was gone, or the account was shut, or the money was lost — nobody knew what was going to happen. He rode as fast as he could, but the streets were clogged with mopeds, cars, and buses. He only really registered the traffic out of the corner of his eye as a panicked jumble of colour.

It was late when they reached the yellow building with the white stucco trim, a proud remnant of the era now coming to a close. Sơn used to take his mother to this building at the end of every month to deposit the dollars paid to them by their American lodger. And each time, she would happily tell him about the big modern hospital they would one day build with the money. But now, a furious crowd of people was gathered in front of an iron gate that could not be opened no matter how hard they tried. Hanging from the front of it was a handwritten sign: *fermée*.

He didn't speak French, but he immediately understood that this wasn't good. They jumped off the moped and began fighting their way through the crowd, with him leading the way and his mother following closely behind, until they finally found themselves at the front. Time seemed to slow as he watched his mother stick her hands through the bars, grabbing at the sign with quaking fingers. She turned it around, and then back again: *fermée*.

'But the clinic,' she whispered. 'Minh's clinic.'

*

The radio was so loud he could hear it from the street. As he came to a stop in front of his house, he wished it could just be silent for a moment. He felt so tired — and endlessly old. With a groan, he stepped off his moped.

'Intense fighting between the Viet Cong and South Vietnamese soldiers continues at the Saigon airport. Eyewitnesses have reported seeing deserters from the South Vietnamese army shooting wildly on National Route 1. Some of the victims are civilians ...'

A dog meandered by. It was quite large, a German shepherd. It had light-brown fur with black patches, and its right front paw appeared to be bleeding. It stared at Sơn, ears pricked up.

Sơn crouched down and began scratching the dog's neck. He had always loved animals. Tail wagging, the dog licked the exhaustion from Sơn's face.

'Where did you come from?' Sơn whispered.

The nametag hanging from the dog's collar read 'Lucy'. A girl, apparently. Sơn looked around for her owner, but people were rushing past him on both sides, their faces empty. Lucy, it seemed, had been left behind in the panic.

'You know what? Just stay with me!'

The dog trotted along beside him as Sơn pushed his moped into the hallway and parked it before heading to the kitchen to get some water. There, he found his father squatting on the floor, his back to the door. He was leaning over the recess in the tile floor where they always did the washing up. How strange, Sơn thought, that his father would be doing the dishes at a time like this.

Then he noticed the smoke rising from behind his father.

'We have breaking news from South Vietnamese president Minh, who has only been in office for the last 48 hours. President Minh has just called on all members of the South Vietnamese army to lay down their weapons. We repeat: All South Vietnamese soldiers are to cease fighting...'

The radio was so loud that it drowned out everything else. Sơn approached his father from behind and saw that he was burning something. The flames crackled as they ate their way through the beige fabric of his uniform, working their way up the sleeve to the shoulder and then the breast. Grey smoke rose from the light-coloured material. It stank even worse than burning hair.

Sơn's eyes started to water, but he didn't dare look away.

'What are you doing?'

The instant he uttered the question, he knew the answer. His father didn't look around. Speaking into the fire, he said: 'Bring me the photo album.'

He addressed Sơn so quietly that he could barely be heard, and he pointed upwards, towards the living room. They must have brought the album back with them from the American Embassy. Sơn ran up the stairs and found it on the floor in front of the balcony, a thick white album as big as an LP. It contained pictures from his parents' wedding, of their family vacations in Vũng Tàu, and of the beautiful red-roofed houses that Minh had sent from Germany. Sơn grabbed it and ran back downstairs.

His father pointed at the fire.

'We have to burn it. It has too many pictures of me.'

As smoke rose into Sơn's lungs, he could feel everything closing in on him. He grew short of breath, his heart racing. He clutched the photo album with both hands, holding on to his family's happiness. He refused to let go.

'We can't burn our memories!' he told his father, begging, then turned his head to the side, unable to hold back a cough.

His father grabbed his shoulder, squeezing gently.

'Give it up, son.'

KIỀU

Uncle Sơn leans forward towards the *Star Trek*-like dashboard of his car and switches on the radio. A woman's voice, as soft and sweet as a sixteen-year-old's, is crooning a cheesy Vietnamese pop song. My father, in the passenger seat next to him, starts humming along softly.

'I know the song, but who's the singer, Sơn?'

'Her name is Lê Vân. She's a big deal in Vietnam right now. She used to be an underwear model, and there are still a lot of sexy videos of her on YouTube. But now that she's dating the head of the state oil company, she's had to change her image. She gave a concert here in California a few months ago and it was sold out!'

'Really? Stars like that never come to Berlin.'

'That's the advantage of living here. It's like Vietnam, but without the grime, poverty, and communism.'

Uncle Sơn laughs, his fingers drumming on the steering wheel. We're riding in a yellow Mercedes SUV so big and pretentious that climbing into it in the parking lot was almost too much for me. He had insisted on picking the three of us up at the motel, exclaiming 'You rented *that* junker?' when he saw our black Chevy. Typical

Vietnamese, I thought to myself. This need to constantly flaunt that you have made it. The yellow polo shirt he's wearing is only a half shade off from the hue of his car.

We've been in Little Saigon for a week and a half now, and today is the first afternoon we are spending alone with Uncle Sơn. Everyone else has to work. He was almost apologetic about it in his WhatsApp message. Unlike Germans, the Vietnamese are herd animals; the larger the group, the more comfortable they feel. I'm also quite happy to be surrounded by others all the time; it distracts me from the unresolved problem of my pregnancy and makes it easier to play the role of the shy niece who is always smiling. My relatives don't expect me to say much about myself or share an opinion; it's enough for me to just sit there and say 'Yes' or 'Mmmh, delicious' from time to time. It gives me the feeling of travelling along on a journey whose direction I have no control over, a small part of something much larger.

'The communists had noble goals,' my father says after a moment. 'They just never got around to implementing them.'

In the rear-view mirror, I can see Uncle Sơn rolling his eyes. 'Are you still defending these people? After they came to power, there was nothing but corruption, re-education camps, and people trying to escape. Believe me, anh, I lived through it.'

'You saw families like ours lose everything after the war. But what about all the other families? The ones who lived in the North? Or those who were torn apart for decades because of the partition? Say what you want about the communists, but at least they reunited the country and secured its independence.'

Uncle Sơn shakes his head, looking upset and resigned at the same time.

'When I was little, Mother always told me to take you as an

example. You were so intelligent. You were such a good speaker. But listening to you now, I just don't get you ...' He sighs. 'Communism turned Vietnam into an unfree country, kept down by mediocre, corrupt Party hacks. Look at the streets here! The businesses. When will Vietnam reach this standard of living? Not in our lifetimes.'

My father turns in the passenger seat to face him. He doesn't raise his voice, instead emphasising his words with animated gestures. It looks like he's giving a speech to an audience of one.

'You have the wrong idea of me, really! I know that you suffered a lot and that the communists made big mistakes. But Vietnam has developed considerably in recent years. Every time I visit Saigon these days, there are new hotels and stores. Many people are better off today than they used to be. That's also part of the truth, is it not?'

My uncle turns his head towards the window on the left and lowers it. The stores of Little Saigon pass by outside. He mumbles his words into the breeze.

'It's funny that you, of all people, are lecturing me about wrong perceptions ... I guess it's easy to be an idealist when you've been so far away for so long.'

Their animosity spreads through the car like an unpleasant odour. Uncle Sơn exhales vociferously and turns up the stereo. As the singing grows louder, it reminds me of our neighbour's cat, the one that always meows loudly at night. Even though I've been exposed to Vietnamese music since childhood, it still all sounds like caterwauling to me. It must be the instruments — the high-pitched hum of the zither, the synthesiser accompaniment, or perhaps the unfamiliar harmonies and melancholic voices. One famous song is about a soldier's wife who waits so long for him to come home after the war that she turns to stone. My father told me about it when I was a child, and even today, it perfectly reflects the image I have of all Vietnamese songs: corny, sad, and with a strange ideal of love, equating it with self-sacrifice.

We pass by a billboard of a black-haired woman in a business suit smiling down at the passing cars. 'Lisa Tran wants to MAKE AMERICA GREAT AGAIN!' it reads. Next to it is a photo of her with Donald Trump, who has his arm around her shoulder and is giving a thumb's up. Tran, apparently, is a local Republican.

'Now *that's* someone who loves his country!' Uncle Sơn says, to no one in particular.

'Trump?' my father replies. 'I've read that a lot of Vietnamese people support him.' He says it carefully, as if he's slowly trying to reconnect with his brother.

'He's different from other politicians,' Uncle Sơn replies. 'He got really rich in the business world. He knows how the economy works. And he's the only one who stands up to China. Of course a lot of Vietnamese people think that's good!'

'Many in Europe have a problem with him. He doesn't act presidential with his constant tweeting and the insulting things he says about other countries. It doesn't go over well abroad.'

Uncle Sơn shrugs his shoulders.

'He doesn't suck up to other countries, that's it! And he speaks his mind because he's honest. What harm will it do if he's in the White House for a few years? Politicians can't be trusted anyway. Why not give him a chance?'

'Kiều said you voted for him. Is that true?'

'Did she?' He looks at me in the rear-view mirror and raises an eyebrow. He sounds annoyed.

I shrug my shoulders. Even if my Vietnamese were smoother, I wouldn't know what to say to him. It's clear that he and I are on different sides of the political divide. Neither of us would be persuaded by the other. Should I lecture him anyway, even though he is older than me and I am 'only' his niece? My mother, sitting next to me in the back seat, puts a hand on my shoulder. *Let it go*, her look says.

'What alternative is there to Trump?' My uncle demands, clearly agitated. 'You can't trust the Democrats; all they do is spread fake news. They won't do anything to stop China — they're far too soft, and they probably even sympathise with them. The only thing on their minds is raising taxes. I'll tell you again, anh: if the leftists come to power here as well, it will be the end of us. California is home to many refugees from South Vietnam. We risked our lives to escape the reds, and we won't let it happen again.'

He shakes his head and accelerates.

'You were too far away to understand. You don't know all that we've lost! What the war did to our family!'

*

Uncle Sơn stops in front of a house at the end of a cul-de-sac with a front yard and purple orchids. We're in an area where white people live, devoid of nail salons or phở restaurants. Without wanting to be, I am impressed by the upper-middle-class ambience. We walk up a small flight of stairs.

'I'm home!'

The anger from earlier seems to have dissipated. Uncle Sơn's voice betrays the giddy delight of a husband who, after a long day at the office, is about to be welcomed home by his wife with his favourite dish.

Instead, the sound of barking erupts, followed by the rapid patter of paws racing through the house towards the door. More barking. He must have dogs. Several of them.

I back away.

Why didn't anyone warn me? Ever since I was attacked by our neighbour's German shepherd as a child, there is no animal I am more afraid of.

Uncle Sơn unlocks the door to reveal three dogs, all barking at him in excitement: a light-coloured golden retriever, a brown cocker spaniel, and a black bulldog. They jump up at him and bark at us, their dank and obtrusive canine smell wafting up into my hypersensitive nose.

I turn to the side and cover my nostrils with a finger.

'I didn't know you had so many dogs, Uncle Sơn!' I blurt out.

He doesn't realise that my comment is meant as an accusation. His voice grows proud and soft.

'I used to just have one dog, named Lucy. Unfortunately, she died after just a few months in America.'

Sadness washes over his face. He buries his hand in the golden retriever's fur and gives him a kiss on the nose.

'Do you like dogs?' He looks over at me as he nestles his head in its fur. 'They're so loyal. Much more faithful than humans.'

I contort my mouth into a smile meant to radiate empathy. 'I know. They're very special.'

I push past him into the living room. To my right, I see a huge aquarium, as tall as a person, with goldfish swimming around in murky water. To my left, bulky Chinese chairs, tables, and benches carved out of dark-brown wood occupy the space. I've seen this type of furniture in temples, but never in homes. Unlike normal sofas and armchairs, they're not upholstered and are hard as a rock. Green jade Buddha statues have been placed on the table and windowsill. It's almost like a museum — everything seems frozen and unused.

'Why don't you get rid of some of this big furniture?' my mother asks. 'There's no room to make yourself comfortable.' She runs her finger over one of the smooth wooden surfaces, grey dust gathering on her fingertip.

Uncle Sơn sits down on a bench as if to prove its utility. Plastic crinkles. The thin red silk pillows that are supposed to provide a bit of comfort are still in their wrapping.

'I can't throw away stuff that Mai bought, can I?' he says gently. He looks at me.

'Do you remember my wife? You met her back when you visited Vietnam. We played cards at our old house that day, and then she came out to dinner with us afterwards.'

I sink down into an armchair. Its excruciating backrest reminds me of the Iron Throne from *Game of Thrones*. Of all the people I met back then, which one was his wife again? I screw up my eyes in concentration.

'She had long, curly hair ...' he adds. His legs are spread wide; he appears to be staring into space.

'I think I remember,' I say, clumsily stringing the words together. My ponderous tongue has a hard time pronouncing the tones correctly, but he seems to understand me anyway.

The scene of the family dinner when Uncle Sơn proudly showed off his wife to my parents appears in my mind. Her hair cascaded in long, tight curls down her back, and she spoke a beautiful-sounding Vietnamese dialect that I was unfamiliar with. She radiated a mixture of kindness and pride that made me like her immediately. We were sitting at a large table in a garden restaurant in Saigon, with colourful lanterns hanging from the trees all around. The adults were drinking beer, and Uncle Sơn laughed a lot. When it came time to order food, he cleared his throat.

'She doesn't eat rice.' He said it the way others might explain their children's obsessive tics: half embarrassed, half protective. Everyone at the table froze. A Vietnamese woman who doesn't eat rice? No one had ever heard of such a thing.

'Does she,' my father finally asked, 'have an allergy?'

'No,' Uncle Sơn replied, 'she just doesn't like rice.'

I remember that there was something rather shocking about this statement — *SHE DOESN'T LIKE RICE?!* — but that she had, at the same time, given me a rare gift. Sitting across from me was a woman who was even more foreign than I. Unlike her, I had no problem eating rice morning, noon, and night; it was she who was abnormal, not I. As much as I could feel her shame at that moment, I was relieved not to have to share it with her. Her status as an outsider transformed me into an equal member of my family. I was grateful for that but, of course, I didn't tell her, because I didn't speak to her; not really, anyway.

'Why didn't you bring her with you when we went out for lobster the other day?' my mother asks. 'Does she not like seafood either?'

SƠN

Saigon, 1975

Wearing his new school uniform, Sơn entered the yellow colonial-style building of his lycée and saw that his class had gathered in the middle of the schoolyard. He was pleased to see their familiar faces, since they had spent the past few months in a kind of forced holiday at home. A lot had changed since the defeat, which they were only allowed to refer to as the 'liberation'. He ran across the schoolyard and stood in the last of the four rows. A red flag with a yellow star flew in the pale sky.

'Good morning!' the teacher said. 'I hope you realise that a new era is now dawning! A better society awaits us, a life without oppression, injustice, or materialism. We all have to work hard to improve ourselves if we are to achieve these glorious goals.'

In contrast to the students, who were wearing grey-black shirts with high collars and matching grey-black trousers, Miss Trà Mi was wearing a red áo dài and white pants. Although she had been strict with the marks she gave Sơn, he had always liked her. She would make brief, witty comments in class or turn a blind eye when he and his friends played football too loudly during recess. Now she seemed completely changed, her lips forming a perfectly straight line. Her forehead was furrowed by a wrinkle he had never noticed before. He found himself wondering where she had spent the last several weeks.

When she opened her mouth again, the words that came out were even stranger than the last, like the phrases you could now read every day in the new newspapers or hear on the radio when yet another blaring speech was broadcast from Hanoi. Sơn let them rush past him like a stiff breeze.

When you stand before the flag ...

... also very important: criticism and self-criticism ...

... bourgeois thinking!

Be thankful for the new books ...

... you must watch the others and declare their mistakes publicly ...

Someone in the front row began clapping. It was Ngọc, the chubby girl who had always been so quiet that she was almost invisible. Now she was wearing a red armband. Sơn had seen many young people dressed like her in recent weeks — they were neither fighters nor North Vietnamese, but called themselves 'the Guardians of the Revolution'. Self-important expressions on their faces, they would march through the streets, exhorting people to obey rules whose origin was unclear: did they really come from Hanoi, or had they just made them up?

Sơn and his classmates' footsteps echoed as they strode across the black-and-white tiled hallways, climbed the stairs to the second floor, and reached their old classroom. He sat down at his desk in the very back by the window and looked down at the schoolyard.

A girl, thin and dark-skinned, took a seat next to him. Her

scratched-up legs were so bony that her kneecaps protruded as perfect circles. Her short, tousled hair framed a small, oval face.

'I'm new here. Is it okay if I take this seat?'

Her accent sounded odd, like the people giving speeches on the radio. Sơn shrugged.

The girl introduced herself as Mai: Mai from Hanoi.

Sơn said nothing.

Miss Trà Mi walked between the rows of students and distributed their new textbooks. They had yellow covers, and the pages were so thin and of such poor quality that the writing shone through: *Introduction to Marxism*.

'You probably know this already,' she said to the girl from Hanoi. Her voice was friendly, so amiable in fact that Sơn felt a brief twinge of jealousy: Miss Trà Mi had never spoken to him like that before.

The teacher turned to him. 'Will you please help her find her way around? Mai recently moved here with her father. He's responsible for reforming the city.'

Sơn immediately understood the warning that resonated in her saccharine tone. The many possibilities — good and ominous — that it contained. Mai's father was important, so she was too. It was the other part that he hadn't understood: what had she meant by reforming the city?

Since Saigon had fallen to the enemy, he no longer recognised it. On the evening of the defeat, he had walked through the streets and discovered countless boots. They must have belonged to South Vietnamese soldiers. The next day, he had seen scores of emaciated fighters from North Vietnam riding around on Soviet jeeps and tanks, waving to a population that eyed them in silence. Vietnam was now at peace, but many seemed torn between fear and relief. Sơn too had yearned for a time when the war would finally be over. Now, though, he found himself wondering what peace might actually mean.

He looked out at the schoolyard, the red flag fluttering gently in the wind. 'If you need any help,' he grumbled, 'just let me know.'

*

After school, the new girl stuck to him like glue. Unlike other girls he knew, she wasn't at all shy around boys; indeed, she seemed a bit boyish herself. With her strange accent, she wanted to talk about things that didn't interest Sơn. They crossed a big street that was as quiet as a cemetery. The city's restaurants, cafés, and stores were all closed, its roaring traffic reduced to a whisper. Only bicycles could still be seen on the roads, whirring about as they tried to figure out their new direction.

'When I was little, my father used to tell me about Ho Chi Minh!' Mai babbled. 'He often said that he had never met anyone in his who life who was wiser and humbler than Uncle Ho. Even though he was president, he lived in a simple hut and always shared his food with those who were less important than him. When others ate only a bowl of rice with salt, he did the same. I thought about that a lot when I was living in the jungle and didn't know when I would see my family again. Whenever there was only rice with salt to eat, I told myself: If it's good enough for Uncle Ho, then it's good enough for me. There's a reason for everything. And he knew what was right.'

Jungle? Sơn thought. Why is she talking about the jungle? He didn't ask.

'I know that you guys in the South didn't know him as well as we did. But let me tell you, anh: I loved this man as I loved my own father. He would have been so happy if he had witnessed the day of liberation. We should be grateful that he fought to set us on the path to freedom. If it wasn't for him, we wouldn't be walking down this street together right now!'

She looked at Sơn as if she were expecting applause.

'Could you ever have imagined this? A girl from Hanoi and a boy from Saigon walking home together after school?'

They arrived at the street corner where Sơn would often buy a coconut after class. The vendor, a cheerful woman with leathery skin and a faded conical hat, had become something of an aunt to him over the years. She would always pick out the biggest fruit she could find, set it on a low plastic stool, and after he had finished drinking the milk, crack it open with her cleaver so he could scoop out the yummy insides. 'Sweet, isn't it?' she had often said, baring her stubby teeth as she laughed.

He glanced around, looking for her. The gnarled trees were still there, but only a puddle was visible under the shade of their crowns. The fruit seller had disappeared, just like John, and his family's savings. Anger welled up inside him. What had he done to end up on the losing side?

He stood in front of Mai, his hands on his hips.

'Do you really want to know if I imagined this? No, I did not! Nor did I wish for us to surrender, or for you to *liberate* us either!'

He spat the words out with disdain. John's betrayal, his father's burning uniform, Miss Trà Mi's twisted sentences — all the disappointments of the past few months burst out of him like a flood breaching a dam. Mai looked at him in surprise. Apparently, she had expected Sơn to be as happy about the new situation as she was. It dawned on him that she had also assumed he wanted to be friends with her.

She took a step forward.

'We fought for *you*! We sacrificed so much so that the country could be reunited!'

'You fought *against* us, and now you want to subjugate us! The Americans fought for us.'

'The Americans occupied you and squeezed you dry!'

'The Americans were with us until the very end!'

'Oh really?' Mai lifted her chin. 'I heard they ran away screaming in the end. Like little girls!'

'Where did they tell you these lies?' Sơn jeered. 'In the jungle?'

If Mai were a boy, he would have tried to beat her up. But she was a girl, and he didn't want to fight girls, even if they were radical North Vietnamese girls. He took a step back, ready to tell her something that would put her in her place once and for all. But to his annoyance, the only thing that occurred to him was that she was right — the Americans *had* run away and abandoned them. But he could never admit that. His mouth snapped open and then snapped shut again. He spun around in a silent rage and ran off.

*

One afternoon, Sơn found his father in the bedroom, his head stuck in the large wood cabinet. He was folding up a pair of grey, pyjama-like garments, carefully placing them in a large green canvas bag.

'Are you leaving?'

His father had barely spoken since the liberation. Most of the time, he just sat smoking in the bamboo chair next to the balcony listening to his silent radio. The batteries had run out on 30 April, but he never bothered to get new ones. At times, Sơn wanted to shake him and ask him why he was acting so strange. It seemed like he was waiting for something.

His father didn't answer him, so Sơn asked, 'If you leave — what will become of us?'

He bent over the bag, which contained two pairs of pyjamas, two shirts, a pair of pants, and underwear. It also held a notepad, a pencil case, and a folded mosquito net.

Why did his father need a mosquito net?

He asked his father — and once again, he received no answer.

His mother walked in carrying a bag in each hand. In one, he could see rice and dry noodles; in the other, pickled vegetables and three pouches of dried, light-coloured meat.

'That should be enough for a month,' she said.

She set the bags down and ran her hands over her pants. A strand of grey hair fell into her face; she undid her braid then retied it. Apart from the day they had tried to escape, he had never once seen her cry or heard her complain. Instead, her eyes had grown hard and unyielding. His father might spend his days in silence next to his radio, but she got up before sunrise to cook, clean, and wait for hours in the food lines. She would do anything to get her children through this, he had once heard her tell their neighbour. *'I'm their mother after all. I have to.'*

She eyed her husband closely.

'Is there anything else you need?'

His father shook his head and zipped up the bag. He was

wearing a loose shirt and khaki pants, the clothes he always wore when going to the authorities.

A sense of foreboding washed over Sơn.

'Are you going to jail?' he whispered.

His father shook his head.

'Re-education camp?'

His father sat down on the bed with him, the mattress squeaking softly. Calmly, he put his right hand on his son's shoulder. Without uttering a word, he nodded.

Sơn's mind began swirling. The older students had spread a number of rumours about the re-education camps. Some said that people were tortured there, while others alleged that no one ever came back. Still others insisted that they weren't all that bad — just extra classes in political ideology.

He grabbed his father's arm.

'Miss Trà Mi said the re-education only lasts three days. Everyone has to be there at seven in the morning and is allowed to return home by three in the afternoon. Why are you taking such a big bag? And so much to eat? It's way too much!'

He unzipped the bag and took out the mosquito net. Whichever rumour turned out to be true, he still had to assume the worst. He hastily unpacked the clothes: the pyjama top, two pairs of underpants, two undershirts.

His father snatched the bag from his lap and slapped his hand. Sơn recognised the angry look on his face — in normal times, it would have come with a sharp exhortation: *'Stop it immediately!'* He almost wished his father would yell at him now. How he longed for the days when bad marks were the worst thing he had to fear. He trembled, with anger and with disappointment.

His father remained silent.

'Those who weren't ordinary soldiers have to do to a different kind of training, a longer one,' his mother explained gently. 'Your father will be back home again in four weeks.'

'And what if it takes longer?' Sơn asked. 'What if they're lying to us? You always said that communists can't be trusted!'

He jumped up and clung to his father.

'You could just hide,' he whispered. 'I know a cave by the Saigon River where you can sleep, and I could come by each day after school and bring you food!'

His father shook him off like a pesky animal. Then he put his things back in the bag, zipped it up, and rose to his feet. With the duffel in one hand and the bags of food in the other, he descended the stairs. He crossed the empty store, stepped out onto Liberty Street, and turned left without looking back even once.

*

At school, everything was now about politics. In geography, they studied Vietnam's socialist brother countries. In mathematics, the word problems revolved around heroic partisan fighters and the number of puppet soldiers they killed. In Vietnamese class, they learned the revolutionary poems of Tố Hữu, the new national poet. They sang communist hymns and practised self-criticism. There were lists for good behaviour and for bad citizens.

Sơn, who had never liked school much anyway, found it harder by the day to sit in his chair in the back row and listen. Miss Trà Mi often seemed robotic as she reeled off sentences that sounded pre-programmed. He began wondering if all these new phrases, all this new rhetoric, was an attempt to transform them into soulless Party foot soldiers. Ngọc, the girl with the red armband, had become the best in class. He, on the other hand, was at risk of being held back next year.

One day, the class took a field trip to a military barracks to learn how to shoot using rubber bullets. Their instructor, a captain in the North Vietnamese Army, told them that Ho Chi Minh loved them and that they needed to show that they were worthy of that love. It was unclear to Sơn how the one thing was related to the other. He knew he wasn't allowed to talk back, but it slipped out anyway: 'What a bunch of damned lies.'

Maybe it was a result of all the pressure built up inside. Even though more than four weeks had passed since his father had been sent to the re-education camp, his family still didn't know where he was or when he would return. Sơn tensely curled his toes together in the last row. He hoped no one had heard him.

The captain straightened up.

'Who dares to insult Uncle Ho!'

The man stood up in front of the group and grabbed the baton hanging from his belt. A wide scar stretched across his left cheek. His nostrils flared.

'Apologise and your punishment will be lenient!'

Keeping his eyes on the class, the man took a step to the right. He waited a few seconds, then stepped to the left. His baton swung back and forth. The rat-tat-tatting of gunfire could be heard at the other end of the field, where older students were firing live rounds.

Slowly, the captain began making his way through the group, parting it into left and right. He was moving like a tiger, his steps intentional and his head bent forward. Sơn closed his eyes. The crunching sound of approaching footsteps grew louder.

'I know exactly who you are!' the captain said threateningly.

Sơn remained silent. Hopefully that too was just a lie.

He could hear his heart pounding, and he prayed that he hadn't caught the man's attention. He tried to calm his breathing.

He heard the sand crunch again, then listened as the tiger's footsteps moved away. At some point, the sound became so quiet that he figured he was safe.

He exhaled. Blinking, he opened his eyes.

The captain was standing in front of the class, his legs spread wide and his right hand on the baton.

'How dare you hide from me! Do you seriously believe you are going to get away with this? And to the others here — are you really going to cover for this coward?' He squinted his eyes. 'You!' He pointed at Mai. 'You're the daughter of our head of state security here in Saigon!'

Mai stepped forward.

'I am,' she replied.

'Which one of them just insulted Uncle Ho? Who called me a liar?'

Mai had earlier been standing right in front of Sơn; she had almost certainly heard him. She stood there with her head bowed.

'Come on, we don't have forever!'

She remained silent.

'Speak, damn it!'

'I don't know, Captain!'

'Think about it again carefully. I think your father would be very disappointed if you failed your marksmanship test, wouldn't you agree?'

He approached the girl and bent down so that his head was level with hers.

'Tell me, comrade.' His voice trembled.

Mai looked up at the man. Finally, a whisper came out.

'It was me.'

*

That night, Sơn went through all the things he wanted to tell Mai in his head, over and over again, trying to find words that would express his admiration for her courage and his shame at himself. (Would he ever have considered sacrificing himself for her? Probably not.) But walking beside her after school the next day, he was too timid to say anything at all. He wanted to thank her, but a simple 'thank you' seemed inadequate, so instead he said nothing. She didn't seem to expect anything from him either, and when he cautiously asked her about her father's reaction, she just laughed. 'My father is a revolutionary,' she said. 'He has far more important things on his mind than me.'

Together, they walked down the street to the river. The sun on the horizon was giving way to evening, bathing the city in a warm, surreal glow. Sơn showed Mai the opulent hotels that now stood empty and the French bakeries that nobody could afford anymore. The sight of the Western buildings, with their bright façades and ornate balconies, still filled him with admiration. Even though he knew this type of architecture was now considered foreign and capitalistic, he enjoyed the feeling for a moment.

They reached the National Assembly, originally constructed by the French as a concert hall, complete with white columns and

Roman statues. There were a few men dressed in green uniforms standing out front.

'This is probably the most beautiful building I have ever seen!' Mai took a few steps towards the stairs and sighed. 'I hope they don't tear it down.'

'Tear it down? Why would they do that?'

Mai shrugged.

'In Hanoi, they always said that the South was very poor and that, following liberation, it would have to be rebuilt.'

'Poor? You people up in the North thought we were poor?'

Sơn leapt up the steps and leaned against the white statue guarding the entrance gate: a bare-breasted goddess with a chiton slung around her waist. From atop the steps, he looked down on Mai with her scratches and abrasions.

'Did you even have the things up North that we have here? Did you have refrigerators, televisions, cars?'

Mai shrugged again.

'We had other things.'

Sơn jumped down to her.

'Like what?'

He looked at her expectantly. She smiled.

'We had values and ideals. They're far more valuable than your refrigerators, aren't they?'

They walked for a while in silence, side by side, before reaching a traffic circle with a huge lotus-shaped pillar in the middle. A large pond surrounded the structure, the water as green as grass. They sat down on the edge of one of the concrete basins that wrapped around the pool and stretched out their legs. Sơn finally asked her the question he had been wondering for weeks.

'What were you doing in the jungle?'

She dipped her index finger into the murky water and traced a circle. Small bubbles formed under the surface, gently bursting as they rose.

'Do you really want to know? It's not a very nice story.'

'That's okay. I don't know anyone else who has been in the jungle.'

'Alright then,' she sighed. 'I don't know if you're aware of this, but the Americans bombed Hanoi heavily for a very long time. It was so dangerous that when I was four, the city administration evacuated all the children. We moved into the jungle and built a camp in a clearing. That's where we slept, cooked, went to school, and learned to shoot. My parents stayed behind in the city, working for the Revolution; my siblings were placed in other camps so that we wouldn't all die at once if a hiding place was bombed. My youngest brother was killed in an attack. He wasn't even six years old. I didn't find out until much later.'

She looked at him.

'Do you know what it means to be a child of the jungle? What it's like to grow up without your family, hoping that the Americans will finally leave you alone so that you don't have to live in the forest like an animal any longer? Did they show you that on your TV?'

Sơn sank his right hand into the green soup, the water cold and soft. He let his hand slide slowly back and forth before pulling it out again. Green algae, fine as hair, had wrapped around his fingers. Not knowing what to say, he remained silent.

'When I was little, I wanted to grow up as quickly as I could so I could fight for the Revolution,' she continued. 'We all did. It was a difficult time, but at least we were all equal. We thought that people all over Vietnam would be happy when the war was over.

How could we have known that so many Vietnamese people would see things so differently to how we do?'

*

A few weeks later, the two went for a walk with Sơn's German shepherd, Lucy. As they approached the end of Liberty Road, they saw a fire — as tall as a man and as wide as a car, its flames dancing around as if they'd been there all along. A Party secretary wearing a wide red armband and a spiky moustache was standing next to the fire while behind him, residents were running out of their homes cradling books and notebooks in their arms. They presented the items to the moustachioed man like offerings to be sacrificed.

After a nod from the official, the people would throw their books into the blaze, the flames crackling greedily as they feasted on the pages.

As Sơn stepped closer, he was able to get a clearer view. There were romance novels. And history books. And English magazines. And American newspapers. And volumes of poetry. And scientific lexicons. And Japanese comics. And French philosophy. And the fundamentals of biology. And old literature. And new literature. And the textbooks Miss Trà Mi had still been using for their lessons at the beginning of the year.

Reactionary books, as he now knew.

Old or foreign books, it was said, were harmful to the Revolution. But Sơn didn't understand how or why. Miss Trà Mi had said something about corrosive thoughts and kept talking until he had almost dozed off at his desk. He gazed into the blazing fire and imagined the letters jumping from the pages, grabbing a hammer, and whacking the Party secretary on the head. Or perhaps they might form grey threads of smoke that would crawl up his nose and poison his brain from the inside.

Mai stepped closer to him, waving the smoke away.

'Definitely an idea from the old man,' she sighed.

'Which old man?'

'My father, of course.'

'The guy with the moustache is your father?'

'What? No!' Mai coughed. 'My father is the head of state security and culture for Saigon.'

'I thought he was responsible for reforming the city.'

'That's what I'm saying!'

Sơn furrowed his brow. 'And it makes the city safer when people burn their old romance novels because … ?'

'How should I know?' Mai shook her head. 'He never tells me anything about what he does. I only find out when yet another ban is imposed.'

In the beginning, Mai had frequently come to Miss Trà Mi's defence, but over the course of their friendship, she had changed. Her new home, her new classmates, and their attitudes were so different from what she had expected. She, who had always believed that Vietnam would become a socialist paradise, now saw that many people feared socialism so much that they were willing to risk their lives to flee from it. She told Sơn that her father was often in a bad mood because things weren't going as expected. That it was almost as bad as it had been after her mother's death a year ago. He worked so much that she hardly saw him anymore — but she was actually relieved about that, because when he did see her, he always had something to complain about and quickly lost his temper.

An elderly man threw a two-volume French dictionary into the fire, and the flames flared again. Smoke rose into their noses, irritating their throats. Lucy barked as if she were afraid of getting burned. The Party secretary looked over at them and raised his hand.

'Either you bring your books over or get lost. This isn't a performance!'

Lucy ran over and barked at him.

'And get this damn mutt away from me!'

Suddenly, the sound of thunder rumbled over the city, and monsoon rains began pelting down from the sky. The water poured in thick drops onto the flames, smothering them. Startled, people retreated into their homes, meaning all further orders went unheeded. Sơn, Mai, and Lucy high-tailed it back to the tailor shop, but they weren't fast enough to avoid getting soaked. They trudged up the stairs dripping wet.

Once in his room, Sơn opened the closet to look for a few dry T-shirts. He pulled out a yellow shirt and handed Mai a red one, which she disappeared with into the bathroom. When she was gone, his eyes fell on the shoebox he had hidden with his underwear.

The box from Minh.

'What actually happens if someone has books at home that haven't been registered?' he asked when she returned.

'It depends on the books. They are fairly lenient when it comes to love poems, but things get trickier with foreign books. My father recently sent someone to jail for hiding French books. He said they were full of colonialist propaganda.'

'Really, to jail?'

'I think it's a bit excessive too. Sure, there are better books and worse books, but for someone to have to go to jail for their taste is pretty harsh. Especially given that I know my father reads foreign stuff himself.' Mai chuckled. 'He doesn't know that I know that, of course.'

Sơn shook his head. The more he heard about the communists, the less he understood them. Even though they always seemed to be speaking about equality for all, things that were forbidden for everyone else were somehow permitted for certain communists. He sighed and stood up.

'I have something to show you.'

He pulled the shoebox out of the closet and set it on his bed. The lid sighed quietly as he pulled it off. On the top was the black notebook that Minh had always mentioned in his letters: *'Sơn, remember my things, and don't snoop around in them!'* He put it aside and pulled out a crumpled paperback; its white cover was yellowing at the edges.

Mai read the title aloud.

'*La Peste*,' she said thoughtfully. 'I think my father has this too. Likely one of the more problematic books, I'd imagine.' Gently, she set it back in the box.

Sơn scratched his head.

'My older brother gave me his books before he left for Germany. He wanted me to keep them for him. He would kill me if I burned them, but I don't want them to cause problems for us either.'

He lowered his voice.

'We still don't know where my father is.'

Mai thought for a second. 'You would have to hide the books in a place where no one would think to look for them.'

'And where might that be? At the police station?' Sơn laughed dryly.

'That's actually not a bad idea.' She tilted her head and squinted her left eye. 'We could hide them at my place!'

'At your place? You might as well gift-wrap them and give them to your father on New Year's!'

'My father is busy with bigger things. Do you really think he has time to snoop around in his daughter's room?' She crossed her arms in front of her chest. 'He would never even think of it!'

Sơn shook his head. 'You're the craziest person I know.'

'I'm not crazy, I just have different ideas from you.'

Sơn wasn't sure if this was about Mai's father, his brother, or something else. But the longer he thought about the alternatives — the risk of going to jail, the prospect of being despised by Minh for the rest of his life — the more the benefits seemed to outweigh them. The way Mai always told it, her father was rarely home; and when he was, he seldom left his study. The risk was likely lower in her home than it was in his.

'If he finds the books, you'll be in big trouble,' he said again, trying to ease his conscience.

'If he finds them, I'll just tell him that one of my capitalist classmates had them and I took them out of circulation for safety.' She grinned. 'And it's even true!'

They shook hands like two businessmen who had just sealed an important deal. Sơn dropped onto his bed, and Mai stuffed the cardboard box into a bag. She whistled as she made her way down the stairs with it. The prospect of pulling one over on her father seemed to put her in the best of moods.

KIỀU

Uncle Sơn slides his wide wedding band from his finger and wraps it in his fist, almost like he's trying to hide it. The way he's sitting in front of us in his living room — legs spread wide and his expression vacantly focused inward — he looks like he's all alone, talking to himself.

'Why didn't I bring Mai when we went out for lobster the other day?' he repeats. 'Because I can't take her anywhere anymore.'

'Did you separate?' my mother asks. 'What a shame!' She sighs. 'A lot of couples get divorced in Germany too. Or they don't even get married in the first place. They all want to protect their freedom, nobody is willing to commit themselves to anyone else. Young women especially are extremely stubborn.'

She shoots me a meaningful look.

Uncle Sơn shakes his head. 'Mai was certainly stubborn, but in a rather different way than you are talking about. She risked her life to go abroad with me. She slept on the living-room sofa with me when we brought over Mother, Linh, and the twins. She never complained, ever!' He pauses and closes his eyes. 'She had been through so much since her childhood that I thought she was invincible,' he mumbles. 'But she wasn't.'

He opens his eyes to look at us again. His eyelids start twitching and he presses them shut again. His voice breaking, he says: 'She died last year. Cancer.'

'*She's dead?*' My mother covers her mouth with her hand. 'But she was still so young!'

She grabs for the back of her wooden chair to hold onto something but misses, and she can't find it on her second try either, clasping her hand in the air. My father sits down next to her so she can use him to prop herself up.

He leans forward towards his brother.

'Why didn't you write me?' he asks. 'Or call? I'm a doctor!' He sounds distraught, and a bit hurt as well.

Uncle Sơn shrugs weakly.

'We discovered it by accident. We wanted to have children, but after half a year, she still wasn't pregnant, so we went to a doctor. She examined Mai and found a different problem: she had breast cancer ...' He pauses for a moment. 'We wanted children and got cancer instead.' He listens to his words as they echo through the living room, as if still in disbelief.

At first, he says, they were hopeful they would be able to defeat the cancer. One night, while in hospital, Aunt Mai had a dream about starting an import-export business and saw it as a good omen. She wanted to get well to turn the dream into reality. The chemotherapy ultimately worked, and the tumour was removed successfully during a long operation. Once she had recovered, she and Uncle Sơn rented a small warehouse in an industrial park and named their company 'Made in America'. Well-off Vietnamese people could order American medicines, clothing, and even cars from the company and have the wares shipped to Vietnam. With the Vietnamese economy growing stronger and stronger, business was thriving. The more people there earned, the larger their thirst for foreign products became.

After five years, Uncle Sơn and Aunt Mai were able to afford a home in this white, middle-class neighbourhood. 'Because of the chemotherapy, we weren't able to have children, but we were so happy. We thought we were living the American dream!'

He lets out a bitter laugh.

Ten years after that first diagnosis, he says in a flat voice, they were hit with another. The breast cancer had apparently come back and metastasised without anyone noticing. As Aunt Mai was confident she would be able to defeat cancer a second time, she insisted on moving her office to their home so that she could work between chemo treatments. She would sometimes even sleep on the floor in front of her desk and get up in the middle of the night to Skype with customers who were in Vietnam and thus in a different time zone. Only after she finished would she come into the bedroom and sleep the rest of the night.

'She was too proud to show how poorly she was feeling. Hardly anyone knew how sick she was,' Uncle Sơn recounts. 'She would always say, "What's the point of telling others about my problems? If they're worried, it will only make the suffering worse."'

I remember the song about the widow who turns to stone and the message that can be found between the lines: the fate of Vietnamese women is to suffer for others until there is nothing left of themselves.

'How could she work in that condition?' I blurt out in Vietnamese. 'Why didn't you make sure she took care of herself?' It's the first time on this trip that I don't care if I make a fool of myself with my garbled Vietnamese.

He runs his fingers through his grey hair.

'I told her that we should take a vacation in Florida, but she didn't want to. I suggested that she should go shopping and buy herself something nice, but she didn't want to. I let her work. I thought it would distract her! We come from a poor country, you understand? She wanted to make sure that I would have enough money to live a worry-free life once she was gone. That was her only wish. How could I have denied her the one thing she wanted?!'

His head sinks forward as he silently wipes away his tears.

'Why didn't I force her to be happy?'

I'm filled with shame as I look at my uncle. Suddenly, I feel remorse over my quick assumptions and petty concerns — my vaunted theories about men and women, delivered from the comfort of my privileged Western life.

How much does it take to understand where you come from?

Perhaps I lack the words to describe it. It may take more to understand. At the same time, I sense that it could be as intuitive a thing as snapping your fingers. Something that is felt rather than said.

'Why didn't you tell us anything?' my mother asks, her voice as wispy as smoke.

He looks at her through reddened eyes.

'If we had seen each other, I would have told you, of course. But we've talked so little over the last several years that it felt strange to me. It's not like you can send a Christmas card and write, "Merry Christmas! Oh, by the way: Mai has cancer."'

I stand up to release the tension within me. In a glass cabinet in the corner of the living room, I discover a black urn with a golden trim, like those I had seen in the temple. The photo shows a woman with a round face wearing a grey stocking cap. Beneath it, the inscription reads: *Võ Hoàng Mai. Born on 8 May, 1961, in Hanoi, died on 20 September, 2016, in Westminster, California.* She passed away just three months before my grandmother. My uncle must have spent his time going back and forth between his dying wife and his dying mother.

He looks grey and tired sitting there in the living room. I wish I could go over, stroke his head, and apologise for all those years that I didn't know him and didn't want to know him.

*

My phone rings in my purse, a call from Dorian. We've been playing phone tag over the last couple of days — and now, of all times, he finally reaches me.

'Can't talk right now,' I write.

'It's important!' he replies.

I excuse myself and head upstairs. There's a guest room on the right and two more rooms on the left. I open the first door and find myself in a bedroom. A black-and-white wedding photo is leaning against the wall, framed in ivory-white satin. Uncle Sơn looks thirty years younger than he does now, slender and proud, his black hair trimmed short. Aunt Mai is wearing an áo dài made of red silk and a golden bridal headdress; she smiles shyly, but her face is bursting with happiness.

I take a few more steps into the room and find myself wading through Uncle Sơn's internal desolation. All kinds of things are strewn across the floor, the desk, and the bed, like toys left behind by heedless children: *Make America Great Again* caps, Vietnamese CDs, cases of wine from Napa Valley, jade necklaces. An open cabinet is full of half-used bottles of medicine and packages of pills.

The scene reminds me of a Netflix documentary about a widow who, after the death of her husband, stuffed her living room with forty nutcrackers and packed three wardrobes with Christmas decorations. It was heart-wrenching to see how she tried to fill the emptiness inside her with shiny objects. How ferociously she defended her Christmas ornaments from being thrown away.

Dizziness wells up inside me, pulling me towards the large bamboo bed standing against an orange wall. I clumsily bump into the bedside table and knock a book to the floor. I'm surprised to see that it's in French. I pick it up and find myself holding an old paperback edition of *La Peste*, the pages yellowed and so thin that they're almost transparent.

Uncle Sơn reads Camus?

Beneath the table, I see a worn shoebox full of more old books. Most of them are in French, but one, the black notebook, is filled with Vietnamese writing. The pages are labelled with dates from 1968, apparently a kind of diary, but some of the entries are several weeks apart. I look more closely: the letters somehow seem familiar to me. They are so straight and narrow, it could be my father's hand.

I shove the notebook into my purse and fall onto the bedspread, breathing in the sticky odour of unwashed sheets. Next to me are two pillows, one of them stained and the other unused. I grab the pillow that must have belonged to my sick aunt, wrap my arms around it, and roll into a ball. I am again overwhelmed by a mixture of nausea and dizziness that apparently comes with being pregnant.

How strange that a baby is growing in my belly right now, even though I never wanted it, planned it, or even gave it permission to be there. For thirty years, I have seen my life as a consequence of choices, the product of correct or incorrect decisions. Only now do I realise just how random it can all be.

My thoughts grow hazy, and I have a vision of myself lying in a coffin in a red dress. I hear my uncle's voice, like an offscreen narrator in a movie: *'We wanted children and got cancer instead.'* Exhaustion overcomes me and I close my eyes for a short rest.

*

The ringing of my telephone jerks me back to reality.

'Hello? Kimmie? I really need to speak to you!'

'Sorry. There was so much going on here.' I sit up to sound more awake. 'Is everything okay?'

'The Toyota heir dropped us,' Dorian responds. His voice sounds anaemic, as if he were deeply hungover.

'What Toyota heir?'

'The guy who wanted to invest in our restaurant! He's launching a start-up and needs his money for that instead. The asshole is leaving us out to dry!'

Through the fog of my mind, it only slowly becomes clear what he is telling me. If the Toyota heir doesn't invest, then David can't finance his restaurant. And if David can't finance his restaurant, then Dorian can't move to Tokyo, which would mean that he has to stay in Berlin.

All in all, not exactly the worst news. Not for me anyway.

'That's terrible!' I respond, because that's what you're supposed to say in this kind of situation. I know that David had been planning to sign the lease for the restaurant space next week, a simple concrete structure with floor-to-ceiling windows and a beautiful Japanese garden. The investor's decision to pull out must be devastating for him.

'It was all just a waste of time,' Dorian laments. 'Without Jiro, we will never be able to afford it. The rent alone is crazy expensive.'

His voice is raised. I've never heard him this disappointed. I immediately have the urge to comfort him and start looking for possible solutions — maybe they can find another investor, or a different, more affordable location — but my freshly awakened egotism holds me back.

'What are you going to do now?' I ask, to cover up my feelings of relief.

'I don't know! David has gone to Tokyo to get a better idea of what's going on. But to be honest, I don't think anything's going to come of it. He doesn't know anyone there except for the Toyota heir.' He sighs. 'It sucks. Just yesterday, I read my first lines of Japanese.'

Ever since we've known each other, Dorian has set his sights on learning all kinds of things — jazz piano, triathlon, computer programming. Usually, he will pursue a new interest obsessively for months on end before suddenly abandoning it to go after something else with the same fervour. However, it's been different with his Japanese lessons. He's been attending weekly classes since the beginning of the year, dutifully doing his homework. It's the one thing he's been really willing to work for, and now it's fallen through. Even though I would never tell him as much, I feel a certain sense of satisfaction. Maybe it's because I found his Tokyo euphoria so hurtful. Or because I have always worked hard for everything in my life and am envious of him. In contrast to me, he has never felt the need to torture himself.

'Try to look at it differently,' I say in an effort to do the right thing and cheer him up. 'You haven't actually lost anything other than time. You can just keep living your life in Berlin until another opportunity crops up. You said yourself that you would miss the bar.'

Dorian keeps silent, then sighs into the phone so loudly that it sounds like a sandstorm. 'I can't keep doing the same thing my whole life. That's too easy. I need something new. A challenge!'

'There are lots of different things you can do to change your life. It doesn't necessarily have to be opening a restaurant in Tokyo.' I notice that my voice has taken on that soft tone that mothers use when trying to calm their children. 'You can also make changes to your personal life.'

Dorian laughs drily. 'Of course. Like I could grow a beard. Or become vegan. Or buy a farmhouse in Brandenburg and remodel the barn. But it's just not the same as trying to build something new in a foreign country!'

'What's so bad about staying in Berlin and improving your life there?'

'You can *always* work on the details of your life,' he says impatiently. 'But I don't care about self-improvement! I want *real* change. Life in Berlin is great and all, but to be honest, I've been thinking for a while now: this can't be all there is. When David told me about his idea, I thought: That's exactly what I've been looking for!'

He falls silent.

'And now the idea is dead,' he says. 'And I'm right back to where I was a year ago.'

I pull up my shirt a bit and lay my hand on my belly. The skin is warm, and a bit tighter than it used to be.

'There's something I've been meaning to tell you.' The words come out slowly. 'I don't know if there is a good or a bad time for it.'

'Did something happen?' he asks.

'No! Or yes. I don't know.'

'What's wrong?' he asks, worry creeping into his voice.

I blurt out the sentence with my next breath.

'I'm pregnant.'

'Pregnant?' he repeats.

Silence.

'Are you sure?'

'I've done three tests.'

'Whoa!'

Silence.

'I've got to let that sink in.'

More silence.

'What are you supposed to say at a time like this? Congratulations?' He laughs nervously.

I say nothing, waiting for what he comes up with next. *You were just as shocked when you found out*, I tell myself. *Give him time.*

'What do you want to do?' His voice is flat.

'I don't know,' I answer, trying to sound noncommittal. 'What do *you* want to do? I mean, it's *our* child.'

'Of course,' he says quickly. 'But you're the one who's pregnant. I really haven't thought about it. Until this morning, my future looked completely different.'

That nervous laugh again.

'Didn't you just tell me that you were looking for a change?' I can hear the tentativeness in my voice, and get frustrated with myself. *It's already starting. You've only just gotten pregnant and here you are in the weaker position.*

'I did,' he responds. 'But I was thinking of something that I choose myself. A crazy experiment like a restaurant in Tokyo. Not a child that dictates a certain lifestyle. It's actually the polar opposite of what I was just talking about!'

I sense a numbness inside of me and sink onto the bed. With my eyes closed, I can see him in Berlin sitting on our vintage sofa pulling on his fingers until they crack. He's almost certainly getting himself a glass of wine — and wondering what he is supposed to say as a man, as the biological father.

He starts over again, and I can hear that he's trying his hardest.

'You have my support, obviously. But to be honest, I never really thought about you getting pregnant. It's kind of sudden.' He pauses briefly before continuing. 'If you want to keep the child, that's fine. But if you don't, that's fine too. I know a few women who decided against it because it wasn't the right time. It's something that has to be carefully thought through, and a kid isn't exactly cheap. Not that I'm trying to push you in a certain direction, I just mean, it would completely change our lives. You know how exhausted and stressed young parents always are.'

Because I don't say anything, he adds: 'But if you still want to keep the child, I'll play along.'

'If you still want to keep the child, I'll play along?'

I'm not sure I spit out that sentence with the same disgust with which it is echoing around in my head. I only know that there is something terribly wrong with it, something cowardly. Deep inside I had been hoping that Dorian would be happy and could give me the courage I need. He should at least have the guts to tell me honestly that a child would be too much responsibility for him and that he doesn't want to become a father for that reason. Why does he keep talking about him and me, but never about us?

My eyes start to itch, and I rub them with my right hand, leaving a wet smear across my face. I drop my phone and roll over on my left side, again grabbing the stained pillow. Pulling up a knee, I hug it with both arms. What a stupid woman I am. So stupid to get involved with this man.

I can hear Dorian's muffled voice coming out of the phone.

'Kimmie? Are you still there?'

'Are you disappointed in me?'

'Did I say something wrong? If I said anything wrong, I'm sorry! I love you! Say something! Tell me what you want from me!'

SƠN

Saigon, 1979

The morning that Sơn and Mai set off on their journey to freedom, they found themselves waiting at a four-way intersection. Roads headed off in all directions: to the market, to the river, to the airport, and to the border. Behind them was a three-metre-tall billboard emblazoned with the image of a smiling Ho Chi Minh. White-haired, bearded, and dressed in a simple, light tropical suit, his arms were spread wide as if to receive a passel of mirthful children. 'Uncle Ho loves every one of us', read the red lettering above the picture.

The intersection, which used to be so wild and chaotic that even the most reckless proceeded with care when crossing the street, now seemed rather tame, as though its heart had stopped beating. It was so quiet that Sơn imagined he could hear the glimmering of the sunlight. He stood there in silence so as not to miss a single sound: the occasional rumbling of an old bus so packed full of people that they looked as though they might capsize at any moment; the sudden roar of a truck that had far too little to haul because there was hardly anything left to sell. Beyond that, though, there was nothing. Time stretched out to infinity.

Behind them were the crushed hopes of a generation of young people that had given up on their future before it had even begun. Ahead of them was a journey that could lead them to their goal of a life abroad. Or to prison. Or to death. It was Sơn's mother who had first uttered the word 'escape', but he had already been thinking of it constantly ever since his night at the American Embassy. Driven by the many stories they had heard of the refugees who had escaped by boat to Hong Kong, Malaysia, or Singapore, or who had been plucked from the waves by ships from elsewhere in the world, he had dreamt over and over again of heading out to sea and escaping to a foreign country.

By the time Miss Trà Mi handed them their diplomas three months earlier, a quarter of his classmates had already vanished. Undeterred by the school's thinning ranks, she continued to talk about the duties they owed to the fatherland — later admitting that such duties could include deployment to Cambodia. Ever since the Vietnamese had liberated the country from Pol Pot at the beginning of the year, they had taken on the role of occupying power in the ravaged country. Sơn carried his loathsome diploma home from school, where he tore it to shreds. That night, he asked his mother for gold.

As dark clouds appeared on the sky above Saigon, Mai started to grow anxious. She swung her arms back and forth, balled up her fists, and started pounding them against each other.

Thwack, thwack.

'Why don't you just hold up a sign: *Hey, police! These two are trying to escape! Arrest them!*' Sơn hissed.

'What escape? I don't think they're coming. How long have we already been standing here? Two hours? Three?'

'My mother knows the guy well. He used to be one of her regular customers. She's already given him a bar of gold.'

'So? It's not exactly uncommon for smugglers to pocket the money and disappear! Hiền's family was ripped off twice. And Quang has been in prison for the last year after getting caught.'

As Mai had grown older, the childhood boyishness had begun to fade. Her face was now longer, making her eyes appear larger and her expression prouder. Her hair fell in loose curls to her shoulders. Sơn could still remember the moment he had noticed her transformation for the first time, half a year earlier: they had been sitting next to the pond with the lotus pillar one evening, a place they frequently visited, when Sơn told her about his dreams of leaving the country.

As it turned out, she had also been thinking of escaping. Her father wanted to send her back to Hanoi, where she was to live with a strict aunt. He didn't like how his daughter had changed, and was convinced her new friends, Sơn in particular, were to blame.

'He doesn't know how to deal with me, so he wants to get rid of me like a dog,' she had said. 'But I'm not a dog, and I'm also no longer a little girl. Wherever you go, I'm coming with you!' Back then, she had quickly brushed aside all of his concerns about how dangerous such an adventure might be and immediately agreed when he suggested they try to make their way to America. She had told him how eager she was to try Coca-Cola. Now, though, Sơn could see that doubts were welling up inside her.

'Any other pep talk you want to share?' he growled.

'I'm just being realistic. We both know that the first try often fails. Sometimes the second and third tries don't work either. Who is this guy, anyway? You're the one always saying that you can't trust anybody!'

Sơn ran his fingers through his hair. He knew she was right. For every story about a fortunate refugee being saved, there was another about an unfortunate refugee being swindled, landing in prison, or drowning in the sea. Maybe it would be better just to go home and think things through again.

At that very moment, a column of trucks rolled up. Two of the vehicles had open beds, while the back of the third was covered with a tarp. It stopped, engine idling, to let them climb into the cab upfront. Next to the driver was the businessman who had frequently ordered Western-style suits from Sơn's mother: Mr Bảy, a man with a high forehead and a passion for Japanese whisky. Ever since the end of the war, he had been using his logistics company to smuggle people out of the country. Sơn's mother had mentioned his 'astonishing contacts with the Viet Cong'.

He used to enjoy relating anecdotes about politicians, soldiers, and spies, peppering them with colourful details and exhibiting a surprising talent for pantomime. Now, though, he merely whispered a couple of curt orders to the two of them: 'Hurry up. Keep quiet. Head to the back with the sacks of rice.' Instead of answering Sơn's question about why he was so late, Mr Bảy merely stuck out his hand to receive two gold-leaf bars from each of them, cardboard-thin and not much bigger than a domino. After weighing them with a tiny scale, he gave one to the driver, who was apparently from Cambodia, and tucked the other three into a small leather pouch hanging from his neck.

They crawled through an opening in the back of the cab into the bed of the truck, sitting on the floor with their knees pulled up to their chins as they bounced through the city centre before turning onto a motorway. Their heads rocked back and forth as thoughts raced through Sơn's mind. With the South China Sea teeming with pirates, his mother had suggested that they flee overland — travelling through Cambodia to Thailand, where the UN had set up a few refugee camps. Those who made it that far had good chances of being flown out to the West. It was a journey through hell, but it could lead to the land of Coca-Cola.

'How do you know the drive through Cambodia will be safe?' Sơn had asked his mother that morning.

'I don't know anything,' she had responded. 'But too many people are dying at sea.'

Sơn pulled out the slender ring she had given him just in case, her wedding ring, the last of the gold she had left. He had been reluctant to take it and had told his mother that he wouldn't give it away no matter what happened. He briefly clenched his hand into a fist as if to squeeze it, before pressing the cool metal against his throbbing eyes. One day, when he was living in America, he would fly his mother over and return the ring to her. He could already see her standing in front of an elegant house — *his* elegant house — hand held to her mouth in happiness and surprise. 'I kept it safe for you,' he would tell her. 'I didn't give it away even in the most dangerous moments.'

They suddenly swerved around a corner so sharp that the ring fell from his hand and jangled onto the bed of the truck. He quickly picked it up and stuffed it into the hidden pocket his mother had sewn into his pants the night before.

*

They were too tense to sleep and too exhausted to talk. As the truck headed West, they lethargically succumbed to their disorientation. In the darkness, Sơn began picturing the people he was leaving behind, kilometre by kilometre: his mother, his siblings, and Miss Trà Mi in her red áo dài. As the memories swirled through his mind, the stench of petrol mixed with the sweet scent of incense, the dry air in the truck transformed into the tangy aroma of a streetside food stall. In the no man's land between departure and arrival, he began recognising for the first time what his homeland meant to him. Already, he felt a sense of longing.

They stopped for the night, but Sơn and Mai were not permitted to leave the bed of the truck. The next morning, they were awakened by the metallic clinking of a rifle. Mr Bảy had climbed into the back and was looking at them through swollen eyes.

'We have to be careful from now on,' he whispered. 'We're in Cambodia. A lot of the roads are mined and there are still some Khmer Rouge hiding in the jungle.'

'We've already crossed the border?' Sơn asked. 'I didn't notice.'

The smuggler laughed contentedly and pulled a beige pack of cigarettes from his pocket. It was printed with the word 'Hero'.

'Have you ever seen these? I call them "the magic bullet from Thailand",' he said, then disappeared back into the cab.

They continued onward more slowly than before as the road was full of cracks and potholes. Through a slit in the tarp, Sơn could see that they were driving over sandy red soil that gave way to overgrown farmland on both sides. Muddy ditches ran through expansive fields full of tall grass and thick bushes. There were no farmers or huts to be seen, just a landscape of pale yellow, green, and red — strangely neglected, as if someone had erased all of the people and animals.

They were repeatedly forced to stop at military checkpoints; each time, Mr Bảy would pull out a pack of Thai cigarettes from his bag, and the truck would be allowed to pass without being searched. Sơn saw that the soldiers' helmets were in the shape of turtle shells and bore a yellow star on a red background. So these were the Vietnamese soldiers who had liberated Cambodia and were now hunting what was left of the Khmer Rouge. The men who were doing the patriotic duty that he was trying to escape.

He crawled back into the darkness and thought about the veterans he had seen begging in the streets of Saigon, hobbling along on wooden crutches, their legs mangled. The mines of the Khmer Rouge, they said, were so treacherous that they didn't kill you, they only maimed you. 'They hate the Vietnamese because we drove away Pol Pot,' one of the veterans had told Sơn. 'They want us to survive so that we return home and become a burden on our families.'

He felt Mai's head sinking onto his shoulder and shifted closer to make her more comfortable. In a quiet murmur, she told him that she had always dreamt of leaving Vietnam.

'When I'm in America, I'll make my own rules and decisions,' she mumbled. 'I'll work in an office. I'll live in a big house and have two children and two dogs. And I'll never eat rice again, only hamburgers and fries.'

'You don't even know if you'll like American food,' he responded.

'I will,' she said, unconcerned. 'There were times when I had nothing to eat but rice and salt. Can you imagine what it's like to eat just that day after day? It makes you dream of having something, *anything* with colour. Why should I do the same in a different country? I'll be able to cook for myself. I'll be free!'

Her words faded into slow, rhythmic breathing. He wrapped his arm around her and laid his head on hers.

Suddenly they braked so hard that Sơn was thrown forward towards the cab. Judging by the temperature, it was early afternoon. They must have managed at least half the journey by now and been somewhere in the middle of Cambodia. The sound of shots rang out, a door was flung open, and the driver was dragged out. Sơn heard men shouting something in Khmer. Two of them pulled Mr Bảy out of the cab while two others tore back the tarp and jumped onto the bed of the truck, Kalashnikovs at the ready.

Sơn saw how their eyes were flickering, bursting with the aggression of those whose lives had been consumed by fighting. He felt a burning pain when one of them jerked him up by his arms, pulled him backwards, and pushed him off the truck. He stumbled and fell to the ground on his belly.

A rat scampered past his face and disappeared behind one of the military pickups the men had used to block the road. They were wearing black uniforms made of coarse cloth and had red-and-white plaid scarves wrapped around their necks — they had to be Khmer Rouge. Their skin was darker than the Vietnamese, and their bodies a bit smaller. The younger ones encircled the prisoners. They couldn't have been older than eighteen, but their faces were etched with a severity that made them look grizzled and worn. The older ones had gathered around a man who was leaning against the pickup, smoking one of the Thai cigarettes. Next to him stood a young girl who was his spitting image. Behind them, Sơn could see a path into the forest lined with grey stones.

He dragged himself to his feet and began looking around for Mai. She was kneeling on the ground, her face contorted in pain. He grabbed her right arm and pulled her up.

'We're staying together,' he whispered. 'No matter what happens, I'm staying with you!'

At a nod from the older man — he seemed to be the group's leader — three of the fighters dragged Mr Bảy over to him. Hands folded as if in prayer, the smuggler began saying something to the leader in Khmer. His voice had a supplicating tone to it, but his pleas, repeated over and over again, seemed to go unheard. The leader knocked his hands to the side with the muzzle of his machine gun and then used it to point at Mr Bảy's pockets and watch. His men quickly searched the prisoner, taking his watch and pulling a bundle of American dollars from his pants pocket before finally finding the pouch with the gold. They swung it back and forth in front of his face, laughing out loud when they heard the jangling from within.

The leader barked a new order at them, and now they grabbed Sơn and Mai. His heart beating wildly, Sơn started thinking about his mother's ring: how could he make sure they didn't find it? He turned around so they couldn't see, pulled out the ring, and placed it in his hand, wrapping his fist around it. He then bent forward and, unnoticed by the others, put the ring in his mouth, balancing it on his tongue.

He and Mai stood side by side in front of the Khmer Rouge leader. He had high cheekbones and deeply recessed eyes, and pointed at Sơn as he said something in his unintelligible, throaty language. As Sơn lowered his head, he swallowed the ring with a bit of saliva. He could feel the metal blocking his windpipe and lifted his chin to try again. He cleared his throat and coughed as the leader uttered a threat. Sơn looked into his eyes and swallowed again before taking a slow, deep breath and standing up straight.

*

After the leader had searched him and yelled at him some more, he ordered Sơn to take off his sandals and give them to one of his men. He then turned to Mai, using his outstretched index finger to brush the hair plastered to her forehead, her face smeared with dust and sweat. She was clutching her left wrist with her right hand. He ordered Mr Bảy to translate his words.

'He wants to know how old you are,' Mr Bảy said tiredly. His voice had lost all energy and his eyes were empty.

Mai lifted her chin. She responded calmly, looking directly into the leader's eyes.

'Tell him that it's none of his damn business.'

Almost unnoticeably, the smuggler shook his head. Even though he was speaking Vietnamese, he lowered his voice.

'Swallow your goddamned pride, girl, or you'll get us all killed!'

Mai remained silent.

Reluctantly, Mr Bảy turned back to the leader and said a few words in Khmer, making supplicating gestures as he spoke. Again, he began pleading, pointing to the two of them and then to himself before folding his hands in front of him again.

The leader raised his eyebrows, apparently amused. Locking eyes with Mai, he pointed his machine gun at Mr Bảy and, without saying a word, pulled the trigger. Sơn swore he saw the bullet leave the muzzle and enter the man's chest. Mr Bảy's shirt burst with red, and his body collapsed to the ground. He landed on the dusty road with a thud.

Sơn felt his hands grow sweaty, and his legs began to wobble. He stepped sideways to get in front of Mai. He was now standing between her and the leader, a human shield, a boy full of fear.

Hands folded, he sank to the ground and began begging the Cambodian for mercy.

'Please,' he whispered, 'let us go. It was my idea. It's not her fault.'

The leader shoved him to the side like a dog. He then grabbed Mai's hair and hit her so hard in the face that she staggered to one side. 'You asshole!' she screamed. 'Let go of me!' He pulled her over to the pickup by her hair. Sơn tried to run after them, but the men pushed him back and again he fell to the ground. Mai was pulled into the bed of the truck and made to sit next to the Cambodian girl.

'I'll come for you!' Sơn called out to her, but his voice was full of dust, a pathetic rasp. From the ground, he watched as the truck bounced onto the road and drove off towards the forest. He could hear them hooting in triumph over their prize, and he could see Mai sat among them, as motionless as a statue.

*

Sơn began walking barefoot down the road in the other direction until it grew so dark that he could hardly see, and his mouth was as parched as the sands of a desert. He climbed down an embankment into a field and dunked his hands into a narrow, stinking ditch. He took them out and the water began slowly running down his arms. In his desolation, he yearned to fall asleep and never wake up again. He had promised Mai they would stay together, but he had failed to protect her. He had told her about the freedom they would find, but he had led her straight into captivity. If only he had never told her about his plans! If only they had turned around at that intersection!

He washed the tears from his face with the muddy water and scooped some of the fluid into his mouth, feeling the sand scratching his throat. He took another gulp and started coughing. Above him, the sky was so black that the world seemed impenetrable.

He awoke in pain. He felt as though someone were punching him in the gut. A new morning had broken, sunlight spreading pale and milky across the fields. For a brief moment, Sơn didn't know where he was, but then everything came rushing back: the journey in the truck, the attack, Mai's stony face in the back of the pickup as it drove away. Groaning, he buckled into the fetal position, his insides feeling like they had turned to stone. He pulled down his pants and squatted on the ground, a liquid mess shooting out of him until he felt something hard blocking his anus.

The ring.

He began crying as he imagined his mother's face.

He cleaned himself up and then crawled up the embankment to the road. If he just kept following this road, he told himself, he would eventually find someone who could help him. He walked as the sun rose high in the sky, the ground under his feet scalding hot, and he was still walking long after the sun had reached its zenith and dusk had started to fall. Two trucks had passed by during the day, but even though he had waved his arms wildly, they had sped past without slowing down.

His legs ached; his body was parched. When he looked at the road, the red sand began to resemble the sea.

Suddenly, he heard the whirring of pedals behind him. He spun around to see a man approaching on a rusty bicycle — gaunt, grey-haired, and wearing one of those turtle-shell helmets of the Viet Cong. On the rack behind him, the man was carrying a basket full of dragon fruit and mini bananas. The fruit looked so luscious and delicious to Sơn that he grew dizzy. He spread out his arms to block the road. The cyclist came to a stop, and Sơn said the only words he knew in Khmer: 'Phnom Penh?'

The rider spread his arms and gestured to the horizon far behind him. Sơn laid his hand on the bike rack. Could the man maybe take him along?

The cyclist shook his head vigorously and set his right foot on the pedal to ride off.

'Stop! Please!'

Sơn pressed his hands together and placed his fingertips on his forehead. The bike rider lifted his head, squinted, pointed to the bicycle, then made the universal gesture for money with his left hand, rubbing his thumb against his index finger.

Sơn thought for a moment. He had given the smuggler all of his gold, and he didn't have the language skills to tell the old man about the attack. The only thing left was his mother's wedding ring.

He glanced around.

The road stretched out endlessly towards the grey horizon in front of him. The sky, slowly filling with dark clouds, arced above him. Somewhere out there was Mai. Mai who had wanted to follow him wherever he went.

He pushed the ring onto his index finger and held up his hand. 'Gold,' said Sơn.

The cyclist grabbed for the ring and flicked it with a finger. He then put it in his half-opened mouth and bit down. His teeth made a crackling noise as they struck the metal.

*

Sơn reached Phnom Penh after two days, during which the sun had darkened his skin and he had consumed the entire cargo of mini bananas. He had managed to get through the checkpoints by acting as though he couldn't speak. If he hadn't been so weak, he would have been shocked by the sight of the capital: Phnom Penh was like a ghost town, with life crawling back only very slowly. He saw rats everywhere, and ruins. The broad boulevards were blocked by barricades, and the grand villas in the city centre were dilapidated and empty. Shoulders hunched, people shuffled in slow motion through the streets, emanating a silent terror. He didn't see anybody laughing, or even speaking loudly. Nobody looked up from the ground in front of them.

He passed by a river, its light-brown water reminding him of the Saigon River back home, and he biked along its embankment in the shade of tall palms. Before long, an abandoned pavilion blocked his path. The curved eaves of its roof were decorated with golden ornaments; homeless children lazed in its shade, occasionally getting up to chase away pigeons. Past it, Sơn could make out a splendid palace with magnificent towers, its orange roofs held up by sculptures of deities. It looked like an optical illusion in the heart of this ravaged city. He dismounted his bike and pushed it up to the gate blocking the entrance. Standing there, he pressed his face between the bars.

Suddenly, Sơn heard people speaking Vietnamese, their voices sounding more energetic and alive than anything he had heard in the last several days. He closed his eyes to listen more closely. Their laughter sounded like music.

'You have the two of hearts again? Who shuffled these cards?!'

'Are you looking for an excuse? I just don't waste the big ones like you do!'

Sơn turned around. At the end of the palace wall, he saw three Vietnamese soldiers sitting on plastic stools. They had taken off their helmets and laid white towels across their necks. In between them was a fourth stool with a pile of cards on it. They must have been playing tiến lên, the card game where two is the highest card. His favourite.

Happily, he ran over to the men.

'Can I join?'

The oldest of the three was just shuffling ahead of the next round. A bright scar ran beneath his right eye. He laughed, as raspy as an exhaust pipe.

'Do you have enough money for the ante? You don't look like it!'

Sơn saw a hat beneath the man's stool full of colourful notes covered in wavy letters. Cambodian money. He took four dragon fruit from his basket and held them out to the man like a sacrifice.

'This is all I have.'

The Vietnamese soldiers were in a good mood. It was their last day in Cambodia and they were feeling generous. Sơn found an old bucket, flipped it over, and sat down with them. In the first game, he came in second. He won the second game with a pair of red aces and almost prevailed in the third as well but was defeated at the last second.

'The boy doesn't play bad at all,' the thin soldier next to him remarked.

In the fourth game, Sơn let the thin soldier win. In the sixth, he again lost a head-to-head battle. When the eighth game rolled around, everyone bet all they had. They were playing with such concentration that they forgot to speak. Finally, the oldest of the group played a two of hearts, his trump. He only had one more card in his hand. He was on the verge of winning all the money.

The thin soldier threw in his hand.

The other soldier fell into a gloomy silence.

But Sơn had four threes. Together, they formed a kind of joker that could beat the man's two.

Slowly, he set his cards on the stool.

'Nobody can beat that, right?'

The oldest one let out the longest string of swear words that Sơn had ever heard. The others grudgingly threw their money into his lap. He carefully smoothed the notes before then stacking them on top of each other. His pile of money was as thick as the pack of cards. His heart was racing.

'So what are you planning to do with all the money?' the old one asked acidly. 'There's nothing to buy in this shithole anyway.'

'I'll give it back to you,' Sơn responded. 'I'll give you everything if you take me with you.'

The old one let out another of his exhaust-pipe laughs.

'You win once and you already want to make a deal! Who are you anyway? What are you doing here?'

He leaned across to Sơn and tapped him on the chest with his index finger.

'You look like a refugee to me! You ran away to avoid serving, didn't you? Listen, boy: we're driving back to Saigon tomorrow morning, and we're certainly not going to be making any detours for someone like you!'

Sơn's heart clenched. He had been hoping for a way out, but the soldiers were only offering to take him back home. Back to where everything had begun what felt like aeons ago.

His fingers caressed the notes as he flipped through the pile of Cambodian money. Maybe he could use it in Phnom Penh to find somebody to take him to Thailand. Maybe he could make it after all.

But what about Mai?

Slowly, he counted out half of his money and placed it in the hand of the oldest soldier.

'I want to go to Saigon too. I have to go meet an acquaintance of mine, the head of the state security service. Don't ask me any questions and just take me along.'

He stood up and brushed the dust from his pants.

'I'll give you the rest when we get there!'

KIỀU

The headache I use as an excuse to get out of the big family dinner on the second-to-last evening of our visit is not fake. I feel like I've been on autopilot ever since that call with Dorian, letting conversations and encounters rush past me without any notice or thought. I'm constantly reliving our phone conversation in my mind, once again feeling that faint hope, then the dull disappointment, and finally the emptiness that followed. He has called me five times since then and written twelve texts. For the first time since we met, I haven't responded.

I am listless and fatigued, my legs feel so heavy it's as if they have been filled with water, and my bra feels two sizes too small. If it weren't for the relationship talk and life-changing decision awaiting me in Berlin, I would have flown back home already. An evening of rest would really do me good.

'We hardly ever get to see our relatives, and you want to skip this? They'll be disappointed!'

My mother is sitting across from me on the shady side of a garden café. Even though her face is concealed by her broad-brimmed pink tulle hat, I have no trouble picturing her expression. It's like in the old days when I wanted to go to a party and she would let her face crumple into a sneer.

'It's just this one night! I'll be there tomorrow when we read the will,' I offer, annoyed by my own obsequiousness. *Why am I even asking her for permission? I understand why you might sometimes have to subordinate your own needs to a group, but do we really have to do* everything *together? The only moments of privacy have been those precious breaks in the bathroom.*

'Your relatives have come up with something special for you,' she announces.

'Oh yeah? Sounds dangerous.'

Over the last several days, it has become far easier for me to talk to my uncles and aunts, the Vietnamese rolling off my tongue much more fluently now. Yet I'm still wary of talking to them about my personal life. Since that one afternoon at Uncle Sơn's, we have never met up with him or anyone else alone. We've only ever been in a group with the extended family, our conversations invariably accompanied by the sounds of eating and various interjections.

'Uncle Sơn knows someone he wants you to meet,' my mother explains, almost as if she were trying to sell me a car. 'He has his own IT business and grew up here. He's like you, except, of course, he speaks much better Vietnamese. Uncle Sơn is bringing him to dinner tonight.'

'He wants to introduce me to a guy?'

I don't know whether to laugh or cry.

'Why not?' she asks, seeming genuinely astonished. 'He's quite tall for a Vietnamese man! Should I show you a picture? Uncle Sơn sent it around on WhatsApp earlier. Even Aunt Linh thinks he's very handsome!'

She pulls out her mobile phone and starts tapping away on it. She too has changed over the course of this trip. Fuelled by the daily comments from our relatives, she seems to have forgotten that in all my years of dating, I have yet to bring home a single Vietnamese man. The boys I met at my parents' karaoke parties were like cousins to me: nice enough and good at school but lacking a certain attraction. I wanted to be German and modern, not foreign and nerdy. I wanted to get ahead in a culture I didn't belong to, one that seemed superior to mine. That, really, was the appeal.

If I fell in love with men, they were Germans. The first had curly blond hair and played guitar, a cool stoner who didn't understand why I let my parents prevent me from doing so many things. The second was a melancholy photographer who was mostly in love with the idea of our romance, not with me as a person. The third was an engineer who knew exactly what he wanted and ended up smothering me with his single-mindedness. The fourth is Dorian. Dorian, who is so talented and free-spirited that he would never sacrifice himself for anyone, not even for me.

'I don't want to be set up, especially not by Uncle Sơn!' I hiss at my mother.

'You should be glad we're trying to help!'

She takes off her hat and starts fanning herself. Her lipstick is the same colour as the tulle, almost garish. She switches to Vietnamese.

'You've always thought you were like the Germans, but you will always be different. When are you finally going to understand that? They have other values than we do! Dorian isn't serious about you! You can't have children with a man like that!'

'Who says I *want* to have children?' I bark back, annoyed that she has once again managed to hit a sore spot. 'Even if I were pregnant right now, I would think twice about whether or not to keep the baby.'

'What nonsense! Are you sixteen? No. Are you sick? No. You have a job and a family that supports you! Why would you even think like that? There is nothing more wonderful for a woman than starting a family of her own!'

She leans over the table and pats my cheek as if I were a stubborn child. The thought that I might have told her the truth just now is so unimaginable to her that she only shakes her head briefly before going back to her phone to find the picture of the guy. I feel the dizziness getting stronger and knock the lawn chair over as I stand up with a jolt.

She raises her left eyebrow.

'What?' she scoffs. 'Another headache?'

*

I rush out of the café and notice out of the corner of my eye that other guests have interrupted their conversations to glance at me with curiosity. In Asian culture, there is this constant fear of losing face, but I suddenly realise that the phrase is misleading. At a moment like this, the face doesn't disappear; it lights up bright red and attracts attention from everyone, like a fire alarm.

I stumble through the small entrance gate and run into a young woman standing next to it smoking. Leaning against the fence, her face is turned to the sun and a cigarette dangles from the corner of her mouth.

'You okay?' she asks.

She pulls a pack of cigarettes out of her pants pocket and holds it out to me. I hesitate. Nothing seems crueller to me than women who smoke, drink, or take drugs during pregnancy. Images run through my head of the baby in my belly choking on the toxic smoke.

Slowly, I pull a cigarette out of the pack and put it between my lips. The flame glows brightly as she ignites it with a silver lighter. I inhale deeply and can feel the nicotine as it rises into in my head, mixing with the dizziness. It's a pleasant sensation, and I feel my anger losing its edge.

Fuck it. Fuck all of this.

'Why is it mostly women who pressure women to have children? So that others suffer the same fate as they did?'

Taken off guard by her candour, I start to cough. I blink as I look at her. She must be a few years older than me, her hair is cut in a short pixie, her eyes framed in black. She has Vietnamese features and a broad American accent. Probably the daughter of immigrants like me.

'I was sitting at the table next to you,' she explains. 'It was impossible not to hear your conversation, sorry. And I'm sorry that I'm always so direct. It's a terrible habit of mine.'

Her voice is so deep and raspy that it's almost soothing. It makes you want to lie down in it like in a warm, soft bed.

'It's okay,' I reply. 'So many people feel the need to tell me what they think, one more hardly matters.'

I close my eyes and try to breathe away my nausea. I slowly start considering her question.

'Mothers probably talk their daughters into having children because they see it as part of the job. They believe that you are only a real woman if you are a mother. At least that's what my mother thinks.'

'I've always considered that to be a stupid ideology.'

'Yeah?'

'Of course! Why should a woman only find fulfilment in marrying a man and getting pregnant with him? Why can't she just be herself? Think about who your mother was before she was your mother. What she was like as an individual.'

For as long as I can remember, my mother has sacrificed everything for the family: her job, her time, and the breadth of emotions at her disposal. She calls me every few days and puts up with my annoyed tone. She also brings me large Tupperware containers full of Vietnamese food whenever we meet. Each time, I tell her she doesn't need to, before taking it and heating it up for dinner the next day — without thanking her, of course. When I was younger, I was blind to her ability to tolerate pain. As I got older, I began seeing it as a call for me to do the same and learn the art of female suffering. I guess that's why she triggers me so much.

'My father once told me she was an activist as a student. I think she changed quite a bit after she had me and my siblings. Her greatest goal is for us to make it in life — if we're happy, she's happy. I can't imagine her without children. Pretty sad, huh?'

Even as I'm talking, I'm surprised at myself. I normally share very little with others. A colleague once confessed to me after a third glass of wine that I have such an 'Asian poker face' that she could never tell what I was thinking. But in front of this stranger, I'm laying all my cards face up on the table.

'You come from a Vietnamese family too,' I add quickly. 'You know what it's like.'

'Of course. Children should do better in life than their parents,' she sighs. 'How many people have been burdened by that expectation?'

'Have they?'

'Have they not?'

'I'm not sure it burdens me.'

'So why are you standing here now, in front of this gate?'

I throw the cigarette to the ground and stamp it out. I'm not sure how to answer that question; perhaps she has gone too far with her impudence. She sees my annoyance and squeezes her eyes so that her face turns into a grimace.

'Did I say something wrong? If I keep doing this, I'll have to apply for the Guinness Book of Records as the woman who puts her foot in her mouth the most. My chances would be pretty good, don't you think?'

I can't help but laugh. What a strange girl! Strange, but interesting. Have I met even one person in the last few years who was able to look behind the poker face? No, probably not.

'Who are you, anyway?' I ask.

'I'm Lee. My real name is Ly Ly, but that was too girly for me.'

'I'm Kim. My real name is Kiều, but that was too Vietnamese for me.'

She laughs.

'But Kiều is much better! Everyone is called Kim!'

*

Lee opens the passenger door of a green convertible and asks: 'Do you need a ride somewhere?' With its scratched-up leather seats and stick shift, the car doesn't fit in at all in this country where everything is new or made of plastic. I give her the address of my motel and climb in, because there's something about her that I find intriguing. A cool wind blows across my face as we drive down Bolsa Avenue, leaving my mother and her expectations behind. I feel awake for the first time in days.

Lee puts on a pair of sunglasses, the wide lenses sitting on her narrow face like the black eyes of a wasp. She leans forward to turn on the radio. The bass booms against the wind, and a woman starts rapping in English before switching to Vietnamese.

'Do you know her?' Lee shouts over the music. 'She's a rapper from Vietnam. She even freestyled for Obama when he was in Saigon.'

'I don't have a clue about Vietnamese music,' I shout back. 'The only thing I know are those love songs my parents always listen to.'

'That schmaltzy shit?' She laughs. 'They play it in all the cafés here too. I call it "the sound of the old generation". Back when my father was still alive, he loved singing war songs with his friends. When we went to Vietnam, he could hardly stand the country because it was so different from how he remembered. As soon as we left the hotel, he would start complaining about how noisy and dirty it was, and of course he hated the communists. At some point, I had enough of his whining and travelled there on my own. That's when I met this rapper. And a few underground poets. The poems were pretty out there, but that's how they are supposed to be, right?'

I hold my face into the wind and can feel the nausea fading away. There are many things I associate Vietnamese culture with, just not rap or underground poetry. I like how she jokes about our parents' generation instead of indulging in the feelings of obligation and guilt that every Vietnamese child is raised on. When I pull out my phone to take a picture, she pushes up her sunglasses and looks at me over the lens of my mobile. Her left eye is a little smaller than the right one. It twitches slightly.

'Let me know the next time you go. I'll give you a couple of recommendations for the kinds of things we are into.'

She says 'we' in the same way football fans say, 'today we are playing Borussia Dortmund' — with that sense of certainty that she and I are on the same team. It's strange how much this little word touches me. Few people have used it around me. Most have said 'you'.

We reach my ugly motel and stop in front of the entrance. She turns the off the engine.

'I guess we're here,' she says.

'A short drive,' I reply.

I unbuckle my seat belt and realise that I don't actually want to get out and be stuck on my own again. Everything seems so familiar with her, and new at the same time; I'd drive all the way to Mexico to savour that feeling a bit longer. 'It was cool meeting you,' I say by way of goodbye. 'Too bad I'm flying back to Germany tomorrow.'

'Tomorrow?' she repeats before starting the engine again. 'Then you definitely need to see the ocean one more time.'

*

The drive to Huntington Beach is either long or short, I don't know; I just feel her sitting next to me, swaying to the music. She's a dancer — what else could she be? — you can see it in the litheness of her body and her graceful movements.

'And what is it that smothers *you*?' I ask, since her directness has removed all barriers, including my reticence towards other people.

She pauses for a moment, as if frozen. Then she rolls her head in my direction. 'I also have a problem with my mother, but it's different from yours. Actually, it might not be that different.'

With the same candour with which she addressed me outside the café earlier, she opens up about her first love and the disastrous dinner-table conversation it led to. She had brought her girlfriend home several times but had only introduced her as a friend. After a few months, though, she went to a Korean barbecue restaurant with her mother and came out. Her mother asked her what she meant by 'relationship' twice before standing up and thanking the heavens that her husband was no longer on this Earth to experience such a thing. Then, she never mentioned it again.

Lee's voice doesn't betray her disappointment, but I can see it in the way she stares out at the road.

'And now? Has she finally come around?'

'We handle it like the military: "*Don't Ask, Don't Tell.*" When I have a steady girlfriend, I take her to my mother's place at some point, because I think it's the right thing to do. But otherwise, we don't talk about it. You know how Asians are.'

'I can imagine.'

I look at her curiously. She's the first lesbian Vietnamese woman I have met — at least the first to talk about it so openly.

'Do you mostly date white women or Asian women?' Even as the question leaves my mouth, it sounds wrong. To my relief, Lee doesn't seem to mind.

'I used to only date white women. Subconsciously, I thought that was cooler. Then something changed. On my first trip alone to Vietnam, I met a second-generation Vietnamese woman from France. We were together for two years. It was fantastic when we saw each other and hell when we didn't. I was really in love with her, but at some point, it just didn't work anymore.'

She turns to me.

'And you? Any preferences in your love life? Let me guess: You only like white guys!'

I feel exposed and think of Dorian and the boyfriends I had before him. At first, I want to justify myself with the fact that there aren't that many Vietnamese in Germany, so the dating pool is quite small. Then I let it go.

Could I, as a Vietnamese woman, be prejudiced against my own people? Probably.

'I've never been with a Vietnamese man,' I say succinctly. 'I haven't even kissed one.'

She laughs.

'Then let me tell you a secret: you wouldn't be able to tell the difference. All saliva tastes the same!'

*

At the ocean, Lee turns out to be one of those people who likes to get as deep into the water as possible. She takes off her baggy jeans and knots her white T-shirt under her breasts, revealing a tattoo resembling a thorny branch winding underneath them. There's a spring in her step as she runs across the light-brown beach. I follow her with heavy legs. She wades ahead into the sea and stops when the water reaches her thighs. It's quiet. No people, no waves; a silence you could happily drown in.

Without taking her eyes off the ocean, she suddenly says: 'I think my mother hopes that I'll eventually come to my senses, find a husband, and have children. She tells herself that I'm just going through a phase.'

'Just because she doesn't accept you being gay doesn't mean that she doesn't accept you,' I reply, suddenly feeling very German and preachy.

She gives me a sideways glance. 'I'm not making it up — it's true! She thinks I'm wasting my life. She sacrificed so much for me. And for what? So I can kiss women?'

'You're too hard on yourself. And on her too.'

'That's easy to say but hard to change.'

'I have a mother too. She's also only human. It took me a long time to figure it out, but I get it now, mostly anyway.'

I take a step to the side so that I'm standing close to her. She dips her hands into the water, rubbing them clean. She has the fingers of a piano player, long and slender. When she stands up straight again, I can smell the salt on her skin.

'When I was a child, I often built sandcastles on this beach. I was always back there, by the palm trees, because my mother wanted to make sure that her skin didn't get too dark. One time, I spent three hours building a castle, only to have a large boy come over and stomp on it. Man, did my mom go after him!'

'A white boy?'

'Does it matter?'

'Yes. No. I'm just curious.'

'It was a Vietnamese boy. Trevor Trúc. She wouldn't have dared to shout at a white boy. But she told Trevor: "One day, someone will break something you care about too."'

'And?'

'When he invited my ex-girlfriend to the prom years later, she first said yes and then ditched him that night to go with me.'

Impressed by her unexpected cruelty, I let out a whistle. The setting sun has turned the sky red, and she's standing there in the gathering shadows of twilight. I feel Lee's gaze on me and take a step to the left, moving to stand by her side.

THE STORY OF MY FATHER (PART II)
MINH

Hanoi, 1980

Minh had to smile as he looked out the airplane window at the slightly overcast S-shaped contours of Vietnam, recalling that moment twelve years ago when he left this country with two dictionaries and two tailored suits. A war, a regime change, and a wedding lay between his departure then and his arrival now. Then he had been a boy who believed that black-framed glasses would make him an intellectual. Now he was a man who knew there was a revolution to complete.

He placed his passport for the Socialist Republic of Vietnam in the pocket of the red airplane seat in front of him and leaned back. A freckled stewardess admonished him to fasten his seat belt, and the captain announced in German and Russian that the plane would soon be landing. The flight from East Berlin had taken eighteen hours, a bit longer than planned because of turbulence from a violent storm that had shaken the plane like a tin can. Children had started crying, adults had moaned in fear, and Hoa had hollered 'At least I'm dying in heaven!' before vomiting into a paper bag. He hadn't flown much in his life — to Germany, of course, then once to Mallorca, and once to Paris — but this had been the worst experience by far.

The thought that he would be landing in thirty minutes and then stepping out onto the soil of his homeland filled him with relief. He had been looking forward to this moment for months. He was wearing a new short-sleeved shirt with his initials embroidered on the breast pocket, and he had been to the barber just before leaving. His suitcase was packed full of aspirin, Leibniz butter cookies, and polo shirts that Hoa had found on sale at the Karstadt department store.

Although he followed the news about Vietnam closely, he didn't quite know what to expect. Ever since the communist takeover, he rarely received mail from Saigon. If his mother wrote to him at all, she would adopt a distressingly formal tone. In her letters, she would address him as 'Dear Sir' and end with 'Sincerely yours'. Her sentences seemed to contain hidden messages. 'The family is doing well, business is going better than before,' she had once written to him. 'Almost as good it was for our old neighbour, Mr Giang. Do you remember?' Giang, as Minh knew well, had lost his house due to gambling debts and become homeless. He could only guess at what his mother was trying to tell him. Was it possible that the new government was reading their correspondence? Apparently, she suspected so.

When he thought of his family, the image was fuzzy, and not just because of his mother's coded communication. He hadn't shared much about his life in Berlin either. What good would it do if she knew about his political involvement? She wouldn't understand him anyway. Their geographical distance had turned into emotional distance, and the longer Minh stayed in Germany, the more unreal his old life in Vietnam began to seem. The fact that a lot had changed at home was clear. But what exactly? He had read numerous essays about the Revolution and penned quite a few himself — yet he could not imagine how it had changed the lives of the people closest to him.

Interflug Flight 990 landed at Noi Bai Airport in Hanoi seventy-five minutes late. From the window, he could see that the sun had parched the fields beneath the flat light of the sky. Only the red of the Vietnamese flag shone strongly to welcome them.

The terminal building resembled a hastily erected shack, and the tarmac was riven with cracks and potholes. They were alone at the airport, with no other planes or people to be seen. Still, they weren't allowed to get up out of their seats yet. Eventually, he saw a thin woman in a conical straw hat hurrying to their plane, pulling a large wooden block on rollers behind her. She disappeared beneath the left wing as she walked under the belly of the plane. Twenty minutes later, she reappeared without the block of wood, apparently having used it to secure the wheels of the aircraft. Squinting into the sunlight, he watched her stooped body as she ambled away. If airports were a gauge of a country's modernity, as he was convinced that they were, then the Socialist Republic of Vietnam must have been roughly on par with Cuba.

*

'I don't think this visit is going to be entirely pleasant,' Hoa said that evening when they were having dinner in their hotel. Called 'The

Victory', there was a portrait of Ho Chi Minh in every room. You could tell by the building's stucco trim and tiled floors that it had been built during the French colonial period, but it didn't seem to have been renovated even once since then. The paint was peeling off the walls, the wood of the tables and chairs was scraped up, and the ceiling fan was rusting. Although it deserved no more than one star by international standards, it cost fifty dollars a day to stay here. All Vietnamese living abroad were required to spend at least one night in the hotel because the government urgently needed hard currency.

Although the restaurant on the first floor had been recommended to them as the best place in town, they were the only guests. The menu listed exclusively European dishes — it was, after all, mainly visitors from the Soviet Union, East Germany, or France who ate here — yet Minh ordered two bowls of phở. The dish originated from Northern Vietnam, and he had often heard that it was particularly flavourful in Hanoi, so he had been looking forward to the meal for days. He stirred the soup expectantly, but to his surprise, it didn't contain a single piece of meat. He seasoned the broth with a bit of fish sauce and hot peppers, but it still tasted like water. The noodles were so doughy that it seemed they must be made of something other than rice.

Hoa had a grimace on her face.

'It tastes terrible! This has to be the worst phở I've ever eaten!'

Minh signalled to the waiter, who was leaning against the counter next to three other young men, letting time flow lazily by. Startled, he shuffled over to them.

'Do you need anything else?'

Minh pointed an accusing finger at the steaming broth.

'The soup is missing the meat.'

'What do you mean?'

'I wanted my phở with beef. Can you take it back to the kitchen and have them add the meat?'

The waiter wiped his hands on his pants. He had to be in his mid-twenties, only a few years younger than Minh, but he acted awkwardly, like a teenager. Going by his accent, he was from one of the villages around Hanoi. A farm boy, Minh thought.

'You want to eat meat?' the waiter asked.

'Yes! As I've already said twice!'

Minh was slowly starting to get annoyed. The people here seemed terribly unprofessional. This would never happen in Germany!

'We don't have any meat,' the waiter finally admitted.

'What do you mean?'

'We're making the soup without meat today.'

'But it's phở!' exclaimed Minh, who could no longer hide his disappointment. 'When did it become a vegetarian dish?' He regained his composure and tried to strike a more conciliatory tone. Of course, things were not going as smoothly here as in Germany. He shouldn't have expected it any other way.

'If you don't have beef, then I'll take chicken.'

The waiter looked around for his colleagues, but no one came to his aid. He wiped his brow with the back of his hand.

'You're from abroad, aren't you?'

'Yes, but so what? I can still tell a real phở from a phoney one!'

'I'm sure you can get meat everywhere in other countries. But it's difficult here in Hanoi.'

He lowered his voice and leaned towards them.

'Yesterday we had a delegation from Moscow here. The meat rations for the week have already been eaten.'

'The Soviet delegation ate it all?' Minh asked incredulously.

'Yes, they come by frequently! They're helping our country rebuild. And they bring along strong appetites for our food and other delights our homeland has to offer.' He chuckled.

Minh decided to ignore the remark.

'And what exactly does their help look like?'

He had read that the Communist Party of Vietnam had based its economic policy on the Soviet model. Many of the ideas for establishing an industrial sector had been copied straight from Moscow, and for that reason they had been labelled inefficient, outdated, or even harmful by Western critics.

The waiter shrugged his shoulders.

'What do I know? I don't talk politics with them, I talk food. I know they like eating fried potatoes with beef, but I don't know what they do. It doesn't really matter, does it?'

*

The next morning, Minh and Hoa began their thirty-hour train journey, cutting through the country from top to bottom, ending in Saigon. As they left, the Interior Ministry employee who accompanied them to the station impressed upon them that it was now called 'Ho Chi Minh City'.

They reached their destination after a long, bumpy, and, above all, sweltering train ride. They hired two rickshaws at the main station, put their suitcases in the first xích lô, and sat down in the second. As they drove through his hometown, Minh found that he could barely recognise it. The hotels and restaurants in the centre were barricaded; the street food stalls and hawkers had disappeared. Neither signs nor street lights illuminated the evening; once the sun had set, he could only see grey.

Where children had once run around and adults had boisterously played cards, people were now scurrying past, jaded expressions on their faces. The women were wearing plain house clothing, the men shirts whose colours were washed out. They rolled past on bicycles, some loaded with heavy sacks, others carrying an entire family. The smell of dust had replaced that of petrol; the cacophony of car horns had given way to the whirring of pedals. Saigon, which Minh remembered as a radiant dancer, now looked like a tired old housewife.

Their rickshaws turned into a side street, and then immediately turned left again. He recognised the French façades and lush tamarind trees that lined the memories of his childhood. But Liberty Street had also changed. Someone had written its new name in red paint on the front window of the now closed Café Brodard: Đường Đồng Khởi, Uprising Street. Although Minh didn't mind the combative tone, it still didn't sound right. When telling others about his youth, he had always spoken of Liberty Road. To use any other name felt like a betrayal of his past.

When they stopped in front of his family's home, a young woman came running up to them and wrapped her arms around his neck, gurgling with pleasure.

'Linh!' he cried. 'How beautiful you are!'

He hugged her and felt like he was reaching into the void. She had to be twenty-six now, but she was as slender as a girl. Her hair was tied into a thick braid with a red rubber band, and she was wearing an áo bà ba, a garment suitable both for home and going out, which she had likely sewn herself. The black trousers were wide cut, the blue-grey top collarless and slightly fitted. She appeared modestly but carefully dressed. After greeting Hoa, she grabbed Minh's hand and pulled him inside. The green grating had been pushed to the side on the right and left, revealing a completely empty store. The shelves, once full of shimmering bolts of fabric, were now covered in a layer of dust. The racks on which the tailored dresses and suits used to hang were gone.

Only a mannequin leaned naked and useless in a corner. A note taped to its plastic belly read: 'For Sale.'

'Is that Minh?'

His mother scurried towards them from the kitchen, and when he saw her, he balked. In his memory, he had preserved the image of an elegant, enterprising woman who preferred wearing an áo dài and would curl her hair on special occasions. Now, though, her hair was streaked with grey, her face worn, and the skin on her fingers cracked. She too wore housewear of relatively good quality, but beneath the brown shirt and black pants, her arms and legs looked bony.

Minh wanted to walk up to her and give her a hug, but he was gripped by the fear of crushing her. After patting him on the shoulder with a wordless smile, she examined him from top to bottom.

'You send your son abroad, and he comes back all skinny! Aren't you eating properly over there?' She pinched his cheek.

Her critique was a welcome relief. Apparently, she hadn't changed that much after all.

She turned to Hoa, who had made a special effort with her clothes and was wearing a flowing white skirt decorated with colourful flowers to go with light eye shadow, her lips shimmering pink. Hoa had insisted that there was no way she could go to the home of a famous dressmaker like his mother in jeans and a T-shirt. Now she seemed uncomfortable in her fancy outfit.

'So you're the woman my son married in Germany!' his mother said matter-of-factly.

She didn't have to utter the words 'without my permission'; everyone present heard them anyway. When Minh had married Hoa a year earlier, he hadn't done so in secret, but he hadn't asked his mother beforehand either, at least not directly.

Vexed by her first, disparaging comment about Hoa, Minh had stopped mentioning her in his rare letters to his family. Then, a week before the wedding, he had sent a brief telegram announcing that he was getting married on Vietnamese New Year. His mother's response came late, and her aggrieved tone (*'When a child is far away, he makes decisions that a mother cannot influence'*) was hard to miss, yet he had decided to take this sentence as a half-hearted blessing. Now he was no longer sure whether his assessment had been correct.

'Do you really think he's that skinny?' Hoa asked in a halting attempt not to immediately surrender to her mother-in-law. 'I try to cook something nice for him when I can. But Germany isn't Vietnam — you have to drive far to find the right ingredients. Most days, I just can't find the time. I have a job too and don't get home until the evening.'

'Is your job more important to you than your husband?' his mother replied. 'I had to run the business because Minh's father was deployed in the war. There was no other way for our family to survive. But you're married to a doctor, you don't have to go to work all day. As a woman, you should take care of your husband and think about having children. You're thirty already, aren't you?'

*

Minh woke up late the next day, his body clock not yet having adjusted to Vietnamese time, and it took him a moment to realise he was back in his old room in Saigon. Although the government had changed, the street bore a different name, and both his father and brother were gone, his bed was still there. Only now did he realise how badly he had missed home.

He wondered about the books he had left behind. Were they still there?

Minh knew from his mother's letters that Sơn had moved to this room after John had moved out. His brother must have hidden the shoebox somewhere. Minh got up and looked under the bed, his hand probing through the darkness beneath the mattress slats, but he found only dust. The shelves on the wall were empty, and the small bedside table didn't have a drawer big enough to hold a box. Which left the wardrobe. He opened the doors and cleared out all the T-shirts and pants he had put away the night before. Nothing. He reached into all the compartments to feel around, but the books were still nowhere to be found.

He sighed. On the way here, he had told Hoa about the diary he had kept in his youth. He didn't remember what he had written in it, but he would have loved to read it again.

Disappointed, Minh called his mother. He wanted to show her something he had bought in Berlin a week earlier: a long-sleeved lab coat with a mandarin collar. It was made of a light cotton-silk blend, lending it a slight shimmer. Minh had discovered it by chance in a specialty shop on Savignyplatz. It had been tailored for an eye surgeon from Singapore, but the man had suffered an accident before starting his job and returned home. Because of its extremely slim cut, it hadn't fit any other customer. But it was so perfect on Minh that the shop assistant had exclaimed: 'You look like a real professor!'

Minh took the garment from his suitcase and held it against the light, the white nearly blinding his eyes.

'What do you think?' he asked.

'It's beautiful,' his mother answered, hesitantly. 'Almost too nice to wear.' She slowly stroked the silky fabric. 'Why did you bring it here?'

'I want to save it for later. I'll be done with my specialist doctor training next year, and then I'm coming back!'

His mother looked at him in surprise. Had she forgotten that he wanted to return to Vietnam? He scolded himself for not visiting her before, but it had been impossible for Hoa to get a visa. Due to a bureaucratic error, the new Vietnamese government had simply transferred Hoa's status as 'traitor to the country' from the old government. The misunderstanding was only cleared up after the development minister of East Germany had intervened.

'You want to live in Vietnam again?' his mother asked.

'Of course! We're going to open a clinic!'

He carefully draped the lab coat on the only hanger he could find in his old wardrobe — a gleaming white promise waiting to be fulfilled. Minh sank onto his bed, and his mother sat down next to him, her shoulder touching his.

'The situation in Vietnam is very difficult, much more difficult than you can imagine.' She spoke cautiously, feeling her way forward, word by word. 'Your father is still in a re-education camp, and God knows when he will return. Sơn has fled for the second time. There hasn't been enough food since the communists have been in power; rations are far too small, and most of the time you don't even get the full amount. I can't wait for the day when we don't have to count every grain of rice. Can you imagine? We live like beggars. Sometimes I almost wish the war was still going on.'

She spoke quietly, as if telling him a secret. Her wrinkled eyelids made it look as though she were crying invisible tears when she blinked. He thought of her strange letters and began to realise just how much she had held back to protect him.

'I didn't know how hard it was for you. You never told me ...' He paused, his voice having begun to waver. The way this conversation was going, disappointment was the only possible outcome. He took off his glasses, cleaned the lenses with the corner of his T-shirt, and then put them back on. After clearing his throat, he started anew. 'Vietnam is experiencing a revolutionary transition, it's only natural that the first stage has been difficult.' He straightened his back and turned his face towards her. 'I'm sure it will get better in the future. We should stick to the plan to open a hospital. It's still a good idea!'

'And how do you suppose we are going to pay for it? The French bank closed and all our money is gone.' She held her left hand out to him. 'You see that? I don't even have my wedding ring anymore.'

He leaned towards her. '*We* can deal with all that, Mother! Hoa works for a bank in Germany, she can contact the French bank and file for compensation. Besides, we have our own savings now. I make plenty of money. Don't worry about that.'

She shook her head slowly. 'The country we knew no longer

exists. We've lost everything. Everything our family has accomplished is gone. Wake up, Minh!'

She rose with a sigh and went back downstairs. As her footsteps echoed on the steps, a long-lost feeling welled up inside him: defiance. Did his mother want to forbid him from coming back and opening a hospital? Why was she treating him like a little boy? Vietnam needed people like him, now more than ever. He was going to do his part, whether she wanted him to or not.

*

The police station where Minh and Hoa had to register as visitors was located in a windowless building riddled with bullet holes. The ceiling lights flickered as they wandered through the corridors asking four different people for the registration desk; no one seemed to be in charge. Finally, they found a police officer who handed them a form to fill out while in the waiting room, saying he would be right back to pick it up. They had to provide all kinds of information: the duration of their stay, the names of all acquaintances they intended to visit, their addresses, professions, and any contacts they might have with the intelligence services of capitalist countries abroad.

Though Minh found the last question strange — of course he wasn't a spy, but if he had been, it's not like he would admit it — he still filled out the form conscientiously in clear, printed letters. He wished he could have written that he had founded an association in Berlin for Vietnamese students who planned to return home after completing their education to help rebuild the country. He wished he had space to write: 'We are proud of the Revolution and consider ourselves to be patriots!' But there was no field for additional comments in the questionnaire, and the formatting was so tight that there was no room for extras.

The room was so stuffy that they stuck to the plastic chairs. There was no fan in sight, so Minh began fanning himself with his papers. They sat there waiting for an hour, then an hour and a half, and finally two hours.

'Didn't you want to pick up these documents?' Minh asked when he finally found the policeman in the hallway next to the bathroom. He was sitting on a red stool, legs crossed, and reading the newspaper.

'Did you fill everything out?' the man asked without looking up.

'Two hours ago, as requested! We were beginning to think there was some kind of a problem.'

Minh waved his papers around, but not wanting any trouble, he didn't dare criticise the officer.

The policeman turned a page.

'The processing of your application is rather time-consuming. If you're in a hurry, I'll have to see what I can do for you.'

'What do you mean by that?'

The man looked up and tilted his head to the side as if to say: *'You know what I mean.'*

Minh was disgusted. The communists had promised time and again that they would end corruption. And now this guy wanted money from him?

'I play by the rules,' he blurted out. 'And I also expect you to process our applications correctly.'

The policeman simply shrugged his shoulders.

'You're welcome to keep waiting if you like. We're open until four o'clock, so if your application isn't ready today, you'll have to come back again tomorrow. Think about it. And could you please step aside? I have to go to the bathroom.'

*

A few days later, Minh came downstairs to the living room in his undershirt and shorts and saw Hoa sitting next to an elderly woman on the tile floor. Her leathery skin was a similar shade of brown to her shirt and her back was turned to Hoa, who was plucking out the white hairs on her head. When they both looked up, he realised they had the same flat nose and round face.

'Minh?' The woman rose, took his right hand in hers, and pressed them together. 'What a bright face you have!' She stroked him with her wrinkled fingers.

'My mother got on the bus in Hàm Tân at two in the morning,' Hoa explained. 'She was downstairs knocking on the door at six.'

Hoa had wanted to visit her family for a few days, but Minh's mother had forbidden her from going. A married woman should live with her husband's family and help with the household, she had said. Though Hoa had been bitterly disappointed, she had complied. But she had apparently found a way to at least see her mother.

Minh's mother walked in with four glasses of tea. She was polite to the visitor, but he could sense that she did not approve. The twins had told him that a couple from the neighbourhood had come to visit a few times. They had a twenty-year-old daughter they wanted to marry off to a Vietnamese man living abroad. The family owned a home next to the old National Assembly that they had somehow been able to save from expropriation.

Hoa's mother, on the other hand, clearly owned nothing. She used to work as a teacher in Huế, but now she lived with Hoa's eight siblings in the Special Economic Zone. They eked out a living there by cultivating fruit and vegetables, which they sold at the market. She had brought four bunches of mini bananas along as a gift.

'Life must be tough where you are,' Minh's mother remarked. 'I've heard that the soil up there is rather infertile.' She gave the woman some tea, placed the other two glasses on the floor next to Minh and Hoa, and sat down cross-legged with them.

'I'm afraid you're right,' Hoa's mother replied. 'We're trying cassava and sweet potatoes at the moment, and they seem to do better. But it is still difficult. The only good thing about poverty is that it makes everyone equal. The whole village is trying to help each other. When I have a good harvest, I take some to our neighbour. She lends the children her bicycle in return so they don't have to walk to school. Three hours each way isn't exactly a short distance ...'

She sipped her tea like a precious wine, and Minh suddenly felt guilty about how often he and Hoa went to the movies in Berlin or ate at that Japanese bistro on Kantstrasse. It was quite cheap, around fifteen marks for the two of them if they shared a cola. But fifteen marks was enough to buy a bike here, and that would spare a child from having to walk six hours to school and back. He looked over at Hoa and sensed that she was doing the same calculations in her head. She wiped her eyes with the back of her hand.

'The mood is terrible in Saigon too,' his mother sighed. 'Half the city is trying to escape.'

'Fleeing isn't something our family would even consider. We neither have the money nor the connections.'

'It's admirable that you're trying to make the best out of a difficult situation,' Minh interjected. 'Perhaps it's wiser to stay here rather than to try to go abroad at any cost.'

His mother glanced at him in irritation, her right eyebrow twitching. With exaggerated politeness, she turned to Hoa's mother and spoke over his head as if he weren't there.

'You know, sister, there are many people who look at our country from the outside but don't really understand what's going on. My husband has been locked up in a re-education camp for five years because he's a political opponent. My second son has been on the run for the past year because he couldn't stand it here anymore. My other children have no chance of studying at university because of their father. How is a family like ours supposed to deal with a situation like this? We have no future here. Anyone who thinks otherwise is either naive or too blinded by ideology to see the truth.'

Minh could feel his head growing hot. Why didn't his mother speak straight to his face? Why did she have to humiliate him in front of others?

Hoa was looking at him in silence, but her gaze said: *Just let it go.*

'Here, everyone who wants to do something with their life is trying to escape,' his mother continued. 'If the street lights had legs, they would run away too!'

Fine, thought Minh, as he turned to address Hoa's mother as well.

'I'm glad people aren't street lamps, because otherwise the lights would go out pretty quickly in this country!' he said defiantly. 'Vietnam must learn to stand on its own two feet to become free and democratic. Anyone who believes that this can happen overnight has a strange notion of politics. Living abroad means that we have access to information that isn't available here. Many of us believe that even though the road may be rocky, it's still the right one. Perhaps it's possible to see this more clearly from the outside than from the inside. In Germany, there's even a saying for this: You can't see the forest for the trees.'

'So *that's* what they are telling you in Germany,' his mother replied venomously. 'The rumours about you two have already made it all the way to Vietnam. A friend of a friend heard that you were seen at a communist demonstration. My oldest son at a *protest*!'

She rose from the floor and began collecting the tea glasses. With a feigned smile, she thanked Hoa's mother for the bananas and informed her that she would have liked to invite her to spend the night, but unfortunately she didn't have a bed to spare. The latter accepted the rebuff with dignity. When Minh ostentatiously tried to place fifty dollars in her hand, she shook her head in silence.

*

One evening, Minh's mother asked him to accompany her to the home of an acquaintance. He was a man with good connections, she explained, adding that he had news from Sơn. While riding in the rickshaw to his home in District 3, she was constantly on the lookout. Just before reaching the destination, she asked the driver to stop at a corner where train tracks crossed the road.

'No one can see that he has a visitor from abroad,' she whispered. 'He works for state security.' Minh was taken aback that she was meeting with a communist intelligence officer of her own accord, but figured she must have her reasons.

It was the first time they had been alone together in days, but even now, Minh didn't ask his mother who had told her about the demonstration, nor did she ask why he had gone. They had come to a tacit agreement to keep the peace during the rest of his visit. It was better to remain silent than to argue.

His mother turned into a narrow side street that bent its way around a number of corners before leading them to a white villa with stately columns. As they walked along the narrow path to the front door, Minh saw two pigs that appeared to be living in a makeshift pen in the garden. An elderly, hunched woman greeted them at the door and announced that Mr Công was expecting them in his study.

Behind a desk of heavy, dark wood sat a man in a green uniform. Perched sideways on the table, he had his right leg crossed over his left and was staring at a map on the wall showing the administrative districts of Ho Chi Minh City. His hair stuck to his forehead in tiny waves, and he appeared to be lost in thought. Minh wasn't sure if Mr Công had even registered their presence, and was about to clear his throat when the man began to speak.

'When I lived up North, I used to tell my wife about houses like this. Once the war is over, I told her, I will take you to my hometown and show them to you. Our children will attend a normal school, we will build a new country. I've been telling her about this new life for so many years ...'

On the wall behind him was a framed certificate recognising his contributions in reforming the city. Above it was a photo, clearly a bit older, showing a bespectacled Ho Chi Minh sitting in a bamboo chair in a garden. Off to the side and partially cut off was Mr Công, handing him some papers. Minh was impressed: he had never met anyone who had known the famous communist leader before.

Mr Công reached for a can of beer sitting on a stack of papers and took a sip.

'Would you like one?'

Minh shook his head. His mother sat down on a chair and folded her hands in her lap.

'In your message, you said that the situation was complicated. Are you well?' she asked.

'Well. Unwell. Who cares about such categories?' he said, throwing his hands in the air. 'In a revolution, only one thing matters. Do you know what that is?'

He leaned over the table.

'The way forward,' he said, before sinking back into his chair. 'And anything that doesn't move forward is pushed to the side. Old ideas, old promises, old South Vietnamese cadres like me. There are still many sacrifices to be made in the name of the Revolution. You should never believe that you have already lost enough!'

This unexpected outburst made Minh uncomfortable. His preference would have been to bid a polite farewell and leave quickly, but the look on his mother's face kept him in line. He sat down in the chair next to hers and saw that there was something on the desk: a photo of Sơn with a young woman whose hair was unusually curly. The two were standing in a clearing, their arms hanging at their sides. Behind them were a number of straw huts and a stream of people, the outline of a mountain range looming in the distance. Although the landscape resembled the mountainous area of central Vietnam, the photo must have been taken somewhere else.

Mr Công followed his gaze and handed him the picture. A bright reflective line mirrored the ceiling light where it curled. He hadn't seen his brother in twelve years, and the last time they had written to each other was two years ago. Sơn's eyes peered out defiantly, his hair shaggy. He was wearing a washed-out white T-shirt and light-blue shorts that were a size too big for him. His skin was dark and uneven, as if it had been exposed to too much dust and sun. He looked much older than Minh remembered. Older and rougher.

'How do you know my brother?' he asked Mr Công.

'Sơn? He went to school with my daughter. I don't know if he's a curse or a blessing! After they fled to Cambodia and she was kidnapped, he came to me. I was furious and wanted to arrest him. Or beat him. Or first beat him and then arrest him! But he's a smart boy, and he implored me to help him find Mai for so long that I eventually gave in. I sent two people back to Cambodia with him, and after two weeks they actually managed to find her. We're on good terms with the Vietnamese army, thank God, so they surrounded the hideout of those Khmer Rouge bastards and captured them ...' Mr Công scratched his face absently. 'I couldn't have known that Mai and Sơn would stay there!'

'They stayed in Cambodia?'

Minh thought back to the images he had seen on the news. The mountains of skulls had reminded him of photos from Auschwitz. If he had known that his brother was living in this hell-hole, he would have moved mountains to get him to Germany.

'I can't tell you for sure, young man. I think they were in Phnom Penh for a while, then they went to the border and, after several failed attempts, managed to cross into Thailand. But it wasn't like Mai could send me a postcard with her itinerary. I told everyone she was dead!'

'Dead? Why did you say that?'

'Listen! I'm a member of the Party! We lock people up who flee. It doesn't look good to have my own child run away.' Fingers splayed, he began fiddling with his beer can. 'If someone had found out ...'

Mr Công closed his eyes briefly, and when he opened them again, Minh could see they had become misty. He had never seen a man cry before and didn't know how to react, so he reached for the nearest document and smoothed out the dog-ears. It was the five-year plan of the Communist Party, adopted at the 4th National Congress in December 1976. *The Socialist Revolution in our country is a process of comprehensive, deep, and lasting revolutionary change. By 1980, the socialist transformation of South Vietnam should essentially be completed ...*

His mother put a hand on the man's arm to calm him, speaking gently as if he were a child.

'You said that one of your contacts had found them in a refugee camp in Thailand. That's where this photo was taken, right? Are they doing okay?'

Mr Công regained his composure and placed a second photo on the table in front of them: a queue of more than a hundred people was winding itself around a long building made of corrugated iron, plastic tarpaulins, and thick bamboo. The children were shirtless and barefoot; some of the adults had plastic buckets with them.

'That's the bathroom,' Mr Công explained, tapping it with his finger. 'Ten toilets for a total of 10,000 people! The stench was so bad that my guy almost got sick when he took that photo.'

In sombre terms, he described an anarchic world where water was so scarce that some women would sell their bodies and men would fight each other for it. A world where the guards ruled over the refugees with the omnipotence of gods, depriving them of what little they still possessed: their last gold, their wounded pride.

'And do you know who the worst ones are?' he shouted. 'Do you know who enjoys raping the women and beating the men the most? It's not the Thai guards. It's the Vietnamese they hired as minders! Our own people!'

His voice was brimming with disgust as he spoke; he had to pause repeatedly to catch his breath. It seemed to Minh as though Mr Công was choking on his own words.

'Is this what we fought for? So that our compatriots could be abused by their Vietnamese brothers and sisters in other countries? Did we spill our blood for *that*?'

His hands were shaking. He had unbuttoned the shirt of his uniform, revealing his undershirt. He opened his mouth to continue speaking, but then closed it again and lapsed into silence.

'I understand your concern,' Minh finally said. 'We're worried too. Do you know how long they'll have to stay in this refugee camp? Maybe we can help them.'

'Help? That's easy to say! Sơn has tried a few times to write to a relative in Germany, but he never answered, can you imagine?' He shook his head. 'The Vietnamese living abroad are strange. As soon as they are gone, they forget their own brothers.'

Minh grabbed him by the arm.

'What do you mean? Sơn has only one relative living in Germany, and that's me!'

'You're the German?'

'Yes! But I never received a letter! Are you sure he sent one?'

'As sure as I am sitting here! Sơn told my contact twice: *"My brother is sitting in his German student residence while I rot here!"* You don't make stuff like that up.'

'But I don't live there any longer! After we got married, we moved into our own apartment.'

Minh fell back in his chair, guilt crashing over him like an avalanche. Because he'd been too cowardly to speak to his family about his marriage, they knew nothing of his new home. And because they didn't know where he lived, Sơn had sent his letter to the wrong address. If only he had told his mother the truth! If only he had written to her more often!

'I didn't know he needed help. If I had known, I would have done something. It was a misunderstanding! A stupid, horrible misunderstanding!'

With red eyes, Mr Công peered over at him.

'And you expect us to believe that?'

'Why would I lie about something like that?'

His mother looked on helplessly. Her eyes had turned the colour of murky water, full of disappointment. He tugged on her arm, but she pulled it away.

'Why didn't you come up with the idea of bringing your brother to Germany yourself?' she asked slowly. 'Why did he have to run away in the first place? Have you and your wife been too busy to think about your family?'

'But you never said anything!' Minh exclaimed. 'You always wrote that you were doing well!'

Even as he uttered these words, he realised how ridiculous they sounded. Of course he had suspected that something was wrong. Of course it came as no surprise that his brother also wanted to leave the country. It had simply been easier for Minh not to think too much about it. In the same way that he eventually acquired a taste for sausage and cheese in Germany, he had also acquired a taste for the freedom that life abroad offered him. By remaining ignorant of what was going on back home, he had been free of the obligations and expectations of his own family. Free to think only of himself.

Mr Công pursed his lips and formed a word that he didn't need to pronounce.

Traitor.

*

Minh spent the rest of his holiday seeing as many friends as he could so as to spend as little time at home as possible. Whenever he looked at his mother's face, he felt he could see that terrible word in it. She never said it out loud, but it echoed in his head. He, who had been sent on a mission by his family, had betrayed them on the way to achieving it. He felt guilty but didn't know how to broach the subject. If he went out in the evening, his mother complained that he was never home. If he did stay at home, they ate in silence.

Only once, after he returned with Hoa from a three-day visit to her family, did his mother erupt in anger. In an act of particular cruelty, she directed her wrath at his wife, not him. Her fifteen-minute lecture on the duties and obligations of a daughter-in-law began even before they entered the house, so that all the neighbours would hear it as well. Hoa, she shouted, now belonged to her husband's family and wasn't allowed to go away for days on end to visit relatives without permission. A good daughter-in-law knows her place and is faithful to her elders. She told Hoa that while she might have forgotten this living abroad, in the end, she owed everything — and she emphasised the word '*everything*' — to the family that had invested so much in Minh.

Red in the face, they both crept upstairs. Minh felt like a

stranger in his own family. 'Only one more week,' he comforted Hoa. 'One week, and then we'll fly home.'

*

On the day of his departure, Minh finally tried to talk to his mother. She was sitting in the bamboo chair next to the balcony, looking out into the lazy afternoon, her fingers stroking the photo of Sơn and Mai. Mr Công had given it to her when she had paid him another visit the day before. Minh put a hand on her shoulder from behind and felt her startle. He had been away for twelve years. When would they next see each other?

'I've been thinking about that conversation the other day. The thing with Sơn,' he said carefully.

'What about Sơn?'

'When I go back to Berlin, I could apply for family reunification. It's not easy, but I could try.'

She looked at him. 'And you're just thinking of this now?'

He set his suitcase down and sat on the floor, cowering next to his mother like a child.

'I always wanted to come back to Vietnam, not bring my family to Germany. We had a plan, remember? I never questioned it, so I always thought we were building something *here*, not over there. I didn't know you had changed your mind, you never told me. But if that's what you want, then I will try.'

I am the eldest son, after all, he would like to have added. *I want to do the right thing.*

But he didn't dare.

His mother remained motionless.

'We don't need your help to leave the country. There's another way now.'

'What do you mean?'

'John recently visited the refugee camp where Sơn is staying. He works for the American Embassy in Thailand now. He promised to get him to the USA.'

'John is unreliable.'

'So are you!'

Her words hit him like a slap in the face. His head fell to the side, heavy and hot.

'It was a misunderstanding!' he shouted.

'Enough of your excuses!' she shouted back.

Minh closed his eyes to avoid having to look at his mother. What was it that he had hoped to find here? A family eagerly waiting for his return? A homeland as warm as his hopes and ideals? He now realised that there were two Vietnams: the one that lived in his memory and the other one that existed in the real world. The two didn't have much in common.

His knees popped as he rose again.

'If you need my help after all, write to me. I'll leave my new address on the table for you.'

He turned away and heard her rise behind him. Downstairs, Hoa was sitting on her big suitcase while Linh and the twins were already waiting at the entrance to the house. His siblings hugged him with sad eyes, but his mother, standing stiffly in front of him, only raised her hand in farewell. After some hesitation, he opened his suitcase once again, took out his white lab coat, and handed it to Linh.

She took the garment in her hands and stroked the soft fabric in delight before burying her face in it. Then she pointed to the naked mannequin guarding the empty store.

'May I?' her expression said.

He shrugged his shoulders. *'As you wish.'*

Carefully, as if she were dressing a queen, she draped the gown around the model's shoulders. She closed the white buttons in deep concentration. When she had buttoned it down to the belly, she removed the sticker and stuck it on her hand. She smoothed out the fabric and took a step back to have a look. The garment was a little tight at the chest, but otherwise it fit as if it had been tailor-made for the mannequin.

Murmuring with pleasure, Linh gave the thumbs up before approaching the mannequin once more. She placed the sticker on the breast pocket.

'For Sale.'

KIỀU

On the final day of our trip, I wake up too early, my body clock apparently having already reverted to German time. My heart is pounding, impatient to get the day started. My parents' snores drift over from the other bed as I quietly get up and begin feeling my way through the darkness.

I have to be with them one last time today when my grandmother's testament is read to the family. Tomorrow, I'm flying back home to my old life.

I open the door, walk down the outdoor staircase, cross the parking lot, and push open the gate leading to the pool area. Day has yet to take over from night, and the pool lies dark and tranquil before me. It's almost as though the people in their beds, the cars in the parking lot, and the streets out in front of the motel are stuck in this moment, patiently trapped as in a photograph. I am suddenly overcome by melancholy. Prior to this trip, I hadn't spoken to my relatives in fifteen years. How long will it be before we see each other again?

Despite the language difficulties, I have come to understand the strange and wonderful meaning behind our family rituals. I see now how routine can forge closeness, while distance creates gaps that are filled with misconceptions or holes. When I get back to Berlin, I will miss something that wasn't there before.

I pull my nightshirt over my head and feel the warm air on my bare skin. I dive into the pool, my hands parting the water as I glide beneath the surface, driving myself forward with my legs. I feel weightless, free of the hindrance of a bathing suit and the inhibiting presence of others. For the first time on this trip, I'm alone. No parents waiting to take me somewhere. No relatives fighting over the perfect restaurant to go to. No questions, obligations, or suggestions that I must agree to, quietly accept, or respond to in some other fashion. The water is so cold that my insides feel warm. I swim until I can no longer stand the tingling beneath my skin.

I lie down on one of the lounge chairs in the darkness, put my feet up, and think back to yesterday's trip to the seaside: the forbidden cigarette that Lee held out to me, the tattoo under her breast, her footprints in the sand. When I told her about Dorian's reaction to my pregnancy and launched into a detailed account of my doubts about our future together, she first fell silent before putting her hands on her hips. 'Are you looking for someone to make the decision for you?' she demanded. 'That's not how it works. I can't take that burden off your shoulders. Grow a backbone! You have to start being you instead of what others want you to be!'

On the way home yesterday, I remained silent. I waved a noncommittal farewell in the motel driveway, intentionally cold, as she cast about for words to salve the wounds she had inflicted. Now regret overcomes me like the rumbling of an approaching storm. Of course I didn't want to hear those words. But she wasn't wrong.

I stretch out on the lounge chair, coming up with five lengthy options for face-saving messages I could write to her, but then grow increasingly frustrated as my internal defences are once again activated. Perhaps directness is best.

'I'm flying out at midnight — am I going to see you again?'

*

In the afternoon, we take our packed suitcases and drive over to Aunt Linh's, her small house standing in a row of beige-coloured homes that all look the same. We walk past languid palm trees and a pool, where I see children swimming. We ring the doorbell of number 68.

No answer.

My mother tries the knob, but it's locked.

I find a half-open window, behind which Aunt Linh is sitting on a leather couch, apparently watching television. It's unclear if there is anyone in the room with her.

I knock on the window.

'Open the door. We're here!'

I wave my arms wildly to attract her attention.

Aunt Linh leans forward for the remote to change the channel. Her face is covered in a white, creamy mask, with fine cracks where it has dried. She looks like a character from a Beijing opera, a creature from a different world.

'She can't hear us,' my mother says, stating the obvious.

'Should we throw something in?' my father asks. 'Maybe a pebble?'

He kneels down and grabs a piece of grey gravel, testing its weight in his right hand.

'I'll try to hit the remote!'

He takes a step to the side, positioning himself in front of the gap in the open window. Squinting his eyes, he extends his left index finger towards Aunt Linh's living room. With his right leg stretched out behind him, he looks like an archer ready to fire off an arrow.

'One,' he says, shaking his right wrist, 'two,' his voice grows louder, 'three!' With a sharp cry, he hurls the pebble into the living room. It pings off the remote control and into the water glass sitting on the table.

Plop. Aunt Linh looks up.

She taps her finger to her forehead.

Her right hand grabs an imaginary knob and turns it to the right. She shakes her head: *'Not like that!'* She then starts again, her thumb pushing a button in the middle before she then turns, her left thumb pointed upwards.

I am always amazed at how much she can say without words.

*

Once everybody has arrived, Aunt Linh sets a gigantic fondue pot on the table, under which she positions a small gas flame. Platters of vegetables, meat, and tofu are brought out of the kitchen. We place the ingredients one bite at a time into small golden baskets and hold them in the broth so they can cook, before then rolling them up in rice paper together with noodles and herbs. It tastes amazing. Grunts of satisfaction can be heard around the table. Uncle Sơn repeats three times that Aunt Linh spent the entire morning in the kitchen preparing the hot pot.

A warm contentment in our bellies, we do the washing up

before heading for the living room to relax. We still have to wait for the lawyer, so we watch Fox News with subtitles to kill time. He was supposed to show up at 6.00 pm with my grandmother's testament, but by the time the doorbell rings, it's almost 7.00.

Uncle Sơn jumps up to let in an African American man who he can't stop patting on the shoulder. The man is sporting a rather unorthodox combination of suit and briefcase together with a bright-red baseball cap, an American flag stitched on the left side. Even though he must be in his late sixties, his black suitcoat is stretched around his bulging biceps. Likely a former athlete.

'*John?* Is it really you?'

My father's voice cracks.

'How long has it been? Fifty years?'

He gets to his feet and lurches towards the man as if he has just rediscovered a long-lost brother. They pat each other on the back, both talking at the same time.

It becomes clear that John is a long-time friend of the family. I can tell by the softer tone of their English that my relatives are relaxed with him, not solicitous as they often are with other Americans. He apparently got to know them when he was a soldier in Vietnam. A few years after the war, he was able to arrange a visa for Uncle Sơn to get him to the United States. He proudly tells my father that after leaving the army, he studied law and ultimately opened a practice.

'I was already thinking about it the first time we met in Vietnam, remember?' he asks. 'It was just an idea back then, not a real plan. But sometimes you surprise yourself.'

He sets the briefcase down, gathering himself for a moment before clearing his throat, almost as if to say that the official part of the evening is now getting started.

'Anyway, I approached your mother about her will after she had been diagnosed with Alzheimer's. She didn't have much to pass on and it didn't take long. But she wanted to leave a letter for you all and asked that I give it to Minh. She said: "*He should read it aloud to the others since he's the eldest son.*"'

John snaps open his briefcase, pulls out a large envelope, and sets it on the coffee table. Padded and yellow, it sits there in anticipation. He turns to my father with a smile.

'She always hoped that you would visit her in the US one day. Now, you're actually here. The first time, right?'

He hands the envelope to my father in such a ceremonious manner that I almost expect him to congratulate my father on his successful career, long marriage, and reunion with his siblings. Instead, he merely nods and steps aside.

My father opens the letter, pulls out four thin, densely written sheets of paper, and begins reading out loud in Vietnamese.

> Dear Minh,
> When you visited us in Saigon those many years ago, you were a grown man with a wife, a degree, and hopes for the wrong country. You were so full of ideals that my own disappointment was all the greater. We had lost our homeland, but you didn't want to see that. As a child, you were able to tell right from wrong, but as an adult, you ran into the arms of the communists. Did Germany change you? Were you away for too long?
>
> After your visit, you stopped talking to me, though you never explained why. Whenever an envelope from you arrived, it was always a check. I looked every time

to see if you might have tucked something else in as well — a brief note or a photo — but you never did. Nothing about your life, apart from the fact that you were able to set aside thousands of dollars for us every year. My oldest son had become a doctor and never neglected to send his mother money. It was a lot, but it was also very little.

The more forgetful I become, the more often I find myself thinking of you. Sometimes I relive the past as though it were happening today. The years in Vietnam blur with the years in America, your visit with your silence. I often find it difficult to tell the difference between what is real and what is memory. The doctors call it Alzheimer's. I can see from the faces of your siblings that they are pained by my condition. But for me, it has brought something to light that was in the shadows for so long.

After Sơn arrived in America, he applied for family reunification so that we could all join him. After just a year, we had all the papers we needed. He had managed to convince somebody to grant us special permission — other families were forced to wait ten times as long. Before we were due to leave, I applied for my annual visit to your father, who had since been transferred to a re-education camp way up in the North. The bus ride to the mountains took two days, and when I finally arrived, I didn't recognise him at first. His arms and legs were as thin as twigs, and he couldn't have weighed more than ninety pounds. His eyes glistened feverishly, and he was constantly coughing. He was sick, very sick, but when I asked him how he was doing, he just shook his head in silence. One of the guards stood a couple steps away from us, watching. He had already confiscated the bag I had brought along containing rice cakes and vitamins.

I whispered: 'We've received our papers!' But your father just gazed at me with no emotion. I took his hand: 'Sơn is waiting for us!' But he just coughed. Finally, he responded: 'I'm a gravedigger now. Do you know what that means?'

In his hoarse voice, he said that he had been assigned to a special group whose mission it was to find and dig up the bones of North Vietnamese soldiers who had fallen in the war. Their only tools were roughly sketched maps and rusty shovels. The work was extremely difficult, and they weren't given enough food to eat. At night, they had so little room to sleep that they had to lie head to toe, squashed in like sardines. Some of the prisoners fell ill and died because there were no doctors and no medicines. Others simply disappeared. Still others were convinced they would never leave the camp. 'I wake up every day believing it could be my last,' he said. 'My dreams each night are filled with bones.'

When the guard came to our table to end our visit, your father slowly stood up and murmured, 'Sơn is a good boy, he always has been.' He followed the man to the exit, turned around one last time, and softly called in my direction: 'Don't wait for me!' Then he was gone.

On the drive back home, I felt numb, almost as if

I had just been to a funeral. It took me a day to admit to myself that your father would likely never leave the camp, and that he would never be able to fly to America with us. What were we to do now? Leave him behind? Or stay in Vietnam and sacrifice the opportunity to start over in another country?

I had almost made it all the way back to Saigon when I turned around and took the bus to Huế. A distant cousin lived there, and I asked her to visit your father once a year. I promised to send her money from the US, not just for him, but enough that she could take care of her family as well.

'What are you going to tell your children?' she asked. 'How are they supposed to start a new life knowing that they've left their sick father behind?'

Back home in Saigon, I told your siblings that your father had died in the re-education camp. 'He rebelled against his guards, so they assigned him to clear a minefield,' I lied. They cried for a week. Then we flew off to America. I watched them learn to drive in California, begin their studies, pick up this foreign language better and better, and bring new friends home. A little over two years later, my cousin in Huế wrote that your father had died of malaria in the re-education camp. I put a new photo of him on the family altar and began wondering if I should finally tell you the truth. But I didn't know how, so I kept silent.

Now, though, the past has returned to me like it never left. The lie from back then has returned like a ghost, haunting my mind and torturing me with questions: Was it wrong to tell you that your father had died? Or was it right to protect you from the truth? I've thought a lot about it, yet I've never arrived at an answer.

You, Minh, used to always approach things with logic, never allowing emotion to distract you. Perhaps you will be able to explain to your siblings that I only meant the best. I wanted you all to do better in life than we did. How would that have been possible with the truth?

Please don't think ill of me. Your father is alone no longer.

Your mother

My father falls silent. The densely written sheets of paper slide out of his hands onto the parquet floor, where they scatter in an anguished jumble. I look at the rigid faces of my relatives and find myself thinking of the black-and-white images from the Vietnam War, the barren expanses of countryside pocked with gaping bomb craters. Emptiness full of rubble and stone.

It's John who breaks the silence. 'Are you okay?'

My father sinks down into his leather recliner and closes his eyes. Speaking more to himself than the others, he asks: 'Should I have written to her? I thought I was doing what she wanted ...'

Not a word from anyone.

It's all rather painful — the letter, the visit, the truth. My relatives launch into nervous activity. Aunt Linh gathers the papers from the floor and begins reading. Uncle Sơn asks how late it is. Aunt Hồng suggests that we go out for dessert. My mother responds by saying:

We really need to leave for the airport soon. John snaps his briefcase shut. Aunt Hồng is going on about some new place that serves chè pudding. My mother relents, apparently deciding that we should take advantage of this last opportunity to go out together. Uncle Hùng rolls his eyes, saying the chè at the new place is too sweet. Aunt Hồng sharply contradicts him: *I'm talking about the new place near the Bella Terra Mall, not the one you always go to. It's on the way to the airport.* Aunt Linh wipes the tears from her eyes. John disappears after mumbling his goodbyes. Uncle Sơn starts jangling his car keys, saying that we really need to get moving, wherever we decide to go.

My phone chimes, a message from Lee.

'Okay — where?'

My mother looks at me like a drowning person catching sight of a passing ship.

'What should we do? You decide!'

They all fall silent.

I suddenly realise that I am the only one here who hasn't experienced a severe letdown today. I hardly knew my grandmother, and never loved her; I'm not beset by questions as to whether she lied to me or betrayed my trust. Even as my relatives are slumped in their seats, I am wide awake and unperturbed, not to mention rather fascinated by this long-concealed family secret. But because I am also aware that such feelings are completely inappropriate, I put on my most stricken expression and try to speak as slowly and profoundly as possible.

'I think chè is the best thing for digesting a shock like this. My God, who would have thought!'

*

I had expected Chè 75 to be a cheap eatery with bland décor, but a short time later, we walk into a café that would be the perfect backdrop for a K-pop video: radiant white walls offset with tubes of neon; pink and purple plastic chairs. A couple of twenty-somethings busy themselves behind the counter, their faces powdered white, their hair dyed blond. The brightly lit display cases are packed with Instagrammable cups chock-full of sweet beans, colourful tapioca pearls, and coconut milk. My mother almost has a heart attack when she sees that they charge seven dollars per serving, so we end up ordering two banana desserts for seven people.

'Unbelievable,' my father murmurs as he slides into the left side of a pink booth.

'It is, isn't it?' Uncle Sơn, who is sitting next to him, responds.

'Would you ever have imagined something like this?'

'That she would keep something that important from us?'

'That she would confess everything in a farewell letter!'

'I wouldn't ever have guessed.' Uncle Sơn sighs. 'But what son *would* think his mother was lying when she says their father is dead? It's just not something you'd suspect!'

'I might have an idea where that came from.'

My father raises the spoon to his mouth, pauses, and then lowers it again, the white plastic disappearing into the light-grey glop. Without taking a bite, he passes the cup to Uncle Sơn, who wordlessly pushes it to me. I have always loved chè, but today the taste is downright heavenly. I can feel the contrast between chopped peanuts, creamy coconut milk, and squishy bananas on my tongue, a delectable interplay of flavour and texture. I dive in like I've been fasting for the last two weeks. My uncle watches me in astonishment.

'Since reading that letter, I've been asking myself if I ever really knew my own mother,' my father mumbles.

'Me too. And I was here with her the whole time! We lived together in a small apartment for so many years!'

'Did you suspect anything?'

'No, never. I remember her changing Father's picture on the family altar. The old one was a photo of him in uniform, the new one was from their wedding. I used to stand in front of it and pray. Strange, isn't it? Do you think a prayer loses its power if the dead person lived two years longer than you thought? On the other hand, he really was dead by then, so he probably heard my prayers anyway.'

My uncle runs his fingers through his hair, but my father says nothing in response. I only ever saw him praying when we visited a temple with others, when it would have been rude not to. I assume he believes in the power of dead ancestors as little as I do. *'When it comes to religion,'* he always said, *'Marx was right, no matter what you might otherwise think of him.'*

'I just can't believe Mother didn't tell us about his true condition,' he remarks, shaking his head.

'I can,' Uncle Sơn replies, lost in thought. 'After the fall of Saigon, I had a few strange encounters with him. Even then, he had changed. He would just sit around at home in his bamboo chair, saying nothing.'

'Sounds like he might have been suffering from some kind of trauma.'

Uncle Sơn shrugs. 'Could be. We didn't really have the right words for it in Vietnam. Whatever the case, it's not hard to believe that he was a broken man after all those years in the re-education camp.'

'Some patients never return to health. As a doctor, I see it every day. Their families are always very emotional, but sometimes it's better to take a rational view of things. If Mother had told me about it, I probably would have understood her decision.'

'You probably would have.'

'And you wouldn't have?' My father lifts his chin. 'She did it for the family. For us, her children.'

Uncle Sơn slumps down into the pink booth, exhausted, his eyes closing almost as if he were falling asleep. 'The thought of Father being left behind all alone is still upsetting. While we were here eating burgers, he was being forced to go out digging for bones. How can a person live with such a secret? How could *she* live with it?' He shakes his head without opening his eyes. 'How could she? Tell me, Minh!'

My father looks at his brother, and then down at his hands. 'I just can't get over the fact that she carried this lie around her whole life. At some point, we were no longer children. We could have handled the truth, right ... ?' He seems lost, like a young boy in a forest looking for the way back home. Never before have I seen him so defeated. I stand up, walk around the table, and lay my hand on his head.

'Dad,' I say gently, in German. 'You didn't speak to your mother for years, remember? And you never told me why. Is it really so hard to see why she couldn't bring herself to tell you the truth?'

*

I discover Lee's slender figure on the way to the restroom, sitting alone at a table on the terrace of Chè 75. She's wearing a white tank top and loose black sweatpants. Her left leg is propped up on a chair and her right leg bounces up and down. She's wearing no make-up aside from dark eyeliner. When she embraces me, I inhale deeply. She smells like she has just showered, and her hair is still damp.

'So good to see you,' she says warmly. 'How was your last day? Any family drama just before you leave?'

I sit down across from her.

'I learned today that my grandmother was pretty badass.'

'Really? I *love* badass women. Tell me everything!'

I tell her all about John's visit and the four-page confession, about the questions that tormented my grandmother, and about the self-reproach now consuming my father. In ten minutes, I have laid out our family secrets like wares at a market stall. I'm not sure why.

'What a lie!' she blurts out. 'So cold-blooded!'

'I think "*lie*" is a bit much,' I reply. 'Yes, her behaviour was atrocious. But in her own ruthless way, she actually meant well.'

'Then what would you call it?'

'I'm not sure. "*Silence*" perhaps?'

She leans forward. '"*Silence*" is, of course, a much nicer word. But isn't that also dishonest?'

The corners of her mouth twitch in amusement as she folds her arms in front of her. The black polish on her fingernails makes it look like she has claws.

I exhale loudly.

She squints her eyes.

'Did I say something wrong again? I'm sorry. I just wanted to tell you that you're protecting your family. Which is a good thing. Good, but also complicated. You might be more Vietnamese than you think you are.'

Not really knowing how to respond, I lift my backpack into my lap and start rummaging around inside. For a moment, I ask myself if I can really trust her with another family secret. But then she might just be the perfect person to help me with this stuff. I pull out the black notebook that I found in my uncle's bedroom and pass it over to her with both hands.

'I suspect this used to belong to my father. I wanted to ask you if you could tell me what he wrote. I can't read Vietnamese.'

She laughs in relief. 'A journalist who can't read. How cute.'

She opens the notebook and starts flipping through the pages, her lips moving silently. She stops on one of the last pages, tracing an entry with her finger and begins reading out loud.

'I'm not afraid of travelling overseas, but these final days at home feel like when, the moment before death, you see your life flash before your eyes and realise how much you love it.'

She looks up. 'Your father is quite dramatic!'

'You think so? He's actually more of a stoic.'

I stand up, move behind her chair, and look at the page. The words are written in Latin letters, but they have a bunch of accents that I am unable to decipher.

'Maybe your father used to be different,' she says. 'He wrote this in 1968, apparently in his last year of high school. I only scanned a couple of pages, but it seems like he lived through some pretty heavy shit.'

'Oh yeah? Like what?'

She starts flipping through the notebook again, and I edge

closer to her so I can follow along. She reads me a story about John, the American, and then another about the night of the Tết Offensive. Sentence after sentence, we plunge into the past until the present has almost dissolved. Leaning into her, I lose myself in my father's stories. When her voice finally fades to silence, I wish that she would never stop talking to me.

Slowly, she closes the notebook, her fingers brushing gently across the cover.

'You should write your family's story.'

'Me?' I say recoiling. 'I hardly know anything about them! I'm just an outsider in the grand scheme of things. Plus, I can't even speak the language properly. The idea of me interviewing my relatives is ridiculous.'

I realise I'm acting all frantic and defensive.

Again, she regards me with that look of amusement, and places her hand on my cheek. Her lips whisper into my ear, her breath loud and ticklish.

'What are you afraid of? That you might discover something about yourself too?'

*

A last-minute panic erupts as we suddenly find ourselves way behind schedule. My relatives launch into an excruciating debate about who should take us from Chè 75 to the airport and how to make up for lost time. My mother is seething like a volcano about to erupt; even though she's not exactly known for being punctual herself, she begins grumbling about my father's 'completely chaotic' family. They finally agree that Uncle Sơn will drive the rental car to the airport and return it as we are checking in for our flight. Befuddled, I stand silently in front of my Aunt Linh. We hug briefly with no bodily contact before I am herded towards the waiting car.

We speed through the night in our black Chevrolet as Uncle Sơn curses about 'these slow hags in front of us'. The red from the cars ahead of us blend with the yellowish light from the skyscraper windows as they pass above us.

I start thinking of Dorian, who has promised to pick me up at the airport in Berlin. He'll probably welcome me with that tender smile I can never resist. I imagine opening the door to our pre-war Berlin apartment and him lugging my suitcase to our bedroom before the two of us sink into the worn leather couch in the living room.

Will he be the one to start talking? Or will I?

We brake abruptly, as if to jolt me out of my thoughts. I see the luminous white letters in front of the glass airport building: TOM BRADLEY INTERNATIONAL. The clock reads 11.14 pm. Our flight is scheduled to take off in less than an hour.

'Hurry up!' urges Uncle Sơn.

He keeps the engine idling and jumps out to unload the luggage. One large suitcase for my parents, a white trolley for me, a flower-patterned bag for my mother, and a blue trolley for my father.

'Leave that one here!' my mother scolds. 'That was the one for the presents. It's empty!'

'I still need it,' my father replies. 'It's not heavy.'

I lift it up, and it is actually quite light. Light, but not empty. Something bulky is rattling around inside.

His books.

'Thank you, Sơn!' he calls out.

I run ahead because the airport is the gateway to the English-speaking world, and I can quickly find my way. Lufthansa counter, baggage drop, security line. We push our way to the front and run through the terminal past the glittering duty-free shops and the cafés lying dormant at this hour. Endless rows of grey chairs stretch out before us, occupied by travellers who are sleeping, fiddling with their mobile phones, or chatting quietly. Gate 30 finally comes into view, and I sprint up to it. The line has almost completely vanished down the jetway, and the stewardess is checking the boarding passes of a young couple. She's wearing a dark-blue uniform and pumps; her hair is tied into a smooth bun. Everything about her is immaculate. She is tall, German, and intimidating.

'Anyone else for Frankfurt? *Last call for Frankfurt!*'

'*Sorry, can you please wait? My parents ...*'

I'm gasping for breath as I stand before her. Inhaling deeply, I switch to German. Ever since I was small, I have been convinced that they treat me better when they hear me speak their language so perfectly.

'My parents have to get on this flight! They'll be here in just a second!'

She glances at her watch, slender and golden. She presses her lips together.

'You're rather late! Boarding begins thirty minutes before take-off!'

We stand waiting next to each other until I finally see my parents, my mother's head bent forward like it always is when she's in a hurry, my father trotting behind her with his blue trolley. I call out to them louder than necessary — '*over here!*' — and then run up to grab my mother by the elbow and push her forward. In a rush, I shove the boarding passes to the stewardess.

'There are only two here,' she says acerbically. 'For Mr Minh Nguyễn and for Ms Hoa Nguyễn. I assume that's you?'

She looks at my parents and then at me.

'And what about yours?'

I clutch my boarding pass with both my hands. 15A, a window seat. My ticket back to my old German life.

'What's wrong with you?' my mother demands. 'Hurry up!'

I take a step back.

'We have to finish boarding,' the stewardess urges, tapping her watch. 'Please give me your ticket!'

I think about my apartment in Berlin and my relatives in California, about the nine time zones separating the two. I think about Lee's questions and my other self that the sea has washed onto the shore.

'I'm staying,' I declare.

My father's eyes open wide. 'You're staying?'

My mother grabs my arm: 'Nonsense! We have to go. Come on!'

I take a step backwards, fold up the boarding pass, and hand it to her. My mother looks at me with such disbelief that I almost feel bad. I lean forward and kiss her on the cheek, and then my father. Unwillingly, they accept a hug.

'Don't wait for me!'

With a pat on the shoulder, I push them towards the jetway. Herded along by the stewardess, they stumble off towards the plane. I wave to them until they finally disappear with their luggage.

Free at last.

*

Back in the departure hall, I find the last shop that's still open, a Starbucks. I dig my wallet out of my backpack and pull out a ten-dollar bill. I have a sudden, overwhelming urge for ice cream, so I order a Mocha Frappuccino with whipped cream and Oreos. The mere thought of the combination of crushed ice, whipped cream, and crunchy cookies warms my belly. I place my left hand on it to calm myself.

The man behind the counter has dark hair and is named Tom Lê. He lazily taps the register before grabbing a paper cup and a pen. Without looking up, he asks me for my name.

'My name is Kiều,' I respond.

He lifts his gaze, narrowing his eyes. I can already hear the question that's coming. He leans over the counter, pen in hand.

'Do you prefer dairy milk, almond, or soy?'

ACKNOWLEDGEMENTS

This book wouldn't have been possible without the memories and stories that others have so generously shared with me. In California: my aunts Lan and Hương and my uncles Đính, Quang, and Vinh. In Vietnam: my aunt Hoa and uncle Lộc, as well as writer Bảo Ninh, journalists Huy Đức and Trương Mai Lan, author Nguyễn Xuân Xanh, businessman Cao Thanh Sơn, and war photographer Hoàng Văn Cường. In Germany: my uncle Bình and the Vietnam experts Gerhard Will and Jörg Wischermann. In Cambodia: human-rights activist Youk Chhang and political scientist Nou Van. I would like to thank them all for helping me gain a better understanding of the distant, momentous times of the Vietnam War.

This book would have been far worse without the questions and suggestions that helped me find my voice and story. Martina Klüver, my German editor at btb/Random House, approached this text with so much passion, it could have been her own. Regina Kammerer, the publishing director, believed in this novel before it took shape. Alfio Furnari motivated and inspired me in a way that went far beyond his job description as a literary agent. Molly Slight, publisher at Scribe in London, gave me the unexpected opportunity to present my novel to the English-speaking world. With much devotion, Charles Hawley and Daryl Lindsey found the right words in English for it. Laura Ali and David Golding helped us refine the translation with their detailed and insightful edits. I would like to thank them all for helping me turn an idea into a novel, and for giving it a new and second life in English. I still can't quite believe it.

Working on this book often felt like an endless journey through uncharted territory. For four years, others accompanied, endured, and encouraged me through this process. Thanks to Cora, Nico, and especially Jochen, who listened to all my ideas and went out alone on countless Sundays and holidays because I had to stay home to write. Thanks to Thi and Đăng, whose story is also told here, although they see so many things differently than I do. My special thanks go to my parents: for translating, for proofreading, and for babysitting Neo. What a gift it is to have this 'Phamily'.